ALSO BY SOPHIE LARK

Brutal Birthright

Brutal Prince

Stolen Heir

Savage Lover

Bloody Heart

Broken Vow

Heavy Crown

Sinners Duet

There Are No Saints

There Is No Devil

BRUTAL PRINCE

SOPHIE LARK

Bloom *books*

Copyright © 2022, 2023 by Sophie Lark
Cover and internal design © 2023 by Sourcebooks
Cover design by Emily Wittig
Cover and internal illustrations © Line Maria Eriksen
Cover image by kues/DepositPhotos

Sourcebooks and the colophon are registered trademarks of
Sourcebooks. Bloom Books is a trademark of Sourcebooks.

Published by Bloom Books, an imprint of Sourcebooks
P.O. Box 4410, Naperville, Illinois 60567-4410
(630) 961-3900
sourcebooks.com

Originally self-published in 2022 by Sophie Lark.

Cataloging-in-Publication Data is on file with the Library of Congress.

Printed and bound in the United States of America.
KP 10 9 8 7 6 5 4 3 2

This book is for every person who's told me Aida inspired them to be strong. Aida is the unbreakable spirit inside all of us. She's the determination to laugh when life is hard and to never, ever be anything but yourself. Stay rowdy, you gorgeous babes.

XOXO

Sophie Lark

SOUNDTRACK

1. "Hate Me"—Nico Collins
2. "You Don't Own Me"—SAYGRACE
3. "Boyfriend"—Selena Gomez
4. "Midnight Sky"—Miley Cyrus
5. "Somethin' Bad"—Miranda Lambert
6. "Sweet but Psycho"—Ava Max
7. "Love the Way You Lie"—Rihanna
8. "Ballroom Blitz"—The Struts
9. "Poison & Wine"—The Civil Wars
10. "Falling Slowly"—Glen Hansard
11. "Make You Feel My Love"—Adele
12. "Gnossienne: No. 1"—Erik Satie

Music is a big part of my writing process. If you start a song when you see a ♫ while reading, the song matches the scene like a movie score.

Spotify   Apple Music

THE GALLOS

1

AIDA GALLO

Fireworks burst into bloom above the lake, hanging suspended in the clear night air, then drifting down in glittering clouds that settle on the water.

My father flinches at the first explosion. He doesn't like things that are loud or unexpected. Which is why I get on his nerves sometimes—I can be both those things, even when I'm trying to behave myself.

I see his scowl illuminated by the blue and gold lights. Yup, definitely the same expression he gets when he looks at me.

"Do you want to eat inside?" Dante asks him.

Because it's a warm night, we're all sitting on the deck. Chicago isn't Sicily—you have to take the opportunity to eat outdoors whenever you can get it. Still, if it weren't for the sound of traffic below, you might think you were in an Italian vineyard. The table's set with stoneware brought from the old country three generations ago, the pergola overhead thickly blanketed by the fox grapes Papa planted for shade. You can't make wine out of fox grapes, but they're good for jam at least.

My father shakes his head. "It's fine here," he says shortly.

Dante grunts and goes back to shoveling chicken in his mouth. He's so big that his fork looks comically small in his hand. He eats like he's starving, hunched over his plate.

Dante's the oldest, so he sits on my father's right-hand side.

Nero's on the left, with Sebastian next to him. I'm at the foot of the table, where my mother would sit if she were still alive.

"What's the holiday?" Sebastian says as another round of fireworks rocket up into the sky.

I tell him, "It's not a holiday. It's Nessa Griffin's birthday."

The Griffins' palatial estate sits right on the edge of the lake, in the heart of the Gold Coast. They're setting off fireworks to make sure absolutely everybody in the city knows their little princess is having a party—as if it weren't already promoted like the Olympics and the Oscars combined.

Sebastian doesn't know because he doesn't pay attention to anything that isn't basketball. He's the youngest of my brothers and the tallest. He got a full ride at Chicago State, and he's good enough that when I visit him on campus, I notice girls stare and giggle everywhere he goes. Sometimes they pluck up the courage to ask him to sign their T-shirts.

"How come we weren't invited?" Nero says, soaked in sarcasm.

We weren't invited because we fucking hate the Griffins and vice versa.

The guest list will be carefully curated, stuffed with socialites and politicians and anybody else chosen for their usefulness or their cache. I doubt Nessa will know any of them.

Not that I'm crying any tears for her. I heard her father hired Selena Gomez to perform. It ain't Halsey, but it's still pretty good.

"What's the update on the Oak Street Tower?" Papa says to Dante while meticulously cutting up his chicken parm.

He already knows damn well how the Oak Street Tower is doing because he tracks absolutely everything done by Gallo Construction. He's changing the subject because the thought of the Griffins sipping champagne and brokering deals with the haut monde of Chicago is irritating to him.

I don't give a shit what the Griffins are doing. Except that I don't like anybody having fun without me.

So, while my father and Dante are droning on about the tower, I mutter to Sebastian, "We should go over there."

"Where?" he says, gulping down an entire glass of milk. The rest of us are drinking wine. Sebastian's trying to stay in tip-top shape for dribbling and sit-ups or whatever the fuck his team of gangly ogres does for training.

"We should go to the party." I keep my voice low.

Nero perks up. He's always interested in getting into trouble. "When?"

"Right after dinner."

"We're not on the list," Sebastian protests.

"Jesus." I roll my eyes. "Sometimes I wonder if you're even a Gallo. You scared of jaywalking too?"

My two oldest brothers are proper gangsters. They handle the messier parts of the family business. Sebastian thinks he's going to the NBA. He's living in a whole other reality than the rest of us. Trying to be a good boy, a law-abiding citizen.

Still, he's the closest to me in age and probably my best friend, though I love all my brothers. He grins back at me. "I'm coming, aren't I?"

Dante shoots us a stern look. He's still talking to our father, but he knows we're plotting something.

Since we've all finished our chicken, Greta brings out the panna cotta. She's been our housekeeper for about a hundred years. She's my second-favorite person, after Sebastian. She's stout and pretty, with more gray in her hair than red.

She made my panna cotta without raspberries because she knows I don't like the seeds and doesn't mind if I'm a spoiled brat. I grab her head and give her a kiss on the cheek as she sets it down in front of me.

"You're going to make me drop my tray!" She tries to shake me loose.

"You've never dropped a tray in your life."

My father takes fucking forever to eat his dessert. He's sipping his wine and going on and on about the electrical workers union. I swear Dante is drawing him out on purpose to infuriate the rest of us. When we have these formal sit-down dinners, Papa expects us all to stay till the bitter end. No phones allowed at the table either, which is basically torture because I can feel my cell buzzing again and again in my pocket, with messages from who knows who. Hopefully not Oliver.

I broke up with Oliver Castle three months ago, but he isn't taking the hint. He may need to take a mallet to the head instead if he doesn't stop annoying me.

Finally, Papa finishes eating. We all gather as many plates and dishes as we can carry to stack in the sink for Greta.

Then Papa goes into his office to have his second nightcap, while Sebastian, Nero, and I all sneak downstairs.

We're allowed to go out on a Saturday night. We're all adults, after all—just barely, in my case. Still, we don't want Papa to ask us *where* we're going.

We pile into Nero's car because it's a boss '57 Chevy Bel Air that will be the most fun to cruise around in with the top down.

Nero starts the ignition. The flare of the headlights reveals Dante's hulking silhouette, arms crossed, looking like Michael Meyers about to murder us.

Sebastian jumps. I let out a shriek.

"You're blocking the car," Nero says drily.

Dante says, "This is a bad idea."

"Why?" Nero can make his voice innocent even when not a single person on this earth believes he's innocent. Of anything. "We're just going for a drive."

"Yeah?" Dante says, not moving. "Right down Lake Shore Drive."

Nero switches tactics. "So what if we are? It's just some Sweet Sixteen party."

"Nessa's nineteen," I correct him.

"Nineteen?" Nero shakes his head in disgust. "Why are they even—Never mind. Probably some stupid Irish thing. Any excuse to show off."

"Can we get going?" Sebastian says. "I don't wanna be out too late."

"Get in, or get out of the way!" I shout at Dante.

He stares a minute longer, then shrugs. "Fine. But I'm riding shotgun."

I climb over the seat without argument, letting Dante have the front. A small price to pay to get my big brother on team Party Crashers.

We cruise down LaSalle Street, enjoying the early summer air streaming into the car. Nero has a black heart and a vicious temperament, but you'd never know it from the way he drives. In the car, he's as smooth as a baby's ass—calm and careful.

Maybe it's because he loves the Chevy and has put about a thousand hours of work into it. Or maybe driving is the only thing that relaxes him. Either way, I always like seeing him with his arm stretched out on the wheel, the wind blowing back his sleek hair, his eyes half-closed like a cat.

It's not far to the Gold Coast. Actually, we're practically neighbors—we live in Old Town, which is directly north. Still, the two neighborhoods aren't much alike. They're both fancy in their own ways—our house looks right over Lincoln Park, while theirs fronts onto the lake. But Old Town is, well, just what the name implies: pretty fucking old. Our house was built in the Victorian era. Our street is quiet, full of massive old oak trees. We're close to St. Michael's Church, which my father genuinely believes was spared the Chicago Fire by a direct act of god.

The Gold Coast is the new hotness. It's all pish-posh shopping and dining and the mansions of the richest motherfuckers in Chicago. I feel like I sprang forward thirty years just driving over here.

Sebastian, Nero, and I thought we might sneak in around the

back of the Griffin property—maybe steal some caterers' uniforms. Dante, of course, isn't participating in any of that nonsense. He just slips the security guard five Benjamins to "find" our name on the list, and the guy waves us on in.

I know what the Griffins' house looks like before I see it because it was big news when they bought it a few years back. At the time, it was the most expensive piece of residential real estate in Chicago. Fifteen thousand square feet for a cool twenty-eight million dollars.

My father scoffed and said it was just like the Irish to flash their money. *An Irishman will wear a twelve-hundred-dollar suit without the money in his pocket to buy a pint.*

The Griffins can buy plenty of pints. They've got money to burn, and they're literally burning it right now, in the form of the fireworks show still trying to put Disney World to shame.

I don't care about colored sparks—I want the bougie champagne ferried around by the waiters, followed by whatever's being stacked into a tower on the buffet table. I'm gonna bankrupt these snooty fucks by eating my weight in crab legs and caviar.

The party is outdoors on the sprawling green lawn. It's the perfect night for it—more evidence of the luck of the Irish. Everybody's laughing and talking, stuffing their faces, and even dancing a little, though there's no Demi Lovato performing yet, just a normal DJ.

I guess I probably should have changed clothes. I don't see a single girl without a glittery party dress and heels. But that would have been annoying as hell on the soft grass, so I'm glad I'm just wearing sandals and shorts.

I do see Nessa Griffin, surrounded by people congratulating her on the monumental achievement of staying alive for nineteen years. She's wearing a pretty cream-colored sundress—simple and bohemian. Her light-brown hair is loose around her shoulders, and she's got a bit of a tan and a few extra freckles across her nose like she was out on the lake all morning. She's blushing from all the attention, sweetly happy.

Honestly, out of all the Griffins, Nessa's the best one. We went to the same high school. We weren't exactly friends since she was a year behind me and a bit of a Goody Two-Shoes. But she seemed nice enough.

Her sister, on the other hand…

I can see Riona right now, chewing out some waitress until the poor girl is in tears. Riona Griffin is wearing one of those stiff, fitted sheath dresses that looks like it belongs in a boardroom, not at an outdoor party. Her hair is pulled back even tighter than her dress. Never did anybody less suit flaming-red hair—it's like genetics tried to make her fun, and Riona was like, *I'm never having one goddamned moment of fun in my life, thank you very much.*

She's scanning the guests like she wants to bag and tag the important ones. I spin around to refill my plate before she catches sight of me.

My brothers split off the moment we arrived. I can see Nero flirting with some pretty blond over on the dance floor. Dante made his way over to the bar 'cause he's not gonna drink froufrou champagne. Sebastian disappeared entirely—not easy to do when you're six six. I'm guessing he saw some people he knows; everybody likes Sebastian, he's got friends everywhere.

As for me, I've got to pee.

The Griffins brought in some outdoor toilets, discretely set back on the far side of the property, screened by a gauzy canopy. I'm not peeing in a porta potty even if it's a fancy one. I'm gonna pee in a proper Griffin bathroom, right where they sit their lily-white bottoms down. Plus, it'll give me a chance to snoop around their house.

This takes a little maneuvering. They've got a lot more security around the entrance to the house, and I'm skint of cash for bribes. Once I throw a cloth napkin over my shoulder and steal the tray abandoned by the sobbing waitress, all I have to do is load up a few empty glasses, and I sneak right into the service kitchen.

I drop the dishes off at the sink like a good little employee, then duck inside the house itself.

Jiminy Crickets, it's a nice fucking house. I mean, I know we're supposed to be mortal rivals and all, but I can appreciate a place decked out better than anything I've ever seen on *House Hunters*. *House Hunters International*, even.

It's simpler than I would have expected—all creamy, smooth walls and natural wood, low modern furniture, and light fixtures that look like industrial art.

There's a lot of actual art around, too—paintings that look like blocks of color and sculptures made of piles of shapes. I'm not a total philistine—I know that painting is either a Rothko or supposed to look like one. But I also know I couldn't make a house look this pretty if I had a hundred years and an unlimited budget to do it.

Now I'm definitely glad I snuck in here to pee.

I find the closest bathroom down the hall. Sure enough, it's a study in luxury—lovely lavender soap, soft, fluffy towels, and water that comes out of the tap at the perfect temperature, not too cool and not too hot. Who knows—in a place this big, I may be the first person to even step foot in here. The Griffins probably each have their own private bathroom. In fact, they probably get tipsy and get lost in this labyrinth.

Once I finish, I know I should head back outside. I had my little adventure; there's no point pushing my luck.

Instead, I find myself sneaking up the wide curved staircase to the upper level.

The main level was too formal and antiseptic, like a show home. I want to see where these people actually live.

To the left of the staircase, I find a bedroom that must belong to Nessa. It's soft and feminine, full of books and stuffed animals and art supplies. There's a ukulele on the nightstand, and several pairs of sneakers were kicked hastily under the bed. The only things not clean and new are the ballet slippers slung over her doorknob by their ribbons. Those are beat to hell and back, with holes in the satin toes.

Across from Nessa's room is one that probably belongs to Riona. It's larger and spotlessly tidy. I don't see any evidence of hobbies in here, just some beautiful Asian watercolors hanging on the walls. I'm disappointed Riona hasn't kept shelves of old trophies and medals. She definitely seems the type.

Beyond the girls' rooms is the master suite. I won't be going in there. It seems wrong on a different level. There has to be some kind of line I won't cross when I'm sneaking around somebody's house.

I turn in the opposite direction and find myself in a large library.

Now this is the kind of mysterious shit I came here for.

What do the Griffins read? Is it all leather-bound classics, or are they secret Anne Rice fans? Only one way to find out...

Looks like they favor biographies, architectural tomes, and yes, all the classics. They've even got a section dedicated to the famous Irish writers of yesteryear, like James Joyce, Jonathan Swift, William Butler Yeats, and George Bernard Shaw. No Anne Rice, but they've got Bram Stoker at least.

Oh, look, they've even got a signed copy of *Dubliners*. I don't care what anybody says—no one understands that fucking book. The Irish are all in on it, pretending it's a masterwork of literature when I'm pretty sure it's pure gibberish.

Besides the floor-to-ceiling shelves of books, the library is full of overstuffed leather armchairs, three of which have been arranged around a large stone fireplace. Despite the warm weather, there's a fire going in the grate—just a small one. Actual birch logs are burning, which smells nice. Above the fireplace hangs a painting of a pretty woman, with a carriage clock and an hourglass beneath it. Between those, an old pocket watch.

I pick it up off the mantel. It's surprisingly heavy in my hand, the metal warm to the touch instead of cool. I can't tell if it's brass or gold. Part of the chain is still attached, though it looks like it broke off at about half its original length. The case is carved, so worn that I can't tell what the image used to be. I don't know how to open it either.

I'm fiddling with the mechanism when I hear a noise in the hallway—a faint clinking sound. I slip the watch into my pocket and dive behind one of the armchairs, the one closest to the fire.

A man comes into the library—tall, dark-haired, about thirty years old. He's wearing a perfectly tailored suit, and he's extremely well-groomed. Handsome but in a stark sort of way—like he'd push you off a lifeboat if there weren't enough seats. Or maybe even if you forgot to brush your teeth.

I haven't actually met this dude before, but I'm fairly certain it's Callum Griffin, eldest of the Griffin siblings. Which means he's just about the worst person to catch me in the library.

Unfortunately, it seems like he plans to stick around a while. He sits in an armchair almost directly across from me and starts reading emails on his phone. He's got a glass of whiskey in his hand, and he's sipping from it. That's the sound I heard—the ice cubes clinking together.

It's extremely cramped behind the armchair. The rug over the hardwood floor is none too cushy, and I have to hunch in a ball so my head and feet don't poke out on either side. Plus, it's hot as balls this close to the fire.

How in the hell am I going to get out of here?

Callum is still sipping and reading. Sip. Read. Sip. Read. The only other sound is the popping of the birch logs.

How long is he going to sit here?

I can't stay forever. My brothers are going to start looking for me in a minute.

I don't like being stuck. I'm sweating from the heat and the stress.

The ice in Callum's glass sounds so cool and refreshing. God, I want a drink, and I want to leave.

How many fucking emails does he have?

Flustered and annoyed, I hatch a plan. Possibly the stupidest plan I've ever concocted.

I reach behind me and grab the tassel hanging from the curtains. It's a thick gold tassel attached to green velvet curtains.

By pulling it to its farthest length, I can just poke it in around the edge of the grate, directly into the embers.

My plan is to set it smoking, which will distract Callum, allowing me to sneak around the opposite side of the chair and out the door. That's the genius scheme.

But because this isn't a fucking Nancy Drew novel, this is what happens instead:

The flames rip up the cord like it was dipped in gasoline, singing my hand. I drop the cord, which swings back to the curtain. The curtain ignites. Liquid fire roars up to the ceiling in an instant.

This actually does achieve its purpose of distracting Callum Griffin. He shouts and jumps to his feet, knocking over his chair. However, my distraction comes at the cost of all subtlety because I also have to abandon my hiding spot and sprint out of the room. I don't know if Callum saw me or not, and I don't care.

I'm thinking I should look for a fire extinguisher or water or something. I'm also thinking I should get the fuck out of here immediately.

The second idea wins—I go sprinting down the stairs at top speed.

At the bottom of the staircase, I plow into somebody else. It's Nero with the pretty blond right behind him. Her hair is all messed up, and he's got lipstick on his neck.

"Jesus, is that a new record?" I'm pretty sure he only met her about eight seconds ago.

Nero shrugs, a hint of a grin on his devil-handsome face. "Probably."

Smoke drifts down over the banister. Callum Griffin is shouting in the library. Nero gazes up the staircase.

"What's that about—"

"Never mind." I seize his arm. "We've gotta get out of here."

While dragging him in the direction of the service kitchen, I can't quite take my own advice. I cast one look back over my shoulder. Callum Griffin stands at the head of the stairs, glaring after us with murder on his face.

We sprint through the kitchen, knocking over a tray of canapés, and then we're out the door, back on the lawn.

"You find Sebastian; I'll get Dante," Nero says. He abandons the blond without a word, jogging off across the yard.

"What the hell?" she says.

I run in the opposite direction, looking for the lanky shape of my youngest brother.

Inside the mansion, a fire alarm starts to wail.

2
CALLUM GRIFFIN

Nessa's party starts in less than an hour. I'm still holed up with my parents in my father's office. His office is one of the biggest rooms in the house, larger than the master suite or the library. Which is fitting because business is the center of our family—the core purpose of the Griffin clan. I'm fairly certain my parents only had children so they could assign roles within their empire.

They certainly meant to have more of us. There are four years between me and Riona, and six between Riona and Nessa. Those gaps contain seven failed pregnancies, each ending in miscarriage or stillbirth.

The weight of all those missing children lies on my shoulders. I'm the eldest and the only son. The work of the Griffin men can only be done by me. I'm the one to carry on our name and legacy.

Riona would be irritated to hear me say that. She's infuriated by any intimation that there's a difference between us because I'm older and male. She swears she'll never get married or change her name. Or bear children either. That part really pisses my parents off.

Nessa is much more pliable. She's a people pleaser, and she wouldn't do anything to annoy dear old Mom and Dad. Unfortunately, she lives in a fucking fantasy world. She's so sweet and tenderhearted that she doesn't have the tiniest clue what it takes to keep this family in power. So she's pretty much useless.

That doesn't mean I don't care about Nessa. She's so genuinely good that it's impossible not to love her.

I'm pleased to see her so happy today. She's over the moon about this party, even though it barely has anything to do with her. She's running around sampling all the desserts, admiring the decorations, without a clue that the one and only reason for this event is to secure support for my campaign to become alderman of the Forty-Third Ward.

The election takes place in a month. The Forty-Third Ward includes the whole lakefront: Lincoln Park, the Gold Coast, and Old Town. Next to the mayorship, it's the most powerful position in the city of Chicago.

For the past twelve years, the seat was held by Patrick Ryan, until he got himself thrown into prison. Before that, his mother, Saoirse Ryan, served for sixteen years. She was much better at her job and demonstrably better at not getting caught with her hand in the cookie jar.

In many ways, being an alderman is better than being a mayor. You're emperor of your district. Thanks to aldermanic privilege, you have the final say on zoning and property development, loans and grants, legislation, and infrastructure. You can make money on the front end, the back end, and in the middle. Everything goes through you, and everybody owes you favors. It's almost impossible to get caught.

And yet these greedy fucks are so blatant in their grift that they still manage to bring the hammer down on themselves.

That won't be me. I'm going to take control of Chicago's wealthiest and most powerful district. And then I'm going to parlay that into mayorship of the whole damn city.

Because that's what Griffins do. We build our empire. We never stop. And we never get caught.

The only problem is that the alderman position is not uncontested. Of course it isn't—it's the crown jewel of power in this city.

The main contenders are Kelly Hopkins and Bobby La Spata.

Hopkins shouldn't be a problem. She's an anti-corruption candidate, running on bullshit promises to clean up city hall. She's young, idealistic, and has no idea she's swimming in a shark tank wearing a meat suit. I'll decimate her easily.

La Spata is a bit of a challenge.

He's got a lot of support, including the electrical workers' and firefighters' unions, plus the Italians. Nobody actually likes him—he's a blustering fuck who spends half his time drunk and the other half getting caught with a new mistress. But he knows how to grease the right palms, and he's been around a long time. A lot of people owe him favors.

Paradoxically, he'll be harder to get rid of than Hopkins. Hopkins is relying on her squeaky-clean image—once I dig up some dirt on her (or invent some), she's sunk.

Everybody already knows La Spata's flaws. They're old news. He's so debauched that nobody expects anything better from him. I'll have to find another angle to bring him down.

This is what I'm discussing with my parents.

My father is leaning up against his desk, arms crossed over his chest. He's tall, fit, with gray hair cut stylishly and horn-rimmed glasses giving him an intellectual look. You'd never guess he came up as a bruiser, smashing kneecaps at the Horseshoe when people failed to pay their debts.

My mother is slim and petite, with a sleek blond bob. She's over by the window, watching the caterers set up on the lawn. I know she's anxious to get out there as quickly as possible even though she won't say anything about it until our meeting is over. She may look like the consummate socialite, but she's as deeply invested in the nuts and bolts of our business as I am.

"Make sure you talk to Cardenas," my father says. "He controls the firefighters' union. We'll need to bribe him. Be subtle about it. He likes to pretend he's above that sort of thing. Marty Rico will need promises that we'll change the zoning on Wells Street so he can put in his condos. We'll waive the affordable housing requirement, obviously. Leslie Dowell will be here, too, but I'm not sure what she—"

"She wants an expansion of charter schools," my mother promptly answers. "Give her that, and she'll make sure all the women on the board of education support you."

I knew she was listening over there.

"Riona can handle William Callahan," I say. "He's had a thing for her for ages."

My mother's lips tighten. She thinks it's beneath us to use sex appeal as a lever. She's wrong. Nothing is beneath us if it works.

Once we've gone down the list of people we'll need to hobnob with at the party, we're ready to break and get to work.

"Anything else?" I say to my father.

"Not about tonight. But sometime soon, we need to discuss the *Braterstwo*."

I grimace.

The Polish Mafia is becoming an increasingly aggressive thorn in my side. Fucking savages who don't understand how things are done in the modern era. They're still living in a time when you solve disputes by cutting off a man's hands and throwing him into the river.

I'll do that if I have to, but I at least try to come to an agreement before it reaches that point.

"What about them?"

"Tymon Zajac wants to meet with you."

That's serious. Zajac is the big boss—the Butcher of Bogota.

I don't want him coming to my office.

"Let's figure it out tomorrow," I tell my father.

I can't have it on my mind tonight.

"Fine." He straightens, tugging the hem of his suit jacket back into place.

My mother gives him a once-over to make sure he's looking sharp, then turns her eyes on me.

"Is that what you're wearing?" She raises one perfectly manicured eyebrow.

"What about it?"

"It's a bit formal."

"Dad's wearing a suit."

"She means you look like an undertaker," my father remarks.

"I'm young. I want to look mature."

"You still need style," he says.

I sigh. I'm well aware of the importance of image. All my suits are custom-made. On the advice of my assistant, I recently started wearing some closely trimmed facial hair. Still, it gets tiring changing your clothes three times a day to perfectly tailor your appearance to the occasion.

"I'll sort it out," I promise.

As I leave the office, I see Riona in the hall. She's already dressed for the party. She narrows her eyes at me.

"What were you doing in there?" She hates being left out of anything.

"We were going over the strategy for tonight."

"Why wasn't I invited?"

"Because I'm the one running for alderman."

Two bright spots of color come into her cheeks—the signal since childhood that she's offended.

"I need you to talk to Callahan for me," I say to smooth it over. To let her know she's needed. "He'll support me if you ask."

"Yes, he will," Riona says loftily. She knows she has the police chief wrapped around her finger. "He's not bad looking. Shame about his breath."

"Don't stand too close, then."

She nods. Riona is a good soldier. She's never let me down.

"Where's Nessa?"

She shrugs. "Running around god knows where. We should put a bell on her."

"If you see her, send her my way."

I haven't actually wished Nessa a happy birthday yet or given her my present. I've been too damn busy.

I jog up the stairs, then all the way down the hallway to my suite. I don't love the fact I'm still living with my family at thirty years old, but it makes it more convenient to work together. Besides, you've got to live in the district to be an alderman. I don't have time for house hunting.

At least my room is on the opposite end of the house from the master suite. It's large and comfortable—we knocked down a wall when I came back from college, giving me my own suite and adjoining office. It's almost like an apartment, separated from everybody else's rooms by the massive library in between.

I can hear guests already starting to arrive down below. I change into my newest Zegna suit, then head back downstairs to mingle.

Everything goes smoothly, as it always does when my mother's in charge. I can see her sleek blond bob across the lawn and hear her light, cultured laugh as she makes a point of circulating through all the most boring and important guests.

I'm working my way down my own list of Cardenas, Rico, and Dowell as each person arrives.

After about an hour, the fireworks start. They've been timed to coincide with sunset, so the brilliant explosions stand out against the newly darkened sky. It's a calm night, the lake as smooth as glass. The fireworks reflect in double on the water below.

Most of the guests turn to watch the show, their faces illuminated, their mouths open in surprise.

I don't bother to watch, taking the opportunity to scan the crowd for anybody I was supposed to talk to that I might have missed.

Instead, I see someone who definitely wasn't invited—a tall dark-haired kid standing with a bunch of Nessa's friends. Towering over them, actually—he's got to be six five at least. I'm pretty sure that's a fucking Gallo. The youngest one.

I'm distracted by Leslie Dowell accosting me again. By the time I glance back at the group, the tall kid is gone. I'll have to speak to security, tell them to keep an eye out.

First, food. I've barely had time to eat today. I grab a few shrimps off the buffet, looking around for a proper drink.

Waiters are circulating through the crowd with flutes of champagne. I don't want that shit. The line at the bar is too long. What I really want is the Egan's Ten-Year Single Malt up in my office.

Well, why the hell not? I already made the rounds of the most important people. I can sneak away for a minute.

I'll come back down when that pop singer gets here. That was a splurge from Dad. I don't know if it was to make Nessa happy because she's his little angel or if it was just to show off. Either way, the guests will love it.

I'll be back with plenty of time.

I head inside before climbing the stairs to my end of the house. I've got a little bar in my office—nothing showy, just a few bottles of high-end liquor and a mini-icebox. I pull out a nice heavy tumbler, throw in three jumbo ice cubes, and pour a heavy measure of whiskey on top. I inhale the heady scent of pear, wood, and smoke. Then I swallow it, savoring the burning in my throat.

I know I should go back down to the party, but honestly, now that I'm up here in the peace and quiet, I'm enjoying the break. You have to have a certain level of narcissism to want to be a politician. You have to feed off the glad-handing, the attention.

I don't give a shit about any of that. I'm powered by ambition alone. I want control. Wealth. Influence. I want to be untouchable.

Campaigning exhausts me.

Instead of heading to the stairs as I intended, I turn into the library.

This is one my favorite rooms in the house. Barely anyone comes in here except for me. It's quiet. The smell of paper and leather and birch logs is soothing. My mother keeps the fire going in the evenings for my benefit. The rest of the house is so heavily air-conditioned that it's never too hot to have a small fire in the grate.

Over the mantel is the painting of my great-great-great-grandmother, Catriona. She came to Chicago in the middle of the potato famine. Fifteen years old, crossing the ocean alone with three books in her suitcase and two dollars in her boot. She worked as a housemaid for a wealthy man in Irving Park. When he died, he left her the house and nearly three thousand dollars in cash and bonds. The papers said they must have had a secret relationship. His kids said she poisoned him and forged the will. Catriona took the house and turned it into a saloon.

She was the first Griffin in America. My parents like to say we're descended from the Irish princes of the same name, but I prefer the truth. We're the American dream: a family rising from a house servant to the mayor of Chicago. Or so I hope.

I sit for a minute sipping my drink, then scroll through my emails. I can never be idle for long.

I hear a sound and pause for a moment, thinking it must be one of the staff out in the hall. When I don't hear anything else, I return to my phone.

Two things happen at the same time:

I smell something that makes the hair rise on the back of my neck. Smoke, but not the clean smoke from the fire—a harsh, chemical smell.

With that, a sound like a sudden intake of breath but ten times louder. Then a flash of heat and light as the curtains ignite.

I jump out of my chair shouting god knows what. I'm confused and panicking, wondering what the hell is happening and what I should do about it.

Then rationality asserts itself.

The curtains are on fire, probably from a spark tossed out of the grate. I have to get a fire extinguisher before the whole house burns down.

That makes sense.

Until a complete stranger leaps from behind a chair and darts past me out of the office.

Realizing I wasn't alone in the library is a rude shock. I'm so surprised that I don't even get a good look at the intruder. All I register is that they're of medium height and dark-haired.

Then my attention is dragged back to the rapidly multiplying flames. They're already spreading across the ceiling and the carpet. In minutes, the whole library will be ablaze.

I sprint down the hallway to the linen closet where I know we keep a fire extinguisher. Dashing back to the library, I pull the pin and spray the whole side of the room with foam until every last ember is extinguished.

When I'm finished, the fireplace, the chairs, and Catriona's portrait are all doused in white chemical foam. My mother's going to be fucking furious.

That reminds me of the other party involved in this debacle. I dash back to the head of the staircase, just in time to see three people making their escape: a blond girl who looks a hell of a lot like Nora Albright, a brunette I don't know, and Nero fucking Gallo.

I knew the Gallos snuck in.

The question is why?

The rivalry between our families goes back almost all the way to Catriona. During Prohibition, our great-grandfathers battled for control of the illegal distilleries in the north end. Conor Griffin won. That money has been fueling our family ever since.

Italians don't go down easy. Every shipment of booze Conor cooked up, Salvator Gallo was waiting to hijack his trucks, steal the liquor, and try to sell it back to him at double the price.

Later, the Griffins took control of gambling at the Garden City racetrack while the Gallos ran a numbers game inside the city. When liquor was legal again, our families ran rival pubs, nightclubs, strip joints, and brothels.

Nowadays, the Gallos have moved into the construction industry. They've done pretty well for themselves. Unfortunately, our interests always seem in conflict. Like right now—they're backing Bobby La Spata for my alderman seat. Maybe because they like him. Maybe because they want to stick their thumb in my eye one more time.

Did they come here tonight to talk to some of the swing-vote guests?

I'd like to get my hands on one of them to ask. But by the time I track down the security we hired for the night, the Gallos are long gone, including the tall kid.

God *damn* it.

I head back to the library to reassess the damage. It's a fucking mess—a smoking, stinking, soggy mess. They destroyed my favorite part of the house.

And why were they even in here anyway?

I search, trying to figure out what they were after.

There's nothing of significance in the library—any valuable papers or records would be in my father's office. Cash and jewelry are stored in the safes scattered throughout the house.

So what was it?

That's when my eye falls on the mantel spattered with foam. I see the carriage clock and the hourglass. My grandfather's pocket watch is missing.

I hunt around on the ground and even in the embers of the birch logs, in case it fell inside the grate somehow.

Nothing. It's nowhere to be found.

Those fucking wops stole it.

I storm back downstairs where the party is just getting going again after the interruption of the fire alarm. Nessa's giggling with some of her friends. I could ask her if she invited Sebastian Gallo, but even she couldn't be clueless enough to do that. She looks so happy despite the commotion. I don't want to interrupt her.

I don't extend the same courtesy to the rest of her friends. Catching sight of Sienna Porter, I seize her by the arm and pull her a little way off from Nessa.

Sienna's a skinny little redhead from Nessa's college. I've caught her sneaking looks at me a time or two before. More importantly, I'm pretty sure she was one of the girls talking to Sebastian earlier in the night.

Sienna doesn't protest my hauling her away. She blushes tomato red and says, "H-hi, Callum."

"Were you talking to Sebastian Gallo earlier?" I demand.

"Uh, well, he was talking to me. I mean, to all of us. Not to me specifically."

"About what?"

"About March Madness, mostly. You know his team played in the first round—"

I shake my head, cutting her off. "Do you know who invited him tonight?"

"N-no," she stammers, eyes wide. "But if you want, I could ask him…"

"What do you mean?"

"I think he's meeting us at Dave & Buster's later."

"What time?" I squeeze her arm a little too hard.

"Uh, ten o'clock, I think?" She winces.

Bingo. I let go of her. She rubs her arm with her opposite hand. "Thanks, Sienna."

"No problem," she says, totally confused.

I pull out my phone and call Jack Du Pont. We've been friends since college. He works as my bodyguard and enforcer when I need one. Since we hired a whole security team for the party, he didn't come over tonight. They've proven themselves to be pretty fucking useless, so it's Jack I want now.

He picks up after one ring.

"Heya, boss."

"Come pick me up. Right now."

3
AIDA

We pile into Nero's car, roaring away from the Griffins' house as quickly as we can without running over any partygoers. Nero and I are whooping, Dante is glowering, and Sebastian looks mildly curious.

Dante demands, "What the fuck did you do?"

"Nothing!" I say.

"Then why are we running like we're about to have ten cops on our tail?"

"We're not. I just got busted in the house…by Callum Griffin."

Immediate alarm from Dante. "What did he say?"

"Nothing. We didn't even speak."

He stares between Nero and me, his thick eyebrows so far contracted that they look like one straight line hanging low over his eyes. Nero tries to seem nonchalant, his eyes on the road. Sebastian looks completely innocent because he is innocent—all he did was drink a Diet Coke with some redhead.

I think Dante's going to drop it.

Then he lunges forward and grabs a handful of my hair, pulling it toward him. Because my hair is attached to my head, this yanks me forward across the seats.

Dante inhales, then shoves me back, disgusted.

"Why do you smell like smoke?"

"I don't know."

"You're lying. I heard an alarm go off in the house. Tell me the truth right now, or I'm calling Dad."

I scowl right back at him, wishing I were as big as Dante, with gorilla arms that look like they could tear you to pieces. Then I'd be a lot more intimidating.

"Fine," I say at last. "I was in the library upstairs. A small fire started—"

"A SMALL FIRE?"

"*Yes.* Quit shouting, or I won't tell you anything else."

"How did this fire start?"

I squirm in my seat. "I might have…accidentally…let the curtains get a little bit in the fireplace."

"*Porca miseria*, Aida," Dante swears. "We just went there to drink their liquor and watch their fireworks, not burn their fucking house down!"

"It's not going to burn down," I say, not entirely confident in that statement. "I told you, Callum was right there."

"That's not better!" Dante explodes. "Now he knows you did it!"

"He may not. He may not even know who I am."

"I doubt that very much. He's not as stupid as the rest of you."

"Why am I included in this?" Sebastian protests.

"Because you're stupid," says Dante. "Even if you didn't do anything tonight specifically."

Sebastian laughs. It's impossible to offend him.

"Where were *you?*" Dante rounds on Nero.

"I was on the main level," Nero says calmly. "With Nora Albright. Her father owns the Fairmont in Millennium Park. He called me a greasy little criminal once. So I fucked his daughter in the Griffins' formal dining room. Sort of killed two birds with one stone, in terms of revenge."

Dante shakes his head in disbelief. "I can't believe you guys. You act like children. I never should have let you go over there."

"Oh, get off it." Nero won't take Dante's shit even if it comes to blows. "Since when are you a good boy? You hate those paddy fucks as much as we do. Who cares if we ruined their party?"

"You're gonna care if Callum Griffin gets that alderman seat. He's gonna tie us up in red tape and shut down every one of our projects. He'll bury us."

"Yeah?" Nero says, dark eyes narrowed. "Then we'll go pay him a visit with a cattle prod and a pair of pliers. Go to work on him until he's more cooperative. I'm not scared of the Griffins."

Dante shakes his head, too irritated to even try to reason with us.

I'm torn. On the one hand, we were a bit reckless. On the other, the look on Callum Griffin's face when his library caught fire was pretty fucking priceless.

"Turn here," Sebastian says to Nero, pointing.

Nero takes a right on Division Street.

"Where do you think you're going?" Dante's still pissed.

Sebastian says, "Some of the kids are gonna hang out after the party. I said I'd meet them."

"Fuck that. You all need to go home."

Nero's already pulled the car up to the curb. Sebastian hops out of the convertible, swinging his long legs over the side as easily as getting out of bed.

"Sorry, big brother," he says genially. "I don't have a curfew. And you're not my mama."

Nero looks like he wants to do the same, but he's stuck driving Dante home. Faced with my angry big brother and the prospect of him ratting me out to Dad, I figure Sebastian has the right idea. I scramble across the seat and jump out of the car.

"Get back here!" Dante shouts.

I'm already running after Sebastian, calling over my shoulder, "I'll be home in a couple of hours! Don't wait up!"

Sebastian slows down when he hears me coming. Even when

he's just ambling, I have to jog to keep up. Those damn long legs of his.

"Was the fire really an accident?"

"More or less." I shrug.

He chuckles. "I didn't even get to see inside the house. Bet it's nice."

"Yeah. If you like pastel."

Sebastian stuffs his hands in his pockets, strolling along. His hair hangs over his eyes. He's got the curliest hair of any of us. He could probably grow it into a 'fro if he wanted to.

"Nessa looked nice."

"Yeah, she's pretty," I agree. "Don't get any ideas—Papa would burst a blood vessel."

"I'm not," Sebastian says. "You know what Mom always said: 'Calm water doesn't need more water—you need wind to move your sail.' I probably need to find a little maniac like you."

I grin up at him. "If I get married, it'll definitely be to someone who doesn't give me any shit. Can you imagine going from being bossed around by Dante to bossed around by somebody else? Fuck that. I'd rather be single forever. In fact, I wouldn't mind that at all."

We're coming up on Dave & Buster's. I can see through the window that Sebastian's friends aren't inside yet.

"What should we do while we wait?" Sebastian asks me.

"Are there any ice cream places around?"

"Didn't you eat at the party?"

"Yeah." I shrug again. "That was a long time ago."

Seb laughs. "I'm not gonna turn down ice cream."

We walk a little farther toward the lake until we find a place that has soft serve. Sebastian gets a cup; I get a cone. We take them out to the boardwalk to eat, walking along the pier so we can look down at the water.

The lake is so big that it looks like an ocean. It has waves just like the sea and storms that blow in. Not right now, though. Right now, the water is as calm as I've ever seen. We've walked all the way to the end of the pier, to the point that juts out farthest over the lake.

Sebastian finishes his ice cream before chucking the cup into the nearest trash can. I'm still working on my cone.

We chat about his classes at school and about mine. I'm taking courses at Loyola—a little bit of everything. Psychology, poli-sci, finance, marketing, history. I like taking whatever I'm interested in at the moment. Unfortunately, I'm not sure how it's gonna all add up to a degree.

I think Papa's getting annoyed with me. I know he wants me to finish up and come work with him full-time. But he's not going to let me do the interesting or difficult stuff—he's already got Dante and Nero for that. He's going to shut me into some boring office doing busywork. And that sounds like a fucking nightmare to me.

I'm the baby of the family and the only girl. There's never been much in the way of expectations laid out for me. Maybe if my mother were alive, it would be different. But I've basically run wild my whole life. As long as I wasn't getting in too much trouble, my father had more important things to worry about.

My brothers are good friends to me, but they have their own lives.

Nobody needs me, not really.

I'm not whining about it. I like being free and easy. Right now, I'm hanging out with Seb, eating ice cream, enjoying a summer night. What more do I need?

That contentment lasts about five seconds. Then I look up and see two men walking toward us. One's wearing a suit; the other, a hoodie and jeans. The suited guy has dark hair, freshly cut, and his hands balled into fists at his sides. The expression of fury on his face is all too familiar, since I last saw it about forty minutes ago.

"Seb," I whisper, making my brother stand up straight.

"Is that Callum Griffin?" he mutters.

"Yup."

"Look who it is," Callum says. His voice is low, cold, and full of rage. He has extremely blue eyes, but there's nothing pretty about them. They're painfully intense, the only color on his person.

I don't know who the guy is standing next to Callum. He looks mean as hell. He's got the build of a boxer, a shaved head, and a slightly squashed nose like he's taken a hit or two. I'm betting he's doled out a whole lot more.

Sebastian moves closer to me and a little bit in front of me, shielding me with his body.

"What do you want?" he says to Callum.

Sebastian isn't nearly as intimidating as Dante or as vicious as Nero. Still, he's taller than Callum and his thug. His voice is as stern as I've ever heard it.

Callum just scoffs. His face is handsome—or at least, it should be. I've never seen such a cold expression. He looks like he hates everything. Especially me.

Not that I can entirely blame him for that.

"What is it with you Italians?" He sneers. "Where'd you learn your manners? You come to a party where you're not invited. Eat my food, drink my liquor. Then you break into my house. Try to burn it the *fuck* down. And you steal from me…"

Sebastian stiffens ever so slightly. He doesn't look at me, but I know he wants to.

I'm also confused what the fuck Callum is talking about. Then I remember the watch still tucked in the front pocket of my shorts. I completely forgot about it.

"Look," Sebastian says, "the fire was an accident. We don't want any trouble."

"Well, that's just bullshit, isn't it?" Callum says softly. "You came looking for trouble. And now you've got it."

It's not easy to rile up Sebastian. Threatening his little sister is a good way to do it. He's bristling, balling his fists in return, stepping all the way in front of me.

"You think you're some kinda tough guy, bringing your boyfriend along?" Sebastian says, jerking his head toward the still-silent boxer. "I've got brothers, too. You better fuck off before I call them here to peel your lily-white skin off."

Not bad, Seb. For someone who doesn't do a lot of threatening, that came out pretty menacing.

I don't need protecting, though. I dart forward so I'm right next to Sebastian and say, "Yeah, fuck off back to your fancy little mansion. You wanna play at being a gangster? You're just a bitch-ass politician. What're you gonna do, rubber-stamp us to death?"

Callum Griffin fixes me with his frozen stare. He's got thick dark eyebrows above ice-pale eyes. The effect is inhuman and unpleasant.

"That's a good point," he says softly. "I do have an image to protect. But it's funny…I don't think there's anyone around at the moment."

The pier is empty all the way along its length. There are people up at the shops on Division Street. But no one is close enough to hear us if I yell.

My throat tightens.

I don't feel afraid very often. I'm scared now. Despite what I said, I don't think Callum is weak. He's tall, powerfully built. And above all, he's staring me down without an ounce of fear. He's not wondering what he should do. He already decided.

He gives a nod to his enforcer. The boxer steps forward, fists raised. Before I can speak or move, he's hit Sebastian four times, twice in the face and twice in the body.

Blood bursts from Sebastian's nose. He doubles over, groaning. He tries to fight back—all my brothers have been trained to fight in one way or another—but where Dante and Nero took their practice to the streets, Sebastian's interest has always been athletic, not violent. With his longer reach, he manages a couple of hits. One of his punches makes the boxer stumble backward. The goon blocks Sebastian's other blows before slamming my brother in the kidney with a punch that makes him crumple and fall to the ground.

The whole fight lasts maybe ten seconds. I'm not just standing there—I try to hit the guy from the side, succeeding in popping him once in the ear. He shoves me back with his hand so hard, I almost fall over.

I launch myself at Callum instead, nailing him in the jaw. He shoves me hard in the chest. This time I do fall back, smacking the back of my skull against the pier railing.

Callum looks a little startled, like he didn't quite mean to do that. His face hardens and he says, "Where's the watch, you fucking degenerates?"

"We don't have your watch." Sebastian spits blood onto the wooden boards of the pier.

I do have the watch. But I'm not giving it to this gaping asshole.

The boxer grabs Sebastian by the hair and cracks him across the jaw. The blow is so hard that for a second, the light goes out of Seb's eyes. He shakes his head to clear it, but he looks dazed.

"Get away from him!" I shriek, trying to pull myself to my feet. My head is spinning, and my stomach turns over. The back of my skull is throbbing. I bet there's a lump the size of an egg back there.

"Give me the watch." Callum's relentless.

The boxer kicks my brother in the ribs to encourage him. Sebastian groans and clutches his side. The sight of this monster beating my youngest and kindest brother is driving me out of my fucking mind. I want to murder both these men. I want to douse them in gasoline and set them ablaze like those fucking curtains.

I don't have any gasoline. So I reach in my pocket and pull out the watch instead. It's heavy in my palm. My fingers clench tightly around it. I hold it up overhead.

"Is this what you're looking for?" I call.

Callum's eyes move to my fist, catch there, and for a moment, his face softens with relief.

Then I cock back my arm, and I fling that fucking watch

into the lake like I'm throwing the opening pitch at Wrigley Field.

The effect on Callum Griffin is incredible. His face goes marble white. "*Noooo!*" he howls.

And then he does the craziest thing of all.

He launches himself over the railing, diving into the water, suit and all.

The boxer stares after his boss in astonishment. He's confused, not sure what to do without instructions.

He looks back down at Seb. Lifting up one booted foot, he stomps it down on Sebastian's knee as hard as he can.

Sebastian screams.

I charge at the boxer. I'm smaller than him, and I weigh a whole lot less, but by getting low and diving at his knees, I actually manage to knock him over. It helps that he trips over Sebastian's outstretched legs.

He falls hard on the pier. I'm punching and pummeling every inch of him I can reach. With his good leg, Sebastian rears back and kicks the boxer right in the face. I jump up and kick him several more times.

This guy is the fucking Terminator. That's not going to keep him down for long; he's already coming to, making grunting sounds. I grab Seb's arm and haul him up. He yells as too much weight comes down on his bad leg.

I sling Sebastian's arm around my shoulder. Leaning heavily on me, he half hops, half limps down the pier. It's like a nightmare three-legged race where the prize is not getting murdered by that boxer or by Callum Griffin once he realizes there's no way in hell he's finding that watch in the freezing-cold, pitch-black lake.

My head is still pounding. The pier seems a mile long. I keep dragging Sebastian along, wishing he weren't so tall and so damn heavy.

As we near the street at last, I hazard a look back over my shoulder. The boxer leans over the railing, probably looking for his boss. He may be shouting something; I can't tell from here.

I hope Callum drowned.

'Cause if he didn't, I have a feeling I'm going to be seeing him again very soon.

4
CALLUM

I don't know what I was thinking, jumping in after that watch.

The moment I hit the water—still fucking freezing, barely warmed by the early summer weather—the cold is like a slap to the face, waking me up.

I'm so desperate that I keep diving, eyes open, searching for a glint of gold in the black water.

Of course, there's nothing to see, nothing at all. The water under the pier is choppy, full of sand and pollutants. Even at midday the sun would hardly penetrate. At night, it might as well be motor oil.

My suit constricts my arms and legs, my dress shoes weighing me down. If I weren't a strong swimmer, I might be in serious trouble. The waves are trying to smash me against the pilings, the pillars sharp with mussels and barnacles.

I have to swim away from the pier before I can stroke back to shore. All that takes enough time that Jack is freaking out by the time I drag myself up on the sand, filthy, soaking, and angrier than I've ever been in my life.

That fucking *bitch*!

I never knew much about the youngest Gallo. Her father keeps her out of the spotlight, and she's not involved in the family business as far as I know.

When we approached her and her brother on the pier, I almost felt guilty. She looked young, barely older than Nessa. And beautiful, which shouldn't have impacted my resolve but did. Dusky skin, dark hair, narrow gray eyes slightly tilted up at the corners... She stiffened as we approached, noticing us before Sebastian did.

I felt a twinge of guilt, seeing how Sebastian stepped in front of her to protect her. That's what I would do for my sisters.

But the girl's height and hair...I remembered the person fleeing the library and began to suspect she was the one who set the fire.

She stepped forward and started yelling with the temperament and vocabulary of a sea-hardened sailor. I became certain she was the one who'd broken into our house.

Instead of handing over the watch, she flung it over the railing. That's when I realized that pretty face disguised the soul of a demon. The girl is pure evil, the worst of the whole family. She deserves whatever she gets.

The question is what am I going to do about it?

Right now, I want to murder every last one of them. But I can't afford that kind of bloodbath right before the election. So I guess I'll just have to do the next best thing—bankrupt the bastards.

They tried to burn my house down—I'm going to burn down the tower they're building over on Oak Street.

That will be the appetizer. The main meal will be wiping out every restaurant and nightclub under their control.

Fantasies of the hellfire I'm going to rain on their heads are the only thing keeping me warm while I stomp down the street in my soggy dress shoes and sopping-wet suit.

Jack jogs along next to me, embarrassed that he let a kid and his little sister get the best of us. He can tell I'm in a murderous mood, so he doesn't say anything to make it worse. He's got a bloody nose himself and a cut over his right eyebrow. Pretty humiliating for someone who won a UFC championship a couple of years back.

My shoes make a disgusting squelching sound. My custom suit smells like a dying starfish.

Fuck that girl!

I've got to change clothes before I literally lose my mind.

I head back to the house, where the party is winding down. I've missed the singer, not that I cared, except to see the look of joy on Nessa's face. Just another cock-up in this shit show of a night.

I've barely stepped foot through the door when I'm met by my furious father.

"Where the fuck have you been? Why didn't you tell me there were Gallos at our party?" He looks down at my clothes dripping dirty lake water on the spotless tiles of the entryway. "And why are you wet?"

"We had a dustup down at the pier, but I'm handling it," I tell him through gritted teeth.

"Unacceptable. Get in my office. Tell me everything."

I'm itching to get back out there and wreak fiery vengeance on those greasy guidos. Instead, I march into the office to give him a report. He's not pleased by a single word of it.

"What the fuck were you thinking?" he shouts, so close to my face that his saliva hits my cheek. "Why are you starting a gang war in the middle of your campaign?"

"They started it!" I yell back. "They tried to burn our fucking house down. They stole grandfather's watch and threw it in the lake! What do you want me to do, bake them a fucking cake?"

"Lower your voice," my father hisses at me. "People will hear you."

As if he hadn't just yelled at me twice as loud.

I take a deep breath, trying to control the anger threatening to spiral out of control. "I told you," I say, quiet and strangled. "I. Will. Handle. This."

"Absolutely not." He shakes his head. "You've already proven your incompetence. Crippling the youngest son? You've lost your mind. You know he's some star athlete? You might as well have killed him."

"Next time I will."

"You're done," he barks.

"That's not your decision!"

He shoves me hard in the chest.

That spikes my adrenaline until I practically explode, vibrating with fury.

I respect my father. He may look like a professor, but he's killed men with his bare hands. I've seen him do it. Yet he's not the only one in the room who can break bones. I'm not the obedient son I once was. We're eye to eye these days.

"Don't. Do that." I seethe.

He won't step back. "As long as I'm head of this family, you'll do what I say."

There are so many things I'd like to say to that. I swallow them. Just barely. "And what do you propose…Father?"

"This is getting out of control. I'm going to call Enzo Gallo."

"Ridiculous!"

"Shut your mouth," he snaps. "You've done enough damage. I'll see what I can do to repair this before both our families end up dead in the street."

I can't believe this. After they spat in our face in our very own house, he wants to call them up and negotiate. It's insane. Cowardly.

My father can see the mutiny in my eyes.

"Give me your phone," he says. He waits, hand outstretched, until I give it to him. It was in my pocket when I jumped in the lake, so it's useless anyway.

"I'm going to contact Enzo Gallo," he repeats. "You will stay here until I send for you. You won't speak to anyone. You won't call anyone. You won't step foot outside this house. Do you understand me?"

"You're grounding me?" I scoff. "I'm a grown man, Father. Don't be absurd."

He takes off his glasses so his pale blue eyes can bore all the way into my soul. "You are my eldest child and my only son, Callum," he says. "But I promise you, if you disobey me, I will cut you out, root and branch. I have no use for you if you can't be trusted. I will strike you down like Icarus if your ambition outstrips your orders. Do you understand?"

Every cell of my body wants to tell him to take his fucking money, his connections, and his so-called genius and shove it right up his ass.

But this man is my father. My family is everything to me—without them, I'd be a ship without a rudder or sail. I'm nothing if I'm not a Griffin.

I submit to his orders.

Inside, I'm still boiling, the heat and pressure building.

If something doesn't change between us soon, I'm going to explode.

5

AIDA

My brothers are in the basement, suiting up. Or at least Dante and Nero are. Sebastian is still at the hospital with my father. His knee is fucked, that much is certain. Ribs are broken, too. I can't bear the look of misery on his face. His season is ruined. Possibly the rest of his career. God, he may not even walk right after this.

It's all my fault.

The guilt is like a shroud, wrapping around and around and around my head. Each glance at Sebastian, each memory of my idiocy, is like another layer wrapping around my face. Soon it will smother me.

I wanted to stay with Sebastian, but Papa snapped at me to go home.

There I found Dante and Nero strapping on bulletproof vests and ammo belts, arming themselves with half the guns in the house.

"Where are you going?" I ask them nervously.

"We're going to kill Callum Griffin, obviously," Nero says. "Maybe the rest of his family, too. I haven't decided yet."

"You can't hurt Nessa," I say quickly. "She didn't do anything wrong." Neither did Riona, but I don't have the same sense of charity toward her.

"Maybe I'll just break *her* knee, then," Nero says carelessly.

"We're not doing anything to Nessa," Dante growls. "This is between us and Callum."

By the time they're ready to leave, they look like a cross between Rambo and Arnold Schwarzenegger in *Predator*.

"Let me come with you," I beg.

"No fucking way," Nero says.

"Come on!" I shout. "I'm part of this family, too. I'm the one who helped Sebastian get away, remember?"

"You're the one who got him in that mess to start with," Nero hisses at me. "Now we're going to clean it up. And you're staying here."

He shoulder checks me on his way by, knocking me roughly against the wall.

Dante is marginally kinder, equally serious. "Stay here. Don't make this worse."

I don't give a shit what they say. The moment they leave, I'm out the door, too. So I follow them up the stairs, not knowing exactly what I'm going to do but knowing I'm not going to be left here waiting like a naughty puppy.

Before Dante is even halfway up the stairs, his phone buzzes in his pocket.

He picks up, saying, "What is it?" in a tone that makes me certain it's Papa on the other end of the line. Dante waits, listening. Then he says, "I understand."

He hangs up, looking at me with the strangest expression on his face.

"What is it?"

"Take off that vest," Dante says to Nero. "Aida, go change your clothes."

"Why? Into what?"

"Something clean that doesn't look like shit," he snaps. "Do you own anything like that?"

Maybe. Possibly not, by Dante's standards.

"Fine," I say. "But where are we going?"

"We're going to meet with the Griffins. Papa said to bring you."

Well. Shit.

I didn't much enjoy my last meeting with Callum Griffin. I'm really not looking forward to a second. I doubt his temper was improved by a swim in the lake.

And what to wear to such an event?

I think the only dress I own is the Wednesday Addams costume I wore last Halloween.

I settle on a gray turtleneck and slacks, though it's too hot for that. It's about the only thing I have that's sober and clean.

Pulling the shirt over my head sets the knot on the back of my skull throbbing again, reminding me of how Callum Griffin shoved me aside like a rag doll. He's strong under that suit. I'd like to see him face off against Dante or Nero—when he doesn't have his bodyguard along for the ride.

That's what we should do—tell them we want a meeting, then ambush the motherfuckers. Callum had no problem attacking us on the pier. We should return the favor.

I'm amping myself up the whole time I'm getting dressed, practically vibrating with tension by the time I slide into the back of Dante's Escalade.

"Where are we meeting them?"

"At the Brass Anchor," Dante says shortly. "Neutral ground."

It only takes a few minutes to drive to the restaurant on Eugenie Street. It's past midnight now. The building is dark, the kitchen closed. Fergus Griffin waits out front, along with two bruisers. Wisely, he didn't bring the shit stain who stomped Sebastian's leg.

I don't see Callum anywhere. Looks like Daddy put him in time-out.

We wait in the SUV until Papa pulls up. Then all four of us get out at the same time. When Dante slides out of the front seat, I see the bulge under his jacket that shows he's still carrying. Good. I'm sure Nero is as well.

As we walk toward Fergus Griffin, his eyes fix on me alone. He looks me up and down like he's evaluating every aspect of my appearance and demeanor on some kind of chart inside his head. He doesn't seem impressed.

That's fine because to me he looks just as cold and arrogant and phony genteel as his son. I refuse to drop his gaze, stubbornly staring straight back at him without a hint of remorse.

"So this is the little arsonist," Fergus says.

I could tell him it was an accident, but that's not strictly true. And I'm not apologizing to these bastards.

Instead, I say, "Where's Callum? Did he drown?"

"Luckily for you, he did not."

Papa, Dante, and Nero close rank around me. They may be angry as hell that I got us into this mess, but they're not going to stand for anyone threatening me.

Dante grunts. "Don't talk to her."

With a little more tact, Papa says, "You wanted a meeting. Let's go inside and have one."

Fergus nods. His two men enter the restaurant first, making sure it really is empty inside. This place belongs to Ellis Foster, a restaurateur and broker who has connections to both the Irish and our family. That's why it's neutral ground.

Once we're all inside, Fergus says to my father, "I think it's best if we speak alone."

Papa slowly nods. "Wait here," he tells me and my brothers.

Papa and Fergus disappear into one of the private dining rooms, closed off by double glass doors. I can see their outlines as they sit together but can't make out any details of their expressions. And I can't hear a word they're saying.

Dante and Nero pull a couple of chairs from the nearest table. Fergus's men do the same at a table ten feet away. My brothers and I sit along the same side so we can glare across at Fergus's goons while we wait.

That keeps us occupied for about ten minutes. Looking at their ugly mugs is pretty boring. Waiting in general is boring. I'd like to get a drink from the bar, maybe even poke into the kitchen for a snack.

The second I start to rise from my seat, Dante says, "Don't even think about it," without looking at me.

"I'm hungry."

Nero has his knife out, and he's playing with it. He can do all sorts of tricks. The blade is so sharp that if he makes a mistake, he'll lop off a finger. He hasn't made one yet.

It may look like he's trying to intimidate the Griffins' men, but it's not for their benefit. He does this constantly. It's pathological.

"I don't understand how you're the one who eats the most out of any of us," Nero says without looking up from his knife.

"I don't!"

"How many times have you eaten today already? Tell the truth."

"Four," I lie.

"Bullshit." He scoffs.

"I'm not as worried about my figure as you are."

Nero is vain about his appearance. With good reason—while all my brothers are handsome, Nero has that male-model prettiness that makes girls' panties spontaneously combust. I don't know a single girl who hasn't slept with him or tried to.

That's a weird thing to know about your own brother, but we're all pretty open with each other. That's what comes of living in the same house for so long, with no mom around to keep them all from treating me like just another little brother.

And that's how I like it. I'm not anti-femininity. I just don't want to be treated like a girl. I want to be treated as myself, for better or worse. Nothing more and nothing less. Just Aida.

Aida who is bored out of her mind.

Aida who is starting to get sleepy.

Aida who is heartily regretting annoying the Griffins, if only because I'm going to be trapped here until the end of time while Fergus and Papa talk and talk and talk…

Then, finally, almost three hours later, the two patriarchs come out of the private dining room, both somber and resigned.

"Well?" Dante says.

"It's settled," Papa replies.

He sounds like a judge pronouncing a sentence. I don't like his tone one bit nor the expression on his face. He looks at me mournfully.

As we head outside, he says to Nero, "Take my car back. I'm going to drive home with Aida."

Nero nods and gets in Papa's Mercedes. Dante climbs into the driver's side of the SUV. Papa gets in the back with me.

I don't like this at all.

I turn to face him, not bothering with my seat belt. "What is it?" I say. "What did you decide?"

Papa says, "You're going to marry Callum Griffin in two weeks."

This is so ridiculous that I actually laugh—a weird barking sound that fades in the silent car.

Papa watches me, the lines on his face cutting deep. His eyes look completely black.

"You can't be serious."

"I'm absolutely serious. This is not up for debate. It's settled with the Griffins."

"I'm not getting married!" I cry. "Especially not to that psychopath."

I look to the driver's seat for Dante's support. He's staring straight forward at the road, his hands clenched on the steering wheel.

Papa looks exhausted. "This feud has been going on too long. It's an ember that smolders and smolders and continually bursts into flame, burning everything we've worked for. The last time we had an eruption, you lost two of your uncles. Our family is smaller than it should be because of the Griffins. The same is true for them. Too many lost on both sides, down through the generations. It's time to change. It's time for the opposite. We'll join together. Prosper together."

"Why do I have to get married for that to happen?" I shout. "That won't help anything! Because I'm going to murder that bastard the moment I see him!"

"You'll do as you're told!" my father barks. His patience is at an end. It's 3:00 in the morning. He's tired, and he looks old. He *is* old, really. He was forty-eight when he had me. He's nearly seventy now.

"I've spoiled you." He fixes me with those beetle-black eyes. "Let you run wild. You've never had to face the consequences of your actions. Now you will. You lit the match that started this blaze—it's you who will put it out again. Not by violence but by your own sacrifice. You'll marry Callum Griffin. You'll bear the children who will be the next generation of our mutual lineage. That is the agreement. You will uphold it."

This is some kind of fucking nightmare.

I'm getting married?

I'm fucking having babies?

And I'm supposed to do it with the man I hate more than anyone on this planet?

"He ruined Sebastian!" I shout, my last-ditch effort to express how utterly revolting Callum Griffin is to me.

"That's as much on your head as his," Papa says coldly.

There's nothing I can say in response to that.

Because deep down, I know it's true.

6
CALLUM

I'm sitting on the back deck, watching the hired staff clean the remnants of trash and supplies from the party. They've been working all night. My mother insisted it all be cleaned up immediately so none of our neighbors would have to see a hint of disarray on our grounds on their way to work in the morning.

My sisters went to bed already—Nessa flushed and happy from the excitement of the evening, and Riona pouting because I refused to tell her where our father had disappeared to.

My mother is still awake, supervising the cleanup efforts, though not actually touching anything herself.

When my father's armored car pulls into the drive, she abandons the workers and joins us back in the office. I feel like I've spent too many hours in here lately. And I don't like the look on my father's face.

"So?" I say at once. "What was the agreement?"

I'm expecting him to say we came to some kind of financial agreement or handshake deal—maybe they'll give us support with the Italian vote in the alderman election, and we'll promise them whatever permits or zoning they want on their next construction project.

When my father explains the actual deal, I stare at him like he sprouted two heads.

"You'll marry Aida Gallo in two weeks."

"That little brat?" I explode. "No fucking way."

"It's already settled."

My mother steps forward, looking alarmed. She lays her hand on my father's arm. "Fergus. Is this wise? We'll be tied to the Gallos in perpetuity."

"That's exactly the point."

"They're filthy fucking gangsters!" I spit out. "We can't have their name associated with ours. Especially not with the election coming up."

"The election will be the first benefit of this alliance." My father removes his glasses, cleaning them with the handkerchief he keeps in his breast pocket. "Your success is by no means assured when you're facing off against La Spata. The Gallos hold the key to the Italian vote. If you're married to Aida when the ballot goes out, every single one of them in this district will vote for you. They'll abandon La Spata without hesitation."

"I don't need her to win!"

"Don't be so sure. You're too confident, Callum. Arrogant, even. If the vote happened today, the results might be a coin toss. You should always secure your victory ahead of time, given the opportunity."

"Fine." I struggle to maintain my temper. "But what about after this month? Do you honestly expect me to stay married to her *forever*?"

"Yes, I do," my father says seriously. "The Gallos are Catholic, the same as us. You'll marry her, you'll be faithful to her, and you'll father children with her."

I shake my head in disbelief. "Mother, surely you have something to say about this."

She looks back and forth between my father's face and mine. Then she tucks a lock of smooth blond hair behind her ear and sighs. "If the deal was struck, we will abide by it."

I should have known. She always sides with Father.

Still, I sputter, "W-what? You can't—"

She cuts me off with a glance. "Callum, it's time for you to become the man you profess to be. I've watched you play around with these girls you date—models and socialites. You seem to deliberately pick the shallowest and most empty-headed girls."

I scowl, folding my arms across my chest. It never mattered who I dated as long as they looked good on my arm and didn't embarrass me at parties. Since I never wanted anything serious, it made sense to find girls who were just looking for fun.

"I didn't know I was supposed to be finding a broodmare. I thought you'd want me to find the right girl and fall in love like a normal person."

"Is that what you think we did?" my mother says quietly.

I pause. I actually have no idea how my parents met. I never asked them.

She glances at my father. "Fergus and I had an 'arranged marriage,' if you want to call it that. More accurately, our parents, who were older and wiser than us, and who knew us better than we knew ourselves, arranged the match. Because they knew we would be good partners for each other, and because it was an alliance that benefited both our families. There were challenges, at first."

A significant look passes between my parents. A little ruefulness and amusement from both of them.

"But in the end, our match is what made us the people we are today," my father says.

This is fucking bananas. I've never heard this before.

"That's completely different!" I tell them. "You were from the same culture, the same background. The Gallos are mobsters. They're old-school, in the worst sense of the word."

"That's part of the value they'll provide," my father says bluntly. "As we've grown in wealth and influence, we've lost our edge. You're my only son. Your mother lost both her brothers. There are precious few men on my side of the family. In pure muscle, we only have what we pay for. You can never be sure of hired guns' loyalties—there's always someone willing to pay more. Since Zajac took over, the *Braterstwo* is becoming a serious threat to us, something we can't necessarily deal with on our own. The Italians have the same problem. With our two families aligned, the Butcher won't dare strike at either of us."

"Great," I say. "But who's going to protect me from my betrothed? That girl is a wild animal. Can you imagine her as a politician's wife? I doubt she even knows how to walk in heels."

"Then you'll teach her," my mother says.

"I don't know how to walk in heels either. How exactly am I supposed to teach her to be a lady, Mother?"

"She's young and malleable," my father says. "You'll train her, mold her into what she needs to be in order to stand by your side and support your career."

Young and malleable? I really don't think my father got a good look at this girl. Young, she may be. But she's about as malleable as cast iron.

"What an exciting challenge," I say through gritted teeth. "I can't wait to get started."

"Good," my father says. "You'll have your chance at your engagement party next week."

"Engagement party?" This is a fucking joke. I just found out about this five minutes ago, and apparently they're already planning the public announcement.

My mother says, "You'll have to agree on your cover story with Aida. Something like, you started dating casually starting about eighteen months ago. It got serious last fall. You'd planned to wait until after the election to marry but decided you just couldn't wait anymore."

"Maybe you'd better just write the press release for me, Mother. Do my wedding vows, too, while you're at it."

"Don't be disrespectful," my father snaps.

"I wouldn't dream of it. Though I doubt the same can be said of my future bride."

That may be the one silver lining of this fucking maelstrom— watching my parents deal with the little hellcat they're bringing into this family.

7

AIDA

My brothers are in uproar over my father's insane plan.

Dante didn't say anything on the drive home, but I heard him arguing with Papa for hours afterward, the two shut up together in the study.

It was pointless. Papa's stubborn as a mule. A Sicilian mule that only eats thistles and will kick you in the teeth if you get too close. Once his mind is made up, not even the trumpets of Judgment Day could change it.

Honestly, Armageddon would be a welcome respite from what's actually about to happen.

The very first day after the deal is struck, I get a message from Imogen Griffin telling me about an engagement party on Wednesday night. An engagement party! As if there's something to celebrate here and not just a slow-motion train wreck.

She also shipped me a ring in a box.

I fucking hate it, of course. It's a big old square diamond on a bedazzled band, chunky and sure to bang against everything. I keep it shut in its box on my nightstand because I have no intention of wearing it before I absolutely have to.

The only good thing in this mountain of shit is that at least Sebastian is doing a little better. He had to have surgery to reconstruct his ACL. We got the best doctor in the city, the same one who fixed Derrick Rose's knee. So we're hoping he'll be up and around again before long.

In the meantime, I've been going to the hospital to visit him every day. I brought him all his favorite snacks—Reese's Peanut Butter Cups, string cheese, and salted cashews—and his schoolbooks.

"Have you ever opened these before?" I tease him, laying the textbooks on his nightstand.

"Once or twice," he says, grinning from the hospital bed.

The little nightie they gave him to wear is ridiculously tiny on his giant body. His long legs stretch out from under it, his bandaged knee propped up with a pillow.

"You don't walk around in that, do you?" I ask him.

"Only when the hot nurse is on duty." He winks.

"Gross."

"You better get used to all things romantic. Since you're about to be a blushing bride…"

"Don't joke about that," I snap.

Seb gives me a sympathetic look. "Are you worried?"

"No!" I say at once, though it's a complete lie. "They're the ones who should be worried. Callum, especially. I'm gonna strangle him in his sleep the first chance I get."

"Don't do anything stupid," Sebastian warns me. "This is serious, Aida. It's not like your semester in Spain or that internship you took with Pepsi. You can't just skip out of this if you don't like it."

"I know that. I know exactly how trapped I'm about to be."

Sebastian frowns, hating to see me upset. "Have you talked to Papa? Maybe if you tell him—"

"It's pointless. Dante argued with him all night. He's not going to listen to anything I have to say."

I look at Sebastian's knee, bandaged to twice its normal size and bruised all the way up the thigh. "Anyway," I say quietly, "I brought this on myself. Papa's right—I made this mess. Now I've got to fix it."

"Don't be a martyr just 'cause my leg got fucked. You marrying that psychopath isn't going to fix it."

"It won't fix your knee. But it may stop anything else from happening."

The silence between us is heavy. By the time Seb leaves the hospital, a lot of things will have changed. For both of us.

I start to say, "I'm really sorry that—"

"Don't apologize again. I mean it. First off, it wasn't your fault."

"Yes, it was."

"Stop arguing! No, it wasn't. We all chose to go to the party. You didn't make that meathead stomp on me. And second, even if it were your fault, I wouldn't care. I've got two knees but only one sister."

I can't help snorting at that. "That's really sweet, Seb."

"It's true. So come here."

I come closer to the bed. Sebastian gives me a side-arm hug. I rest my chin on his hair, which is messier and curlier than ever. It feels like lamb's wool.

Seb says, "Quit beating yourself up about it. I'll be fine. You just figure out a way to get along with the Griffins. Going into this like you're going into battle is only going to make things harder."

That's the only way I know how to do it, though—head down, covered in armor. I approach everything as a fight.

"They've planned some god-awful engagement party tomorrow night…"

"I wish I could come," Sebastian says wistfully. "Them and us, all forced to dress up fancy and be nice to each other. I'd love to see it. Take pictures for me at least."

"I don't think they'll show up in a photo. Bunch of blood-sucking vampires."

Sebastian shakes his head at me.

I ask him, "You want any water or anything before I go?"

"Nah. But if the hot redheaded nurse is out there, tell her I look all pale and sweaty and probably need a sponge bath."

"No way," I tell him. "And also, still gross."

"Can't blame a guy for trying." He leans back against his pillow, propping up his head with his arms.

All too soon, it's time for the Griffins' stupid engagement party. I feel like these people would throw a party for the opening of an envelope. They're so ridiculous and showy.

I'm supposed to behave myself and put on a good face. This will be the first test of my compliance.

I wish I had someone to get ready with. I loved growing up with all brothers, but it's times like this that a little feminine company wouldn't go amiss.

It would be nice if I had someone to assure me I don't look like half-melted sherbet in this stupid dress. It's yellow with scallops along the hem. It looked all right on the mannequin, but now that I'm trying it on at home, I feel like a little kid all dressed up for Easter. All I need is a straw basket over my arm.

Papa nods in approval when he sees it. "Very good."

He's wearing a suit. Dante has on a black T-shirt and jeans, and Nero's wearing a leather jacket. My brothers are refusing to dress up on principle. A silent protest. I wish I could do the same.

We drive together to Shoreside, where the Griffins are hosting the party. The restaurant is already packed with guests. I recognize more people than I expected—our families run in some of the same circles, and I did go to the same school as Nessa and Riona, though I was between the two of them and not in the same grade.

I wonder if Callum went there, too. Then I crush that thought. I don't care where Callum went. I'm not curious about him in the slightest.

Our upcoming nuptials don't seem real to me at all. I feel like the punishment is the lead-up—the pretense that this is actually going to happen. Surely one or both our families will call it off at the last minute when they see we've learned our lesson.

Until that happens, I just have to grin and bear it. Put on a phony face of cooperation so they can see I've had my wrist successfully slapped.

The only thing keeping me going is my morbid amusement that Callum Griffin is going to have to pretend to be in love with me tonight, just like I'm going to have to do with him.

It's a joke to me, but I get the impression that for a stuck-up bastard like him, this will be pure torture. He probably thought he would marry some perfect prissy Hilton or Rockefeller heir. Instead, he gets me on his arm. He has to pretend to adore me, while the whole time, he's dying to wring my neck.

Actually, this could be the perfect opportunity to put the screws to him. He won't be able to do anything in front of all these people. I should see how far I can push him before he snaps.

First, I need a little refreshment to get me through this pony show.

I shake off my father and brothers, heading straight to the bar. Shoreside may be a bit snooty, but it's got a fun resort kinda vibe, and they're famous for their summery cocktails. Especially the Kentucky Kiss, which is bourbon, lemon, fresh strawberry purée, and a splash of maple syrup, poured over ice with a dumb little paper umbrella on top.

When I order it, the bartender shakes his head regretfully. "Sorry, no Kentucky Kisses."

"What about a strawberry daiquiri?"

"No can do. We can't make anything with strawberries."

"Did your truck get hijacked on the way up from Mexico?"

"Nah." He fills a shaker with ice and starts making a martini for somebody else while I scan the drink menu. "It's just for this party—I guess the dude is allergic?"

"What dude?"

"The one gettin' married."

I set my menu down, alight with interest. "He is?"

"Yeah, his mom was makin' a big deal out of it. Sayin' no straw-berries for anybody in the whole place. Like someone's gonna try and hide one in his drink."

Well, now they may...

"Very interesting," I say. "I'll take one of those martinis."

He pours the chilled vodka into a glass and slides it to me. "Take this one. I can make another."

"Thanks." I hold it up in a cheers motion.

I leave him a five-dollar tip, tickled to think the political robot has a weakness after all. Shiny red kryptonite. Another thing to needle him about.

That's my plan, until I actually see Callum.

He really does remind me of a vampire. Lean, pale, dark suit, eyes inhumanly blue. An expression both keenly sharp and highly disdainful. It must be difficult for him to be charming for his work. I wonder if he watches actual humans and tries to emulate them. If he does, he's failing miserably. Everyone around him is chatting and laughing, while he's gripping his drink like he wants to crush it in his hand. He's got large hands, long, slim fingers.

When he catches sight of me, he shows some emotion at last— pure, unadulterated hatred. It burns out of him in a straight line directly at me.

I walk right up to him, bold as brass, so he knows he can't intim-idate me.

"Better watch it, *my love*," I whisper. "We're supposed to be celebrating our engagement. Yet you look completely miserable."

"Aida Gallo," he hisses back. "I'm relieved to see you're at least aware of the concept of dressing up, even if your execution is trash."

I keep my smile firmly plastered in place, not letting him see that stung a little. I hadn't realized until I walked right up to him how much he towers over me, even with these stupid heels. I'm kind of wishing I hadn't stood so close. But I'm not going to take a step back now. That would show weakness.

And anyway, I'm used to scary-looking men, thanks to my brothers. In fact, Callum Griffin doesn't have any of the scars or permanently swollen knuckles that hint at what my brothers get up to. His hands are perfectly smooth. He's just a rich kid after all. I have to remember that.

His eye is drawn to the showy ring on my left hand. I put it on for the first time tonight, and I already feel strangled by it. I hate what it means, and I hate how it draws attention. Callum's lips almost disappear as they blanch at the sight of it. He looks nauseated.

Well, good. I'm glad it makes him suffer, too.

Without warning, Callum wraps his arm around my waist and jerks me close. It's so sudden and unexpected that I almost haul off and smack him, thinking he's attacking me. It's only after a squealing blond girl runs up to us that I catch on to his game.

She's about five two, wearing a pink sundress with a matching silk scarf around her neck. She's trailed by a bearded man carrying a large Hermès bag that I can only assume doesn't belong to him, since it really doesn't match his polo shirt.

"Cal!" she cries, grabbing his arms and stretching on tiptoe to kiss his cheek.

All this is par for the course at Shoreside. It's Callum's reaction that astonishes me.

His chilly expression transforms into a charming smile, and he says, "There they are! My favorite newlyweds. Any tips for us now that you're on the other side?"

It really is incredible how the politician's mask slides into place on his handsome face. It looks totally natural—except for the rigidness of his smile. I had no idea he was so good at this.

Makes sense, I guess. But it's disturbing how easily he puts on the cheerfulness and charm. I've never seen anything like it.

The woman laughs, resting her manicured hand lightly on Callum's arm. I can see her engagement ring, the rock almost tipping her hand sideways. Jesus Christ, I think I just found the iceberg that sank the *Titanic*.

"Oh, Cal!" she says with a twittering laugh. "It's only been a month for us, so all I've learned so far is that you shouldn't register at Kneen & Co.! What a nightmare trying to return the things we didn't want. I asked for the Marie Daage Aloe custom dinnerware, but I immediately regretted it once I saw the new spring pattern. Of course, you don't care about that—you'll probably leave it all to your fiancée to handle."

Now she spares me a glance. The tiniest of lines struggles to appear between her eyebrows, valiantly fighting against the mass amounts of Botox attempting to smooth it back out again.

"I don't think we've ever met. I'm Christina Huntley-Hart. This is my husband, Geoffrey Hart."

She holds out a hand, limp and overhand. I have to fight the urge to bow and kiss it with a big smack like an earl in an old-timey movie. Instead, I just give it a weird sideways squeeze before letting go as quickly as possible.

"Aida," I reply.

"Aida…?"

"Aida Gallo," Callum supplies.

That forehead line struggles to reappear again. "I don't think I know the Gallos… Are you members at the North Shore Country Club?"

"No!" I say, matching her voice in pitch and phoniness. "Should we join? I fear my tennis game has been suffering ever so much…"

She stares like she has a slight suspicion I'm making fun of her but doesn't believe that could possibly be true.

Callum's hand tightens painfully around my waist. It's hard not to wince. "Aida loves tennis. She's so athletic."

Christina smiles uncertainly. "Cal—remember when we played together in Florence? You were my favorite doubles partner of that trip."

It's funny. I couldn't give two shits if Christina Cuntley-Hart wants to flirt with Callum. They might have fucked last week for all I know. But I find it pretty fucking disrespectful that she's doing it right in front of my face.

I look over at poor Geoffrey Hart to see what he thinks about it. He hasn't spoken one word so far. He's got his eye on the television over the bar, which is playing highlights from the Cubs game. He's holding Christina's purse in both hands with an expression on his face like this month of marriage has been the longest thirty days of his life.

"Hey, Geoff," I call, "did they let you play, too, or did you just carry the rackets?"

Geoffrey gives a little snort. "I wasn't on that particular trip."

"Too bad. You missed seeing *Cal* score with Christina."

Now Christina's definitely pissed. She narrows her eyes, nostrils flared. "Well," she says flatly. "Congratulations again. Looks like you've got quite the catch, Cal."

As soon as she sweeps away with Geoffrey in her wake, Callum lets go of my waist and seizes my arm instead, digging his fingers into my flesh.

"What the fuck do you think you're doing?"

"Are those your actual friends? She should have just gotten one of those little dogs for her purse. Geoff is an awkward accessory…"

"Grow up." Callum shakes his head in disgust. "The Huntleys organized a massive fundraiser for me last year. I've known Christina since grade school."

"Known her? Or fucked her? Because if you haven't done it yet, you'd better get to it before she starts humping your leg in public."

"Oh my god." Callum presses his fingers against the bridge of his nose. "I can't believe this. I'm marrying a child. And not a normal child—a demon hell spawn, like Chucky or the Children of the Corn..."

I try to jerk my arm away from him. His fingers dig in harder. I'm going to have to really make a scene to get loose, and I'm not quite ready to blow this thing up just yet.

Instead, I signal to the nearest waiter and take a glass of champagne off his tray. I take a sip before saying to Callum, quietly and calmly, "If you don't let go of me, I'm going to throw this drink in your face."

He releases me, paler than ever from anger.

He leans right into my face. "You think you're the only one who can fuck with my plans? Don't forget you're going to be moving into *my* house. I can make your life a living nightmare from the moment you wake up in the morning until I allow you to lay your head down again at night. I really don't think you want to start a war with me."

My hand is itching to fling that champagne right in his face, to show him exactly what I think of that.

I manage to restrain myself. Just barely. I smile up at him and say, "Amid chaos, there is also opportunity."

Callum stares at me blankly. "What...what the fuck are you talking about? Does that mean you're going to make the best of this mess?"

"Sure. What else can I do?"

Actually, it's a quote from *The Art of War*. Here's another one I like:

"Let your plans be dark and impenetrable as night, and when you move, fall like a thunderbolt."

8
CALLUM

After that first bit of brattiness, Aida calms and starts to behave herself. Or at least she does her best. She puts on a smile and chats with reasonable civility to the stream of guests who come up to congratulate us.

It's pretty fucking awkward explaining to friends and family that I'm about to marry this girl they've never even heard of, let alone met. Again and again, I tell them, "We kept things private. It was romantic, keeping it between the two of us. But now we can't wait anymore; we want to get married."

I see more than a few people glance down at Aida's stomach to see if there's a reason we're in such a rush.

Aida puts those rumors to rest by drinking her weight in champagne. As she reaches for another glass, I snatch it out of her hand and slug it down myself instead.

"You've had enough."

"I decide when I've had enough," she says stubbornly. "It takes more than a little glorified ginger ale to get me drunk."

She's already less steady on her high heels, and she was none too steady to begin with.

I'm relieved she wore a dress, though the one she picked looks cheap and overly bright. What's wrong with these people? Don't they have the money to buy decent clothes?

Her brothers look like complete thugs. One's wearing a fucking T-shirt and jeans; the other's kitted up like James Dean. Dante is skulking around the room like he expects a bomb to go off any minute, and Nero's chatting up the bartender like he's planning to take her upstairs. Maybe he will, that sleazy shit. I'm pretty sure he fucked Nora Albright in my house.

At least Enzo Gallo is properly attired for the occasion, and properly mannered. He seems to know almost as many people here as I do. Not the new-money socialites, but anybody deeply connected to old Chicago. They shake his hand with respect. Maybe my father wasn't entirely wrong about the benefits of this alliance.

My parents come over to check on us, Madeline Breck alongside them. Madeline is almost seventy years old, Black, with close-cropped gray hair, a plain suit, and sensible shoes. She's got a calm and intelligent face. If you were stupid, you might think she's a friendly grandmother type. In actuality, she's one of the most powerful people in Chicago.

As president of the Cook County Board of Commissioners, she controls the purse strings of massive publicly funded projects, from parks to infrastructure. She also has an iron grip on the liberal Democrats of Chicago. Without ever appearing to stick her finger in the pie, she manages to get whomever she wants appointed to key positions like city treasurer or state's attorney.

She's shrewd and subtle and not at all someone I want to cross. So I'm almost sick at the thought of Aida saying something obnoxious in front of her.

As she approaches, I hiss to Aida, "Behave yourself. That's Madeline—"

"I know who she is," she interrupts, rolling her eyes.

"Madeline," my father says, "you know our son, Callum. He'll be running for the alderman seat in the Forty-Third Ward in a few weeks' time."

"Excellent," Madeline says. "It's about time we had someone in there with some vision."

"What sort of vision are you hoping for?" I ask her. "Maybe someone who can keep Lincoln Park in one piece?"

She smirks. "Who told you I was against the remapping?"

"A little bird. If I become alderman, I won't want Lincoln Park chopped up and portioned out. Luckily, I'm close personal friends with the head of the rules committee."

"Jeremy Ross is stubborn," Madeline says, peering at me over her glasses like she thinks I don't actually have any sway over him.

"He's stubborn as hell, but he owes me a favor. And not a small one either."

"Well, I only want what's best for the neighborhood," she says magnanimously.

"Of course. I feel exactly the same. Lincoln Park has history. We can't allow it to be farmed out to other districts that won't see it as a priority."

"That's the spirit," she says, patting my arm. "Nice to meet you, dear," she says to Aida, then walks away.

I'm a little confused about why she ended our conversation so abruptly. I'm pretty sure we both want the same thing.

Aida takes another swig of the drink she swiped from somewhere. "You know she doesn't give a fuck about Lincoln Park."

My father whips his head around. "What are you talking about?"

"She gets kickbacks on the garbage service in the Forty-Fourth and Thirty-Second Wards," Aida says, as if it's obvious. "You add half of Lincoln Park to that, and you double the value. She's just opposing the remapping in public because it's unpopular."

A glance passes between my parents.

"I better talk to Marty Rico," my mother says.

As they split off to confirm, Aida laughs softly.

"How did you know that?" I ask.

"Looks like the Griffins aren't so well-connected after all," she says. "I guess nobody was talking about it at the North Shore Country Club."

"How would you get her to come around, if you're so smart?" I demand.

"Why should I tell you?" Aida narrows her gray eyes at me, taking another sip of her drink. She looks sly and malicious when she does that, like some sort of jungle cat high in the branches, about to drop on my head.

"Well," I say, "in another week's time, what's mine is yours. Which means my successes…and my failures…will all be on your shoulders, too. So it makes sense for you to help me."

She sets her empty glass on the nearest planter, color coming into her cheeks. "You think I'm going to be some little woman standing behind you, working to help launch your bright, shiny star?"

"I don't *need* your help," I tell her, "but if we're going to be stuck together, we might as well work together."

"I'm not your accessory!" she says hotly.

"Oh, you've got something better to do with your time? As far as I can tell, you don't do shit in your own family's business. You just fuck around taking classes at Loyola. What do you care about, besides sneaking into other people's parties?"

She stares up at me, angry and, for once, silenced. At last she mutters, "I don't have to explain myself to you."

A weak retort, compared to her usual. I must have struck a nerve. So I push her just a little further. "I doubt you'd have anything to say."

She's quivering with anger. Aida has a temper—I really shouldn't needle her like that, especially not in a public place where I've got more to lose from her flying off the handle than she does.

She surprises me by taking a breath, squaring her shoulders. "You're trying to goad me. I'll tell you the answer because it doesn't matter, and you won't be able to do it anyway. Madeline Breck cares about making money, end of story. She gets a chop out of a hundred different utility and construction deals. But if she's passionate about anything, it's cops shooting people. If you can convince her you're actually going to do something about that, you might get her on board. But you can't 'cause then you'll lose the support of the police union and probably the firefighters, too."

That's…not the worst idea in the world. Aida's probably right. But she's also right that it would be difficult to impress Madeline without pissing off the police union.

"That's actually pretty smart."

"Oh, thank you! I'm so honored."

Right as she's in the middle of rolling her eyes, Aida catches sight of someone coming toward us. She whips around like she's going to find somewhere to hide, despite the fact this party is in our honor and she's dressed about as subtly as a sunflower.

Oliver Castle strolls over, his hands stuffed in his pockets, a big stupid grin plastered across his face. I've known him since college. Never been a fan. He was a football star, and he's obviously still been eating like one, despite the fact he works at his father's investment firm now. His big, beefy frame is just starting to get soft, though he still looks strong. He's extra tan, probably from some recent trip he's sure to tell me all about.

As he draws close, I see his attention is entirely fixed on Aida.

"I couldn't believe it when I heard."

"Hey, Ollie," she says, turning around unenthusiastically.

Ollie?

"I'm hurt, Aida. You get engaged, and you don't even call to tell me?"

"Why would I call you?" she says flatly. "I spent three months ignoring your messages and calls. When you're trying to train a dog, you can't give it a single treat, or it'll keep barking and slobbering on you forever."

I expect Oliver to be offended. He just grins and sidles all the closer to Aida until he's towering over her. It's pissing me off how close he's standing and how he hasn't even acknowledged me yet.

"There's the bite I love," Oliver says. "Never change, Aida."

"I didn't know you two knew each other."

"Oh, we go way back," Oliver drawls, still looking at Aida.

I step between the two of them, partially cutting off his view. "Well, I guess we'll be seeing you at the *wedding*, then," I say, not bothering to hide the irritation in my voice.

"I guess so." Oliver finally spares me a glance. "Funny, I never pictured you two together. Aida's so wild. I didn't think she'd let one of the glitterati put a ring on her finger."

"Just because you didn't manage it doesn't mean no one else can," I growl.

Aida interrupts. "As thrilling as this is, I think I'm gonna go get some food."

She pushes past me, leaving us alone together.

Without Aida, the tension dissipates. I find myself annoyed that I'm even talking to Oliver, let alone getting riled up about the fact he apparently used to date my fake fiancée. Why should I give a fuck who Aida dated before me? She could have banged the whole Bears starting lineup, and what would it matter? Our arrangement is business, nothing more.

Still, it pisses me off when Oliver says, "Good luck, Griffin. She's a live one."

"I doubt you know a fucking thing about what she is or isn't," I snap.

Oliver raises his hands in mock apology. "Sure, sure. I bet you've got it totally under control." He's giving me a wicked grin, like he can't wait to see how Aida's going to fuck up my life. Unfortunately, I think he may be right.

I go find Riona—she'll know the scoop on this.

"You know Oliver Castle?" I ask her.

"Yeah." She tucks back a lock of her bright red hair. She has her phone out, checking work emails in the intervals between socializing. Riona got her law degree, mostly to prove she could. Now she works for the firm that handles all our business interests.

"Did Castle use to date Aida?"

Riona raises her eyebrows. They're as red as her hair. "*Yeah*," she says, like I asked her if sushi's made of rice. "They dated for over a year. He was *obsessed* with her. Completely head over heels, making a fool of himself, barely working, chasing her everywhere she went. She went to Malta on vacation, and he ditched his job in the middle of some huge acquisition. His father was furious."

"So what happened?"

"She dumped him out of nowhere. Nobody could figure it out. Oliver's a catch—only child, going to inherit Keystone Capital. Plus, he's good-looking, charming enough… She dumped him on his ass, wouldn't tell anyone the reason."

"Well, he's a fucking moron, for one."

Riona stares at me. "Is that *jealousy*?" she says in disbelief.

"No." I scowl. "I just don't like finding out that my *fiancée* dated that ape. This is the problem with marrying a fucking stranger!"

"Lower your voice," Riona says coldly. "None of us likes this, but since our parents have apparently gone insane, we've got to make the best of it."

At least Riona's on my side.

It's a shame my father always pits us against each other, because I do respect her. She's disciplined, hardworking, intelligent. But she's always nipping at my heels, waiting for me to fail so she can take my place.

Well, that ain't happening. I'm powering through this, no matter how many trust-fund idiots Aida dated before me.

"Listen," I say to Riona. "I've got to get in good with Madeline Breck. Can you work some kind of deal with Callahan?"

I explain the whole thing to her.

William Callahan is the chief of police in my district. It'd be better if I could get the superintendent of the whole city on my side, but it's a start at least. To show Madeline Breck I've got sway with the cops.

Riona listens, skeptical. "That's a tough sell."

"Try, at least."

She nods, resolute. That's the perfectionist in her. She can't turn down an assignment.

She leaves to talk to Callahan again, and Dante Gallo takes her place. He's got one of those faces that always looks unshaven, with dark shadows all around his lips and jaw. He's got a brutal, uncut look to his face and frame. Hunched and defensive, like a fighter. I'm not intimidated by him—I'm not intimidated by anyone. But if I had to face off against one of Aida's brothers, I wouldn't want it to be Dante.

I already know why he came over here to talk to me.

Sure enough, Dante looks me in the eye, saying, "My father may be handing Aida over to you people, but don't think for a second that we're forgetting about her. She's my baby sister. If you lay one finger on her in a way she doesn't like—"

I cut him off. "Save it. I have no intention of abusing Aida."

"Good," he growls.

But now it's me who takes a step closer to him. "Let me tell *you* something. When she says those vows to me, she becomes my wife. She belongs to me. What happens to her isn't your concern anymore. She answers to me. What goes on between us is my business, not yours."

Dante's shoulders hunch all the more. He clenches two fists the size of grapefruits. "She'll always be my business," he snarls.

"I don't know what you're worried about. I'm pretty sure she can take care of herself."

Dante scowls. "Yes, she can. That doesn't mean she's unbreakable."

I look across the room to where Aida's talking to Nero. He apparently didn't close the deal with the bartender. Aida seems to be ribbing him about it. While I watch, she throws back her head and laughs so loud that I can hear it all the way over here. Nero scowls and punches her hard on the shoulder. Aida just laughs harder.

"She'll be fine," I say to Dante.

"Treat her with respect," he says threateningly.

"Worry about your own side of the family," I say coldly. "If we're chained together, you fucking savages need to learn to act civilized. I'll kill every last one of you before I let you drag us down."

"Just so long as we understand each other." Dante turns and stomps away.

I look around for another drink.

In the past week, I've had enough of the Gallos to last me a lifetime. And we're only getting started in our new "close-knit" relationship.

Dante can take his protective older brother schtick and shove it up his ass.

He thinks Aida has some vulnerable side?

I doubt it.

She's an animal, just like her brothers.

Which means she needs to be broken.

Oliver wasn't able to tame her—she ran right over him. Made a fool of him, publicly. Well, she's not doing that to me. If Aida is a rock, then I'm the fucking ocean. And I'm going to beat against her, over and over, wearing her down one pebble at a time. Until I've broken her up and swallowed her whole.

9

AIDA

The whole next week is wasted on idiotic wedding planning. Imogen Griffin handles most of it because the Griffins are control freaks and my family doesn't give a shit what the wedding looks like. Still, she expects me to approve seating arrangements and flowers and meal plans like I give a crap about any of it.

Spending time with Callum's family is bizarre. I still can't shake the feeling they're going to jump me anytime I'm alone with them. Yet there's this make-believe between us where they pretend like all this is genuine. I'm supposed to play along like I'm actually some blushing bride-to-be.

I can't figure out Imogen. From the outside, she looks like your typical wealthy socialite: blond, perfectly coiffed, always speaking in cultured tones. But I can tell she's intelligent, and I suspect she's much more heavily involved in the Griffins' business than she lets on.

The wedding will be small since it's taking place so quickly. She still insists I need a proper dress. That's why I'm in Bella Bianca, trying on wedding gowns in front of Nessa, Riona, and Imogen.

I don't have any female family members to invite, not that I'd want to involve them in this farce anyway.

Nessa is the most excited, pulling down dress after dress for me to try on, then clapping and squealing over each one. They're all puffy princess dresses and ball gowns, ridiculously exaggerated like a cartoon brought to life. Half the time, I get lost in the tulle. Nessa has to pull down the layers and turn it all around, then zip me up.

Even though I hate every single dress, I can't help laughing at her infectious energy. She's so sweet, with her big green eyes and her pink cheeks.

"Why don't you try some on, too?" I ask her.

"Oh no." She shakes her head, blushing hard enough to drown out her freckles. "I couldn't do that."

"Why not? There are a million of them. It'll go way faster if you help me."

"Well…"

I can see she's dying to do it. I shove one of the puffiest dresses into her arms.

"Come on, let's see it."

Nessa goes to change. Sighing with resignation, I pull on dress number sixty-seven. It weighs about a hundred pounds and has a train longer than Princess Diana's.

Nessa comes out looking like the dancer she is, her slender neck rising from the bodice of the gown, the skirt as puffy as a tutu.

"What do you think?" she says, twirling on the raised dais. Now she looks like one of those music box ballerinas.

"I think you're the one who should be getting married. It suits you way better."

I reach out my hands so we can dance around together. Our skirts are so huge that we have to bend way over to even reach each other. Nessa falls off the dais, landing unharmed in the massive puff of her own skirt. We both burst out laughing.

Riona watches us, unsmiling. "Hurry up. I haven't got all day to spend on this."

"Just pick one, then," I bark back at her. "I don't give a shit which dress I wear."

"It's your wedding dress," Imogen says, in her calm, cultured voice. "It has to speak to you. It has to resonate. Then someday you can pass it down to your own daughter."

My stomach lurches. She's talking about some fictional daughter I'm supposed to have with Callum Griffin. The idea of waddling around pregnant with his baby makes me want to rip off this skirt and sprint out of the store. This place is stuffed with so much pure-white tulle and beading, sequins, and lace that I can barely breathe.

"I really don't care." I press my hand against my side. "I'm not that into dresses. Or clothes in general."

"That's obvious," Riona says tartly.

"Yeah," I snap, "I don't dress like Corporate Barbie. How's that working out for you, by the way? Does your dad let you take notes during his meetings, or do you just stand there looking pretty?"

Riona's face turns as red as her hair.

Imogen interrupts before Riona can retort. "Maybe something a little simpler would appeal to you, Aida." She motions to the attendant, requesting several dresses by number and designer name. She obviously did her research before she came. I don't care what she picked out. I just want this to be over. I've never pulled up so many zippers in my life.

I don't know what happened to my mother's dress. But I do know what it looked like—I have a picture of her on her wedding day. She's sitting in a gondola in Venice, right at the bow of the boat, the long lace train trailing over the edge, almost touching the pale green water. She's looking right at the camera, haughty and elegant.

Actually, one of the dresses Imogen selected is a little like my mother's—caplet sleeves trailing off the shoulders. A fitted bodice with a sweetheart neckline. Old-fashioned lace but no puffiness. Just simple smooth lines.

"I like this one," I say hesitantly.

Imogen agrees. "That off-white suits you."

"You look *stunning*," Nessa says.

Even Riona doesn't have anything disparaging to say. She just tilts up her chin and nods.

"Let's wrap it up!" I say.

The attendant takes the dress, fretting over the fact we don't have time to get it altered before the wedding.

"It fits fine," I assure her.

"Yes, but if you took it in just a little at the bust—"

"I don't care." I shove it into her arms. "It's good enough."

"I've booked girls to do your hair and makeup the morning of the wedding," Imogen tells me.

That sounds like way more fuss than necessary, but I force myself to smile and nod. It's not worth fighting over—there'll be plenty of things to brawl about later.

"Callum booked a spa day for you before the wedding," Imogen says.

"That's really not necessary."

"Of course it is! You'll want to relax and be pampered."

I don't like relaxing or being pampered.

This is how Imogen Griffin gets her way, I'm sure—telling you how it's going to be with a light tone and polite smile on her face. Acting like any resistance would be the height of uncouthness so you're shamed into going along.

"I'm busy," I tell her.

"It's already booked. I'll send a car around at nine to pick you up."

I'm about to say, *I won't be there*, but I force myself to take a deep breath and swallow the instinctive rebelliousness. It's just a spa day. They're trying to be nice in their own pushy, prissy way.

"Thank you," I say through gritted teeth.

Imogen gives me a tight smile. "You'll be the perfect bride."

It sounds more like a threat than a compliment.

Each day whips by faster than the one before. When the wedding was two weeks away, it seemed like a lifetime. Like anything could happen to call it off.

But it's only three days away. Then two. Then it's actually happening tomorrow, and I'm waiting outside my house for Imogen's stupid town car to pick me up to take me to some spa day that I neither want nor need.

They want to pluck me and exfoliate me and rub off all my rough edges, make me some smooth, soft little wifey for the scion of their family. The great Callum Griffin.

He's their JFK, and I'm supposed to be their Jackie Kennedy.

I'd rather be Lee Harvey Oswald.

Still, I stuff down all my irritation and let the driver take me to a posh spa on Walton Street.

It's not so bad to begin with. Callum really did book the works. The aestheticians soak my feet and paint my fingers and toes. They have me sit in a giant mud bath with a completely different sort of mud plastered all over my face. Then they put a conditioning wrap on my hair and oil me up like a Thanksgiving turkey. They cover me in hot stones, then take them off again and rub and pummel every inch of my body.

Since I don't give a fig about being naked, this is my favorite part. I've got two ladies with their four hands all over me, rubbing and massaging and working out every last stress-induced knot that's burrowed its way into my neck, my back, and even my arms and legs. Seeing as Callum is the one who initiated that stress in the first place, I guess it's only fitting that he should pay to have it rubbed out again.

It's so delightfully relaxing that I start to fall asleep, lulled by the women's hands on my skin and the faux ocean sounds being pumped through the speakers.

I wake to blinding pain in my crotch region. The aesthetician stands over me, holding a waxing strip bearing the little hairs that used to be attached to my body.

"What the fuck?" I shriek.

"It can sting a little," she says in a completely unsympathetic tone.

I look down at my lady bits, which are now completely bald on the left side. *"What the hell are you doing?"*

"Your Brazilian," she says, slapping another wax strip down on the right side.

I smack her hand away. "I don't want a fucking Brazilian! I don't want to be waxed at all."

"Well, it was on the service list." She picks up her clipboard and hands it to me, like that's going to ease the burning fire on the newly bald and horribly sensitive parts of my groin.

"I didn't set the damn service list!" I shout, tossing down the clipboard. "And I don't want you practicing your torture techniques on my crotch."

"The wax is already set," she says, pointing to the strip she just slapped down. "It has to come off one way or another."

I try to pry up the edge of the cloth strip. She's right. It's already good and adhered to what little hair I have left.

The aesthetician looks down at me with zero sympathy in her cool-blue eyes. I think these women get off on inflicting pain. I could easily see her swapping out her white smock for a leather corset and riding crop.

"Get it off, then," I say grumpily.

With one quick jerk, the aesthetician rips off the strip, leaving another stripe of smooth pink skin.

I shriek and let out a string of expletives, some English and some Italian. The aesthetician doesn't flinch. I'm sure she's heard it all.

"All right, that's enough!"

"You can't leave it like that," she says, wrinkling her nose.

Cazzo! I've got about two-thirds of my pussy waxed, with little patches of hair in odd places. It does look fucking awful. I don't care for Callum's sake, but *I* don't want to have to look at that for weeks until it grows out again.

I can't fucking believe his nerve, booking a bikini wax along with everything else. He thinks he owns my pussy already? He thinks he gets to decide how it looks?

I should wait until he's sleeping, then slap hot wax on his balls. Give him a taste of his own medicine.

Grimly, I say, "Finish it off."

It takes three more strips and a whole lot more swearing to get off the remaining hair. When they're finished, I'm completely bald, the cool air touching me as it never has before.

It's fucking humiliating. It's…whatever the feminine version of *emasculating* would be. I'm like Samson. Callum stole my hair and stripped me of my power.

I'm going to get back at him for this, that conniving, perverted fuck. He thinks he can wax my pussy without consent? He doesn't know what he started.

The aestheticians go back to massaging me. Inside, I'm fucking fuming.

I'm already planning all the ways I'm going to make Callum's life a living hell.

10
CALLUM

IT'S MY WEDDING DAY.

It's nothing like I pictured, but then, I never spent much time picturing getting married. I expected it to happen eventually, but I never really gave a shit about it.

I dated plenty of women—when it was convenient. I've always had my own plans, my own goals. Any woman had to fit in with that, or I'd cut her loose the minute she became more trouble than she was worth.

In fact, I was dating someone when my father arranged this whole thing with the Gallos. Charlotte Harper and I had been together for about three months. As soon as I found out that I was "engaged," I called her to break it off. And I felt…nothing. I didn't really care if I saw Charlotte again or not. There's nothing wrong with her—she's pretty, accomplished, well-connected. But when I break up with a woman, I feel the same as when I throw away an old pair of shoes. I know I'll find a replacement soon enough.

This time the replacement is Aida Gallo. I'm supposed to love, cherish, and protect her until the end of her days. I'm not sure I can do any of those things, except maybe keep her safe.

Here's one thing I do know: I'm not going to put up with her fucking nonsense once we're married. It's like my father says: she needs to be trained. I'm not going to have some wild, disobedient wife. She'll learn to obey me, one way or another. Even if I have to grind her to powder under my feet.

I smirk a little, thinking about her "spa day" yesterday. The point of that, obviously, was to get her ready for tonight. I'm supposed to consummate the marriage, and I'm not fucking some messy little ragamuffin in flip-flops and jean shorts. I expect her to be properly groomed, head to toe.

I love the idea of her being primped and cleaned and waxed to my specifications. Like a little doll, built just the way I like it.

I've already showered and shaved, so now it's time to put on my tux. But when I check the hook in the closet where I expect it to be hanging, there's nothing there.

I call down to Marta, a member of our house staff.

"Where's my tux?"

"I'm sorry, Mr. Griffin," she says nervously. "I went to the shop to pick it up like you said, but they told me the order had been canceled. A box was shipped here instead, from Ms. Gallo."

"A box?"

"Yes, shall I bring it up?"

I wait impatiently in the doorway while Marta jogs up the stairs, a large square garment box in her hands.

What the hell is this? Why is Aida fucking with my tux?

"Leave it," I say to Marta. She sets the box gingerly on my couch.

I wait until she's gone, and then I open it.

On top is an envelope, with messy handwriting I can only assume belongs to my fiancée. I rip it open, pulling out a note:

Dearest betrothed,

It was so kind of you to see to all my pre-wedding grooming yesterday. What a stimulating and unexpected experience it was!

I've decided to return the favor with a gift of my own—a little piece of my culture for your wedding day.

I'm sure you'll do me the honor of wearing this for our wedding ceremony. I'm afraid I couldn't possibly say my vows without this reminder of home.

Forever yours,
Aida

I can't help snickering at her description of the spa. My smile freezes on my face when I pull apart the tissue paper and see the tux she's expecting me to wear.

It looks like a fucking clown suit. Made of shiny brown satin, it's covered in garish embroidery on the shoulders, lapels, and even the back of the jacket. It's a three-piece suit complete with a vest, not to mention a lace pocket square and cravat. The only person I can picture wearing this is Liberace.

My mother hustles into the room, looking flustered. I can see she's already dressed in an elegant sage-green cocktail gown, her hair a smooth pale cap, tasteful gold earrings dangling from her lobes.

"What are you doing? Why aren't you dressed?" she says when she sees me standing there with a towel tied around my waist.

"Because I don't have my tux."

"What's that?"

I step aside so she can see. She plucks up the lace cravat, holding it distastefully between her forefinger and thumb.

"A gift from my soon-to-be bride." I hold out the card.

My mother reads it in a glance. She frowns, then says, "Put it on."

I bark out a laugh. "You have to be joking."

"Do it! We don't have time to get another tux. And it's not worth blowing this whole thing up over a suit."

"This isn't a suit. It's a fucking embarrassment."

"I don't care!" she says sharply. "It's a small wedding. Hardly anyone will see."

"Not happening."

"Callum…enough. You're going to have a hundred more battles to fight with Aida. You need to pick the important ones. Now get moving, we need to leave in six minutes."

Unbelievable. I thought she'd lose her mind over this, if only for the way the brown will clash with her carefully curated cream, olive, and gray color scheme.

I pull on the ridiculous suit, almost choking on the smell of mothballs. I don't even want to know where Aida dug this up. Probably her great-grandfather was buried in it.

The important thing is how I'm going to punish her for this.

She's made a serious mistake, poking the bear over and over. It's time for me to wake up and give her a good slap.

She'll get what's coming to her tonight.

As soon as I'm dressed, I hurry down the stairs to the waiting limo. The one carrying my mother and sisters already left—it's just me and my father.

He raises an eyebrow at my suit but doesn't say anything. My mother probably already briefed him.

"How are you feeling?"

"Fantastic," I say. "Can't you tell?"

"Sarcasm is the lowest form of humor," he informs me.

"I thought that was puns."

"This will be good for you, Cal. You can't see it now, but it will be."

I set my teeth, imagining taking out every one of my frustrations on Aida's tight little ass later tonight.

I feel sacrilegious walking into the church—like god might strike us down for this unholy union. If Aida pisses me off enough, I'm going to dunk her in the holy water and see if it sets her aflame.

It's easy to see which side of the aisle is mine and which is Aida's—all those dark, curly-haired Italians versus the horse-mane hues of the Irish: blond, red, gray, and brunette.

The groomsmen are Aida's brothers; the bridesmaids, my sisters. We have equal numbers because only Dante and Nero are standing up—Sebastian is sitting in the front row in a wheelchair, his knee bulky from the bandage under his slacks.

I don't know if he actually needs the wheelchair or it's just a *fuck you* to my side of the family. I feel a twinge of guilt, then push it away, telling myself the Gallos are lucky they got off that easy.

The sage-green bridesmaid dress suits Riona very well, but not Nessa—it makes her look pale and a bit sickly. She doesn't seem to mind. She's the only one smiling up by the altar. Dante and Riona are glaring at each other, and Nero is looking at Nessa with an expression of interest that has me about five seconds away from wrapping my fingers around his throat. If he says one word to her, I'm going to bash his pretty face in.

The church is full of the heavy scent of cream-colored peonies. The priest is already standing at the altar. We're waiting for Aida.

The music starts. After a moment's pause, my bride comes walking up the aisle.

She's wearing a veil and a simple lace dress that trails after her. She has a bouquet in one hand, but she lets it hang by her thigh, using her other hand to hold the skirt of her dress. I can't see her face behind the veil, which drives home more than ever that I'm marrying a stranger. There could be anybody under there.

My bride stops in front of me. I lift the veil.

I see her smooth, tanned skin and her clear gray eyes, heavily lashed. I have to admit, she looks beautiful. The reveal of her face illuminates how lovely those features really are when they're not screwed up in some demonic expression.

It doesn't last long—as soon as she catches an unencumbered view of my suit, her face lights up with malicious glee.

"You look *amazing*." She snickers.

"I'll get you back," I calmly inform her.

"I was already getting *you* back for that bullshit you pulled at the spa!"

The priest clears his throat, wanting to start the service.

"When you're married to me, I expect you to maintain yourself at all times."

"The *fuck* I will," Aida snaps, loud enough to make the priest jump.

"Is there a problem?" He frowns at us.

"No problem at all. Start the ceremony," I order.

Aida and I continue to snipe at each other in muttered tones while the priest drones his way through the vows.

"If you think I'm gonna be some little porn star for you—"

"That's just bare-minimum standards—"

"Yes, it certainly was *bare*—"

We break off when we realize the priest is staring at us.

"Callum Griffin and Aida Gallo, have you come here freely and without reservation to give yourselves to each other in marriage?"

"Yes," I snap.

"Oh yes," Aida says in the tone of voice my father would classify as "the lowest form of humor."

"Will you honor each other as man and wife for the rest of your lives?"

"Yes," I say after a moment's hesitation. The rest of our lives is a very fucking long time. I don't want to picture it right now.

"Yes," Aida says, looking at me like she's planning to make the rest of *my* life as short as possible.

"Will you accept children lovingly from God and bring them up according to the law of Christ and his church?"

"Yes," I say. I'd get Aida pregnant right this second, purely because of how furious it would make her. That would be one way to tame the beast.

Aida already looks so annoyed that I don't think she's going to answer the question. Finally, through stiff lips, she mutters, "Yes."

"Then say your vows," the priest instructs.

I seize Aida's hands and squeeze them as hard as I can, trying to make her flinch. She stubbornly sets her face, refusing to acknowledge the pressure on her fingers.

"I, Callum Griffin, take you, Aida Gallo, to be my wife. I promise to be true to you in good times and in bad, in sickness and in health. I will love you and honor you all the days of my life."

I spout the words quickly, having memorized them on the car ride over.

Aida looks at me for a moment, her gray eyes more serious than usual. In a flat tone, she repeats the vow back to me.

"I pronounce you man and wife," the priest says.

That's it. We're married.

Aida tilts her lips up for a chaste kiss.

To show her who's boss, I seize her by the shoulders and kiss her roughly, forcing my tongue into her mouth. Her lips and tongue taste sweet. Tart and fresh. Like something I haven't tasted in a very long time...

Strawberries.

I can already feel my tongue going numb. My throat starts to swell, my breath coming out in a whistle.

The church whirls around me in a kaleidoscope of color as I slump to the floor.

That fucking *bitch*!

11
AIDA

My husband spends the night in the emergency room. I guess that strawberry allergy was pretty serious after all. It doesn't make up for the weeks Sebastian spent at the hospital or the months of rehab and the loss of his basketball season, but it's something.

It also allows me to skip the farce of the wedding photos, the dinner, the dancing, and all the other nonsense in which I wanted no part. It was bad enough having to spout all those lies in a church, in front of a priest. I'm not religious, but that didn't make it any better. The pious nonsense was the cherry on the bullshit sundae.

Callum and I were supposed to go to the Four Seasons to consummate our union. That's another thing that doesn't end up happening. I go up to the honeymoon suite alone, kick off my shoes, ditch the itchy lace dress, and order enough room service that the concierge sounds very concerned when I tell her I only need one fork.

All in all, it's a pretty glorious night. I try every kind of cake on the menu while watching old episodes of *Law and Order* and *Project Runway*.

The morning isn't quite as cheerful. I have to pack my bag and head over to the Griffin mansion on the lake. Because that's where I'll be living now. That's my new home.

I'm deeply bitter toward my father and brothers as I climb in the cab. They're at home in the house I was born in, the place I've lived every day of my life. They get to stay there, surrounded by family, while I have to march into the lion's den. I have to live in the middle of my enemies for the rest of my life. Surrounded by people who hate and distrust me. Never truly comfortable. Never really safe.

The Griffin mansion looks gleaming and formidable. I hate the manicured lawn and the sparkling windows. I hate how everything in their lives has to be so perfect, so soulless. Where are the overgrown trees or the bushes you plant because you love the way the flowers smell?

If you told me their garden was full of plastic plants, I wouldn't be surprised. Everything they do is for appearance, nothing more.

Like how Imogen Griffin stands in the doorway to greet me. I know she doesn't give a shit about me, except for how I'm going to help promote her son's career and maybe provide her with grandchildren.

Sure enough, as soon as I'm inside, the mask drops.

"That was some stunt you pulled," she says through pale lips. "I assume you knew he was allergic."

"I don't know what you're talking about."

"Don't insult me." Her eyes bore into mine, alight with blue fire. "You could have killed him."

"Look," I say, "I didn't know he was allergic. I don't know anything about him. We're strangers, remember? We may be married today, but I feel the same as yesterday—like I barely know you people at all."

"Well, here's something you should know about me." Imogen's voice is sharper than the ladies of the country club have ever heard it. "As long as you're part of this family, I will help you and protect you. But everyone here pulls their weight. We work together for the betterment of our empire. If you threaten what we're building, or if you endanger any member of the family, when you lay your head down that night, you'll never lift it again. Do you understand me?"

Ha. That's the Imogen Griffin I was looking for. The steel behind the socialite.

"I understand the concept of family loyalty," I tell her. Seeing myself as part of the Griffin family—that's another thing entirely.

Imogen stares me down a minute longer, then nods. "I'll show you your room."

I follow her up the wide curving staircase to the upper level.

I was here once before. I already know what lies to the left: the girls' rooms and the master suite belonging to Imogen and Fergus.

Imogen turns right instead. We pass the library, which shows no hint of smoky ruin. I can't resist peeking inside. Looks like Imogen already renovated, replacing the carpet and repainting the walls. They're pale blue now, with shutters over the windows instead of curtains. Even the fireplace got a facelift: a new white stone facade and a glass enclosure for the grate.

"No more accidents," Imogen says drily.

"Much safer," I agree, not sure whether to laugh or be embarrassed.

We walk down a long hallway to another private suite, similar in size to the master. When Imogen opens the doors, I realize we're in Callum's room. It's got exactly the sort of dark masculine decor and attention to order I would expect of him. It smells entirely of man—cologne, aftershave, soap, and a hint of his skin from the bed that hasn't been slept in. Little goose bumps rise on my forearms.

I was expecting the Griffins to give me my own room. Sort of like royals in the olden days, living in their separate suites. I thought, at worst, Callum would have to visit me in the night now and then.

Apparently, they actually expect us to share a room. To sleep side by side in that wide low bed. Brushing our teeth at the same sink in the morning.

This is so fucking weird.

Callum and I haven't had one conversation that wasn't furious or threatening. How am I ever going to close my eyes at night?

"I'm sure there's plenty of space for your clothes," Imogen says, eyeing my small suitcase. "Will your father be sending over the rest of your things?"

"Yeah."

It's just a couple of boxes. I don't have that much stuff. Plus, I didn't want to bring anything personal over here. My tiny little christening dress, my mother's wedding ring, old photo albums—all that can stay in the attic at my father's house. There's no reason to move it.

"When will…Callum be back?" I ask Imogen hesitantly.

"He's here right now," she says. "Resting down by the pool."

"Oh. Okay."

Shit. I was hoping for a longer reprieve before I saw him.

"I'll leave you to get settled in," Imogen says.

It doesn't take long to stash away my toiletries and clothes. Callum considerately cleared out the space under one of the sinks in the bathroom, and half the massive walk-in closet.

He really didn't need to leave one whole side empty. My clothes look ludicrously lonely, dangling in the space.

Not that Callum has that many clothes himself. He's got a dozen identical white shirts and three blue ones, suits ranging from charcoal to black, and a similarly uniform casual wardrobe. His clothes are hung with robotic precision.

I touch the sleeve of one of three identical gray cashmere sweaters. "I've married a psychopath."

Once I've unpacked, there's really nothing left to do except look for Callum.

I slink downstairs, wondering if I should maybe apologize. On the one hand, he totally had it coming. On the other, I did feel a little guilty when his whole face swelled and he was clutching and clawing at his throat.

I'd snacked on strawberries all morning, thinking it would give him hives. Maybe ruin a few of our stupid wedding photos.

The actual effect was far more dramatic. If Imogen Griffin hadn't had an EpiPen stashed in her Birkin bag, I might be a widow right now instead of a wife. She ran to her son, jamming the uncapped needle into his thigh, while Fergus called an ambulance.

However, when I reach the pool deck, I see Callum looks completely recovered. He's not resting at all but swimming laps. His arm cuts through the water like a knife, brilliant droplets sparkling in his dark hair. His body looks lean and powerful as he dives under the water, pushes off the wall, and rockets half the length of the pool before having to come up for air.

I sit on one of the deck chairs, watching him swim.

It's actually pretty amazing how long he can hold his breath underwater. I guess the Griffins must be part dolphin.

I watch him swim a dozen more laps, only realizing how much time has passed when he stops abruptly, leaning his arms on the edge of the pool and shaking water out of his eyes. He looks up at me, fixing me with an unfriendly expression. "There you are."

"Yup. Here I am. I put my stuff in your room." I don't call it *our* room. It doesn't feel like that at all.

Callum looks equally irritated at the prospect of sharing quarters.

"We don't have to stay here forever," he says mutinously. "After the election, we can start looking for our own place. Then we can have separate rooms if you prefer."

I nod. "That may be better."

"I'm going to finish up," Callum says, readying himself to push off the wall again.

"Okay."

"Oh, but one thing first."

"What?"

He beckons for me to come closer.

I walk over to the side of the pool, still distracted by the question of whether I should say sorry or not.

Callum's hand shoots up and closes around my wrist. With a jerk, he yanks me into the water and wraps his iron arms around me.

I'm so surprised that I yelp, letting out a breath instead of sucking one in. The water closes over my head, colder than I expected. Callum squeezes me hard, pinning my arms against my sides so I can't move them at all.

The pool is too deep for my feet to touch. Callum's weight drags me down like an anvil. He's squeezing me like a snake, crushing me against his body.

I squirm and struggle, but there's nothing for me to kick against, and my arms are pinned. My lungs are burning, heaving, trying to force me to inhale, even though I know I'll suck in a mouthful of chlorinated water.

My eyes open involuntarily. All I can see is bright teal, turbulent with useless struggle. Callum is going to kill me. He's going to drown me right now. This is the last thing I'll ever see—the last bit of my air, rising to the surface in silvery bubbles.

I'm twitching, jerking, starting to go limp as inky spots burst in front of my eyes.

Then he finally releases me.

I pop to the surface, gasping and coughing. I'm exhausted from fighting him. It's hard to tread water with my soaking-wet jeans and T-shirt dragging me down.

He rises next to me, just out of reach of my flailing arms.

"You—you *fuck!*" I shout, trying to hit him.

"How do you like having your air cut off?" he says, glaring at me.

"I'm going to feed you every fucking strawberry in the state!" I shriek, still choking on pool water.

"Yeah, you try that. And next time I'll tie a fucking piano to your legs before I throw you in the pool."

He swims to the other side and climbs out before I've even made it to the edge.

I wait until he's gone to pull myself out of the pool, sopping and shivering.

To think I was going to apologize to him.

Well, I learned my lesson.

Callum doesn't know who he's playing with. He thought I messed up his house before? I live here now. I'll see everything he does, hear everything. Then I'll use what I learn to destroy him.

12
CALLUM

I stomp inside the house, my entire body shaking with rage.

The nerve of that fucking girl, showing up here with her suitcase like she didn't just try to kill me. Like I didn't spend my wedding night in the hospital with a fucking tube shoved down my throat.

She humiliated me in front of everyone—first with that suit and then by making me look weak, fragile, utterly pathetic.

That allergy is the most embarrassing thing about me. It makes me feel like some little kid with bottle-cap glasses and a snotty nose. I hate that it's so irrational. I hate that I can't control it. I hate that I have such a ridiculous vulnerability.

I don't know how she found out about it, but the fact she sussed it out and used it against me makes me absolutely fucking furious.

I pulled her under the water to give her a taste of her own medicine. See how she likes clawing and gasping for air, helpless against the necessity of breathing.

It made me feel better. For a minute.

But it also made me feel something else.

Her body, twisting and writhing against me… It wasn't supposed to be sexy.

"Cal," my father calls as I pass the kitchen doorway.

I glance into the kitchen, seeing him seated at the counter eating one of the meals the chef keeps prepared in the fridge.

"Where's Aida?"

"Out by the pool," I tell him, crossing my arms over my bare chest. I didn't bother to grab a towel. I'm dripping all over the tiles.

"You should take her out somewhere tonight. A nice dinner. Maybe a show."

"To what purpose?"

"Because of your…accident…yesterday, you didn't make use of the honeymoon suite."

"I'm aware of that," I say, trying to keep the sarcasm out of my voice.

"You need to seal the deal, so to speak. You know a marriage isn't finalized until it's consummated."

"So you want me to fuck her tonight, is that your point?"

He puts his fork down next to his plate, fixing me with a cold stare. "No need to be crude."

"Let's call a spade a spade. You want me to fuck this girl, despite the fact we hate each other, despite the fact she tried to kill me yesterday, because you don't want your precious alliance to fall apart."

"Exactly," he says, picking up his fork once more and spearing a grape out of his Waldorf salad. "And don't forget, this isn't *my* alliance. It benefits you more than anyone."

"Right," I say bitterly. "It's been a real joy so far."

I stalk upstairs, stripping off my swim trunks and running the shower as hot as I can stand it. I take a good long time soaping myself, washing my hair, letting the water pound down on my shoulders.

I'm aware I'm supposed to "make Aida my wife" in every sense of the word, but I doubt she's going to be in the mood for that after I half drowned her. I've never been one for grand romantic gestures, but even under the most liberal interpretations, I don't think waterboarding counts as foreplay.

In fact, I doubt she'll even agree to go to dinner with me. Which is fine by me. She probably eats with her hands. She'd only embarrass me if I took her someplace nice.

Even after I hear Aida coming into the room, I stay exactly where I am, enjoying the hot shower. She can stand out there and shiver her ass off for all I care.

I can hear her moving around but can't see what she's doing. I've been in here so long that the glass enclosure of the shower is opaque with steam.

Aida startles me by pushing her way inside, completely naked.

"Hey!" I say. "What the fuck are you doing?"

"Showering, obviously. Some asshole pulled me into the pool."

"I'm already in here."

"Really?" She fixes me with an unimpressed stare. "Thank you for informing me of that fact. That's the kind of razor-sharp observation and inside information that's sure to secure you the alderman seat."

"Sarcasm is the lowest form of humor," I say to her in my father's most insufferable tone.

"Taking lessons in humor from you would be like asking a dog how to perform an appendectomy," she replies.

She elbows past me to grab the shampoo.

Her bare arm grazes my stomach, and I become acutely aware that we haven't actually seen each other naked before now.

I'm used to girls who keep their bodies torturously slim by any means necessary—diet, pills, Pilates, and even surgical intervention. Aida obviously doesn't bother with any of that. From what I've seen, she eats and drinks whatever she likes, and she probably hasn't seen a running shoe in years. As a result, she's curvy, with a soft stomach and a big ass.

But I have to admit…her figure is pretty fucking sexy. She'd probably hate to hear me say this, but she kinda has that classic bombshell look—like I could slap a fur bikini on her and she'd be Raquel Welch in *One Million Years B.C.*

It makes me curious what it would feel like to grab a handful of that soft flesh, to watch her ride on top of me. To throw her around and manhandle her, without worrying she's going to snap like a stick figure.

Her smooth light-brown skin looks even better when you can see more of it. The hot shower is bringing a pink flush to it, particularly across her chest. I'm trying not to stare at her breasts, but the way the soap suds slide down the chasm between them is so distracting...

The warm water runs down her body to the delta between her thighs. I can see her freshly waxed pussy, completely bare, looking softer than velvet. The fact it's waxed for me, under my instructions, is incredibly erotic.

Aida is so wild and rebellious, making her do anything is an incredible feat. She's determined to spite me, to do the opposite of whatever I say.

The more she rebels, the more I want to control her. I want to bend her to my will. I want to make her do whatever I say, for my pleasure...

My cock hangs heavy and swollen between my legs. Aida's lashes flutter as she glances downward.

She looks away, rinsing shampoo out of her hair. Soon enough, her eyes are drawn back down.

I know I'm in good shape. I work out every morning: sixty minutes of weight training, thirty minutes of cardio. Our chef makes macroportioned meals to ensure the perfect protein, carb, and fat intake. All that has led to a well-muscled physique.

Aida's eyes linger over my abs and the member continuing to swell under her gaze. It's standing out from my body now.

"See something you like?"

"No," she says, stubborn as ever.

"You fucking liar."

I step closer to her so my erect cock brushes against her bare hip. My thigh slides between hers, slippery with soap. I thrust one hand into her hair, wrapping the wet rope around my palm and then tugging her head back so she has to look up at me. "You fucked up our wedding night. You know we're not actually married until we sleep together."

"I know that," she says.

"You haven't been eating anything else poisonous, have you?"

Before she can answer, I press my lips hard against hers.

When I kissed Aida at the church, it was only to finish that stupid ceremony. Now I'm kissing her because I want to taste her mouth again. I want to press my whole body against hers and run my hands over that silky tan skin.

She's incredibly soft. I don't know how someone with the personality of a cactus can have the softest lips, shoulders, and breasts I've ever touched. I want to run my hands over every inch of her.

At first, she's stiff and unyielding, not wanting to respond to me. As my thigh grinds against her bare little cunt, and as I take her breasts in my hands, she gasps and her lips part, allowing me to slide my tongue inside her mouth.

Now she's pressing back on me, grinding her pussy against my leg. She's kissing me back, deep enough that I can taste the lingering tang of chlorine on her lips.

I slide my hand down her belly, all the way down to her bald pussy. I rub my fingers over the perfectly smooth lips, loving how bare and exposed she is. Then I part her folds and find the tiny nub of her clit, swollen from the heat of the shower. I circle my middle finger around it before reaching down to test how wet it's making her, then returning to the most sensitive spot.

She gasps when I touch her there and squeezes her thighs around mine, rubbing and pressing against my palm with her cunt.

I slip a finger inside her, making her moan. She moans right into my mouth, a deep and helpless sound.

I knew it. She's a horny little slut. She likes sex as much as I do.

That's perfect. Because if she wants it, if she needs it, then she has to come to me. And that's one more way I can control her.

I rub her and finger her until her legs start to shake. Her breath quickens. Her thighs squeeze tight as she gets closer and closer to climax.

Right when she's at the edge, I stop touching her and withdraw my hand.

"Don't stop!" she gasps, opening her eyes and glaring at me.

"If you want to come, then suck my cock first," I demand.

She looks down at my cock, so hard that it juts straight out from my body.

"Fuck no," she says. "I'll just do it myself."

She leans back against the shower wall, putting her hand between her thighs. Her fingers slide between her pussy lips. She exhales softly. I grab her by the wrist and yank her hand away.

"Hey!" she shouts, eyes flashing open again.

"Suck me off, or I'm not letting you come."

She glares at me, cheeks flushed from heat and from the denied orgasm. I know it's boiling inside her, spinning around like a cyclone. I'm sure it's nagging at her, making her ache and throb.

I put my hand on her shoulder and push her down to her knees.

Reluctantly, she grips the base of my cock.

Her lips part, and I see the gleam of her teeth. I wonder for a moment if I've made a horrible mistake. I'd really rather not lose my dick to the temper of my new wife.

Then her warm, wet mouth closes around my cock, and my brain short-circuits. If I thought her lips were soft before, I had no idea how they could feel on the painfully sensitive head of my cock. They slide over and around, completely enveloping me. Her tongue flicks against the underside as she gently licks and sucks.

Fuuuucking hell, she's good at this. It's no wonder Oliver Castle was obsessed with her. If she sucked his cock like this just one single time, I could imagine him following her to the ends of the earth to get it again.

She slides her hand up and down the shaft, her mouth and

fingers working in tandem. Her other hand reaches underneath to gently cradle my balls, stroking the underside of the sac.

All these sensations together rocket me toward orgasm…

Until she drops my cock and stands again.

"That's all you get."

God, her obstinance is infuriating. If I said the grass is green, she'd call it purple just to spite me. I really should take this opportunity to teach her a lesson.

But she and I both want the same thing in this moment, a rare instance of our impulses aligning. We want it so bad that desire outweighs malice.

Aida puts an arm around my neck, steadying herself while she lines the head of my cock up with her entrance. She wraps both legs around my waist as my cock slides all the way inside her.

I grip her thick ass with both hands, digging my fingers into her cheeks. I hold her up as she starts to ride me, her arms locked around my neck, her soap-slippery body grinding against mine.

As hot as the shower is, her pussy is even hotter. It clenches around my cock, squeezing me on the inward and the outward motion of the thrust.

I was wrong in my assumption that Aida isn't athletic. She's riding me with the vigor and enthusiasm of a sexual Olympian. I'm used to girls who pose themselves in the most attractive position possible, then lie back to let you fuck them. I've never been with someone so…eager.

As she gets closer to the edge, she rides me even harder, her pussy a vise around my cock. She slams down on me over and over. The intensity of the strokes and the heat of the shower make me dizzy.

But there's no fucking way I'm tapping out. I press her back against the glass wall and fuck her all the harder, determined to prove I can dish it back to her twice as heavy.

When her eyes start to roll back, I feel a surge of triumph.

"Oh my god…oh my god…oh…Cal…"

I'm wringing the climax out of her. It's going on and on, drawn out by every stroke of my cock. It's so fucking sexy seeing that rebellious expression wiped off her face, watching her submit to the pleasure surging through her body.

I'm doing this to her. I'm making her feel this. Whether she hates me or not, whether she wishes it were anyone but me, she's helpless to resist it. She loves the way I'm fucking her.

With that thought, I explode inside her.

I mean, I really explode. The orgasm is like an atom bomb, hitting me without warning. My balls are ground zero, and the shock wave rockets through every last neuron, all the way out to the tips of my fingers and toes. In the wake of that sensation, my brain can't send any other signals. My body goes limp. I have to put Aida down before I drop her.

I collapse against the opposite shower wall, both of us panting and flushed.

Aida refuses to meet my eye.

It's the first time she hasn't been able to look at me. No matter how I've tried to stare her down, she's always been up to the challenge.

Now she's rinsing off slowly, pretending to be totally absorbed by her cleaning routine.

She called me *Cal*. She never did that before. Except to make fun of me at the engagement party.

"So that's it," I say to her. "It's official."

"Right," she says, still not looking at me.

I like her embarrassment. I like that I've found this chink in her armor.

"Good to know you're not completely awful at sex."

She glares back at me, her eyes bright and ferocious once more. "Wish I could return the compliment."

I grin.

Aida, you little liar. Keep it up, and I'm going to wash your mouth out with soap. Or maybe something even better...

13
AIDA

Living with the Griffins is strange, to say the least.

The only person who seems happy to have me there is Nessa. We weren't exactly friends at school, but we were cordial enough, from a distance. We know some of the same people, so now we can talk about all the weird shit they got up to since graduation.

I think Nessa likes having me there because I'm the only person who doesn't behave like an Ambition Bot. I'm willing to actually talk at breakfast, not just work and eat in silence. Plus, we're both taking classes at Loyola, so we can ride to school together in Nessa's Jeep.

Nessa is a genuinely kind person, something you don't see a lot of in the world. Plenty of people act nice, but it's just manners. Nessa gives away all her pocket money to homeless people, every single day. She never talks shit about anybody, even people who totally deserve it, like her siblings and her most vapid friends. She listens when people talk—I mean, really listens. She's more interested in you than in herself.

I don't know how a bunch of sociopaths managed to raise a girl like that. Actually, it's kind of tragic because the Griffins look at her kindness as a failing, like some mild disability. They joke about how soft she is, how innocent.

I know Callum cares about her, but she's a pet to him, not an equal.

Nessa welcomes me with open arms, glad to have another sister. Especially one who's slightly less of an asshole than Riona.

I don't know shit about having a sister. All I know is what I see in movies: braiding each other's hair, stealing each other's clothes, sometimes hating each other, sometimes crying on each other's shoulders. I don't know if I could do any of those things without feeling idiotic.

But I'm glad to have Nessa as a friend. There's a peacefulness to her personality that helps smooth some of my rough edges.

I spend more time with her than I do with my new husband. Callum is working insanely long hours in the lead-up to the election, and I'm usually already asleep in our shared bed by the time he comes in.

Maybe it's on purpose. We haven't hooked up again since our official "consummation" of the wedding.

That had taken me by surprise. I barged into the shower because I was cold and tired of waiting, and I wanted to show him he couldn't intimidate me, not by half drowning me and certainly not with a little nudity.

I didn't expect him to kiss me. And I definitely didn't expect him to touch me that way…

Here's the problem. I like sex. A lot. And I'm used to getting it pretty frequently. So, unless I'm going to start cheating on my brand-new husband, which is a really bad idea for a variety of reasons, there's only one place to get my fix.

And it's not exactly like I have to grin and bear it. Callum is hot. He's cold, arrogant, and a total control freak—he's already chewed me out five times this week for leaving clothes on the floor, spattering the mirror while I'm brushing my teeth, and not making the bed when I get up an hour after him. But none of those things change the fact the man is genetically blessed. His face, his body, and that cock…none of it is hard to look at.

He's got some skills, too. He doesn't fuck like a robot. He can be gentle, he can be rough, and above all, he's extremely perceptive. He reads me like a book. So I wouldn't mind exploring this whole married-sex thing a little further. But he's been too busy—or avoiding me.

Of course, when he does finally need my help, he asks in the most obnoxious way possible, which is by not asking at all.

He corners me in the kitchen where I'm trying to toast a bagel. The Griffins' toaster keeps popping it back up again because it probably hasn't been used in ten years. I'm the only one in this house familiar with the concept of carbs.

"I have a fundraiser tonight," Callum says. "Be ready at seven."

"Sorry," I say, jamming down the lever on the toaster and holding it in place. "I've already got plans."

"Doing what?"

"*Lord of the Rings* marathon. All three movies, extended version. I won't be finished until tomorrow around noon."

The toaster makes an angry clicking sound. I hold the lever in place, determined to brown my bagel even if it makes the machine explode.

"Very funny." Callum narrows his pale blue eyes at me. "Seven o'clock, and make sure you're not late. I expect proper hair and makeup. I've already laid a dress out on the bed."

I let the bagel pop up, nicely browned at last. Then I spread a nice thick layer of cream cheese, glomming on even more when I see Callum's expression of disgust.

"Do you have my lines ready for me, too? Maybe you should just hang a placard around my neck with whatever you expect me to say."

I take a huge bite of my bagel, enjoying it all the more because I know Callum probably hasn't let himself eat one in years.

"If you could refrain from cursing every third word, that would be a start," he says, his fingers twitching involuntarily. I'm pretty sure he's dying to snatch the bagel out of my mouth. He's holding back because he doesn't want to antagonize me before the fundraiser.

"I'll damn well try, sweetheart," I say around a mouthful of bread.

He glares at me and stalks off, leaving me alone in the kitchen. Well, not totally alone—I still have plenty of snacks.

I make a bowl of popcorn so I can at least start *The Fellowship of the Ring*.

As I head toward the theater room, I see Riona coming from the opposite direction, carrying a stack of folders. She looks flustered and stressed, as per usual. I don't know why she's always knocking herself out trying to impress these people—it's pretty clear her parents see Callum as the star of the family and her as a supporting character at best. Yet the more they push her to the side, the harder she fights for them to notice her. Watching it bums me out.

Not that I have much sympathy. Riona was a grade-A bitch at school. Queen of the mean girls. The only reason I didn't get more shit from her is because I was younger and therefore beneath her notice.

That's pretty much how she acts having to live in the same house with me. So I can't resist poking at her now and then.

"You wanna join me?" I hold up the popcorn bowl. "I'm about to watch *Lord of the Rings*. Ever seen it? There're some characters I think you might really identify with." Specifically, the ones that eat human flesh and are born out of muddy egg sacs.

Riona gives a dramatic sigh, annoyed I'm even talking to her. "No, I don't want to watch a movie at three o'clock in the afternoon because I'm not a fucking child. I have work to do."

"Right." I nod vigorously. "I forgot you're the secretary for your whole family. Really important stuff."

"I'm a *lawyer*," Riona says with icy dignity.

"Oh." I give a fake grimace. "Sorry about that. Well, don't worry, I won't tell anybody."

Riona shifts the heavy folders against one hip, cocking her head to the side so she can look me up and down with that patented mean-girl stare.

"That's right," she says softly. "Everything is a joke to you. You get traded like a baseball card, and you don't care, right? You don't care that your family abandoned you. That they sold you to us."

That puts a sick little knot in my stomach, but I'm not going to let Riona see it. I force myself to keep smiling and even pop a piece of popcorn into my mouth. It feels as dry as cardboard against my tongue.

"At least I'm a Topps Mickey Mantle," I tell her. "I doubt you'd be an '86 Jose Canseco."

Riona stares at me, shaking her head. "You are so fucking weird."

Eh…that's probably true.

She shoves past me, hurrying down the hallway.

I head into the theater, settling down in my favorite seat in the middle row.

Riona's a bitch. Her opinion means less than nothing to me.

But it keeps bothering me all the same. I can't even pay attention to the dulcet tones of Sir Ian McKellen, my favorite old-man crush.

The truth is I do feel abandoned. I miss my father. I miss my brothers. I miss my own house, which was old and shabby and stuffed with ancient furniture, but I knew every bit of it. It was safe and comfortable, with memories attached to every surface.

I eat my popcorn without tasting it, until I can finally lose myself in the fantasy world of elves and dwarves and good-hearted hobbits.

Around 6:30 p.m., I figure I should start getting ready. I shut the movie off and head upstairs to see what monstrosity Callum laid out on the bed for me.

Sure enough, when I unzip the garment bag, I see a tight silver-beaded dress that looks stiff and dowdy and fucking awful. Right as I'm wrinkling my nose at it, Callum comes into the room, already dressed in a spotless tux, his dark hair combed back and still damp from his shower.

"Why aren't you dressed?" he says angrily. "We're supposed to be leaving in twenty-five minutes. Jesus Christ, you haven't even done your hair yet."

"I'm not wearing this," I tell him flatly.

"Yes, you are. Put it on. Immediately."

"Did you steal this out of Imogen's closet?"

"*No*," he snarls. "I bought it specifically for you."

"Good. Then you can return it."

"Not until after you wear it tonight."

"Not happening." I toss my head.

"Get in the shower," he barks. "We're going to be late."

I walk toward the shower, moving deliberately slowly just to annoy him. I don't need more than half an hour to get ready; I'm not a fucking pageant queen.

Still, I'm tempted to stand under the warm water forever just to let him stew. I'm definitely not wearing that dress—I can wear the yellow one I wore to the engagement party.

Callum will probably pop a blood vessel at the idea of a person wearing the same outfit two entire times.

When I step out of the shower, I see he picked up the clothes I'd left in a crumpled heap on the bathroom floor. Nice.

I wrap a big fluffy towel around myself—say what you will about the Griffins, but at least they have excellent taste in linens—then I stroll into the closet to find my dress.

My entire side of the closet has been completely cleared out. Empty hangers dangle at odd angles—some of them still swaying from the wild stripping that occurred here.

I pull open the drawers—empty, too. He's taken every last stitch of my clothing, down to my underwear.

When I turn around, Callum's shoulders fill the doorway, his arms crossed over his chest and a smirk on his handsome face. "Guess it's the dress or nothing."

"I pick nothing, then." I drop the towel in a puddle around my feet, folding my arms across my chest in imitation of his.

"Understand this," Callum says quietly. "You're coming to that dinner tonight, even if I have to throw you over my shoulder and carry you like a caveman. You can be wearing the dress when I do that, or I swear to god, Aida, I will haul you there naked and make you sit in your seat in front of everyone. Don't fucking test me."

"That'll embarrass you more than me."

I can feel the color rising in my cheeks. Callum's eyes look wilder than I've ever seen them. I actually think he's serious—that's how determined he is to bend me to his will over this stupid dress.

The seconds tick by. Seconds that are making us later and later for this fundraiser, but Callum isn't budging out of the doorway. This is the hill he's choosing to die on: that ugly beaded dress.

"Fine!" I bark at last. "I'll put on the stupid dress."

The smirk on his face makes me want to take it back immediately. Or else punch him in the eye. If I have to go to the dinner in that lame-ass dress, then he can go there with a nice fucking shiner.

I'm so mad, I'm almost shaking. I step into the stiff, scratchy dress and stand there while Callum zips up the back. It feels like he's lacing a corset. I have to suck in my tummy, and then, once it's zipped, I can't let it out again. Which makes me kind of regret all that popcorn I ate.

"Where did you hide my underwear?" I demand.

Callum's fingers pause at the top of the zipper. "You don't need any underwear."

That fucker. He's getting off on this! I knew it!

Sure enough, when I turn around, there's a hungry look on his face, like he wants to rip the dress right off me again. But he won't do that. He's going to savor watching me walk around in it all night. Knowing he's making me do it. Knowing I'm not wearing any panties underneath.

I'm so infuriated, I could scream. Especially once he holds up the shoes he expects me to wear.

"How am I even going to get those on?" I shout. "I can't sit down in this fucking straitjacket."

Callum rolls his eyes.

Then he does something that surprises me.

He gets on his knee in front of me, placing my hand on his shoulder for balance. He lifts my foot and slides the stiletto onto it, like he's Prince Charming and I'm Cinderella. His hands are surprisingly gentle as his fingers touch the arch of my foot. He buckles the strap, then puts the other shoe on my opposite foot.

When he stands again, we're close to each other, so much so that I have to tilt my head to look up at him.

"There," he says gruffly. "I'll send Marta up to help you get ready."

Marta is a catch-all personal assistant to the family. She also happens to be good with hair and makeup, so she frequently helps Riona and Nessa get ready for events. Imogen does her paint job herself or else goes to a salon.

"Whatever," I say.

Callum heads downstairs to find Marta. I start hobbling back to the bathroom on the sky-high heels.

I don't know if it's the lack of underwear or something else, but I can feel an uncomfortable wetness between my legs. Every step I take in that tight dress makes my pussy lips rub together. I'm warm and throbbing, and I keep thinking about that look of arousal on Callum's face. How stern he was when he ordered me to put on the dress.

What the fuck is happening to me?

It must just be the fact I haven't gotten laid in over a week. There's no way I could be turned on by Callum ordering me around. That's crazy. I fucking hate being bossed.

"Aida?" a voice says behind me.

I yelp and spin around.

It's just Marta, holding her makeup bag. She's about thirty years old, with big brown eyes, dark bangs, and a soft voice.

"Callum said you needed a little help getting ready?"

"Right. Y-yes," I stammer.

"Take a seat." She pulls a chair up in front of the mirror. "We'll have you ready in no time."

14

CALLUM

AIDA COMES DOWN THE STAIRCASE, CLINGING TO THE RAILING, twenty minutes late but looking utterly stunning. Marta pulled her hair up into a slightly retro updo that plays up that classic bombshell look. Her eyes are lined with kohl, making them look almost as silvery as the dress.

I like the fact Aida can barely walk in the stilettos. It gives her a vulnerable air and makes her cling to my arm for the walk to the car.

She's quieter than usual. I don't know if she's annoyed about me stealing her clothes or if she's nervous about the night ahead of us.

I feel calm and more focused than I've been in weeks. Just as my father predicted, the Italians are throwing their full support behind me now that Aida and I are officially married. La Spata is sunk, and I've already dug up some fantastic dirt on Kelly Hopkins from her college years, when she was neck-deep in a cheating ring, selling ready-made thesis papers to wealthier and lazier students. Poor little scholarship student, forced to compromise her morals to get her degree.

That's what you always find in the end—no matter how pure people pretend to be, when the screw gets tight, there's always a place they crack. That'll shoot an arrow through her pretensions of moral superiority. Which leaves the field clear for one candidate: me.

The election is only a week away. Almost nothing can fuck this up for me now.

As long as I can keep my wife in line.

I see her sitting across from me in the back of the town car. She looks calm enough, watching the buildings stream by out the window. She doesn't fool me. I know how unruly she is. I might have slipped a bridle over her head for the moment, but she's going to try to buck me off again the moment she gets the chance.

The crucial thing is to keep her in line during this party. After that, she can mutiny as much as she likes. Several Italian business owners, CEOs, investors, and union reps will be here tonight. They need to see my wife at my side, obedient, supportive.

We drive to the Fulton Market District, which used to be full of meat-packing plants and warehouses and has now gentrified into hotels, bars, restaurants, and trendy tech companies. The fundraiser is at Morgan's on Fulton, in the penthouse at the very top of the building.

We make our way toward the elevator through the art gallery on the main floor. It's stuffed floor to ceiling with paintings of various styles, in varying levels of skill. Aida pauses by one particularly hideous modern piece in shades of peach, taupe, and tan.

"Oh, look. Now I know what to get your mother for Christmas."

"I suppose you prefer *that*." I indicate a dark and moody oil painting of Cronus devouring his children.

"Oh yes." Aida nods somberly. "Family portrait. That's Papa when we leave the cupboards open or forget to turn off the lights."

I give a little snort. Aida looks startled, like she's never heard me laugh before. She probably hasn't.

As we reach the elevator at last, somebody calls, "Hold the door!"

I put my arm out to stop it from closing. Then immediately regret it when Oliver Castle pushes his way inside.

"Oh," he says, spotting us and giving an arrogant toss of his head. His hair is longish, thick and sun streaked. He's got a tan and a hint of a burn, like he's been out on a boat all day. When he grins, his teeth look too white by comparison.

His eyes crawl over Aida's body, which is lusciously hourglass shaped in the tight beaded dress. It pisses me off how blatant he's being. My arrangement with Aida may not be romantic, but she's still my wife. She belongs to me and me alone. Not this overgrown rich kid.

"You really went all out, Aida," he says. "I don't remember you dressing up like that for me."

"Guess it wasn't worth the effort." I glower at him.

Oliver snorts. "Guess Aida was using her *effort* for other things…"

I get a vivid image of Aida sliding her tongue up and down Oliver's cock like she did to mine. Jealousy hits me like a sack of mud. It knocks the air out of me.

It takes everything I have not to grab Castle by the lapels of his velvet dinner jacket and throw him up against the wall.

The elevator lurches, stopping at the top floor. The doors part. Oliver saunters out without a glance back at us.

Aida watches me with her cool-gray eyes.

I don't like this new quiet Aida. It makes me nervous wondering what she's up to. I like it better when she blurts out whatever she's thinking as soon as it comes into her head. Even if it really pisses me off.

The penthouse is a large open room, stuffed full of potential donors getting sloshed on free liquor. Of course, it's not really free— I'm going to milk every one of these fuckers for every last bit of support I can get out of them. In the meantime, they're welcome to gorge themselves on high-end cocktails and fancy finger foods.

One whole side of the room is composed of sliding glass doors, currently thrown open to the rooftop deck. The guests mingle back and forth, enjoying the warm night air and the breeze off the lake. The deck is strung with glowing lanterns.

Right now, neither the flawless setup nor the excellent turnout is giving me any pleasure. I march over to the bar and ask for a double shot of whiskey, neat. Aida watches me down it in one gulp.

"What?" I snap, slamming the empty glass back on the bar.

"Nothing." She shrugs her bare shoulders, turning away from me to order her own drink.

Trying to get the thought of Oliver and Aida out of my mind, I scan the crowd, looking for my first target. I've got to talk to Calibrese and Montez. I spot my mother talking to the state treasurer over by the food. She's been here for hours, overseeing the setup and greeting the first guests as they arrived.

Then I see somebody who definitely wasn't invited: Tymon Zajac, better known as the Butcher. Head of the Polish Mafia and a major fucking pain in my ass.

The *Braterstwo* controls most of the Lower West Side, right up to Chinatown, Little Italy, and the wealthier neighborhoods to the northeast that are controlled by the Irish—a.k.a. me.

If there's a hierarchy to gangsters, it goes something like this: at the top you've got your white-collar gentrified gangsters who use the levers of business and politics to maintain their control. That's the Irish in Chicago. We run this city. We've got more gold than a fucking leprechaun. And we make as much money legally as illegally—or at least in that nice gray area of loopholes and backdoor deals.

Which doesn't mean I'm afraid to get my hands dirty—I've made more than one person in this city disappear. But I do it quietly and only when necessary.

On the next rung down the ladder, you've got gangsters with a foot in both worlds—like the Italians. They still run plenty of strip clubs, nightclubs, illegal gambling, and protection rackets. But they're also involved in construction projects that form the bulk of their income. They hold heavy sway over the unions for the carpenters, the electrical workers, the glaziers, heavy-equipment operators, ironworkers, masons, plumbers, sheet metal workers, and more. If you want to get anything built in Chicago, and you don't want it to burn down halfway through, or get "delayed," or have your materials stolen, then you have to hire the Italians as your foremen or pay them off.

Lower still, you've got the Polish Mafia. They're still participating in violent crime, in loud and obvious and attention-grabbing shit that causes problems for those of us who want to keep up the perception of a safe city.

The *Braterstwo* is still actively running drugs and guns, boosting cars, robbing banks and armored cars, extorting, and even kidnapping. They get their dirty deeds published in the news, and they're constantly pushing the boundaries of their territory. They don't want to stay in Garfield, Lawndale, and the Ukrainian Village. They want to push into the areas where the money is. The areas I own.

In fact, Tymon Zajac showing up at my fundraiser is a problem in itself. I don't want him here as an enemy or a friend. I don't want to be associated with him.

He's not the kind of guy who blends in. He's nearly as broad as he is tall, with wheat-colored hair just starting to gray, and a craggy face that might be scarred from acne or something worse. Hatchet-like cheekbones frame a Roman nose. He's carefully dressed in a pinstripe suit, a white bloom in the lapel. Somehow those natty details only serve to emphasize the roughness of his face and hands.

Zajac has a mythos around him. Though his family's been in Chicago for a century, he came up on the streets of Poland, operating a sophisticated car-theft ring from the time he was a teenager. He single-handedly tripled the number of exotic car thefts in the country, until the wealthy Polish hardly dared buy an imported car because they knew it'd disappear off the streets or even out of their own garages within the week.

He rose through the ranks of the Wolomin near Warsaw, until that gang became enmeshed in a bloody turf war with the Polish police. Around the same time, his half brother Kasper was murdered by the Colombian drug lords helping to smuggle cocaine, heroin, and amphetamines into Chicago. The Colombians thought they could start dealing directly in the city. Instead, Zajac flew into Chicago for his brother's funeral, then organized a two-part retaliation that left eight Colombians dead in Chicago and twelve more slaughtered in Bogota.

Zajac did the killings himself, holding a cleaver in one hand and a machete in the other. That earned him the nickname *the Butcher of Bogota.*

The Butcher took his brother's place as the head of the Chicago *Braterstwo.* Since then, not a month has gone by without him chipping away at the edges of my empire. He's old-school. He's hungry. And I know he's here for a reason tonight.

That's why I've got to speak to him, though I'd rather not be seen with him in public. I wait until he moves to a less obtrusive part of the room.

"Taking an interest in politics now, Zajac?"

"It's the true syndicate in Chicago," he says in his low, gravelly voice. He sounds like he's been smoking for a hundred years, though I don't smell it on his clothing.

"Are you here to donate, or do you have a comment card for the suggestion box?"

"You know as well as I do that wealthy men never give their money away for nothing." He takes a cigar out of his pocket and inhales the toasted scent. "Care to smoke one with me?"

"Wish I could. There's no smoking in the building."

"Americans love to make rules for other people that they never keep themselves. If you were here alone, you would smoke this with me."

"Sure," I say, wondering what he's driving at.

Aida appears at my side, quiet as a shadow.

"Hello, Tymon," she says.

The Polish Mafia has a long and complicated history with both my family and Aida's. During Prohibition, when the Irish and Italians battled for control of the distilleries, there were Poles on both sides. In fact, it was a Polack who carried out the Saint Valentine's Day Massacre.

More recently, Zajac has done business with Enzo Gallo—mostly successfully, though I heard rumors of a conflict over at the Oak Street Tower, with reports of shots fired and a hasty laying of the foundation, possibly with a body or two concealed underneath the cement.

"I heard the happy news," Zajac says. He gives a significant glance to the ring on Aida's finger. "I was disappointed not to receive an invitation. Or an inquiry from your father beforehand. You know I have two sons of my own, Aida. Poles and Italians work well together. I don't see you learning to love corned beef and cabbage."

I cut across him. "Be careful how you speak to my wife. The deal is done, and I doubt any offer you would have made then or now would interest her. In fact, I doubt you have anything to say to either of us."

"You might be surprised." Zajac fixes me with his fierce stare.

"Not likely," I say dismissively.

To my surprise, it's Aida who keeps her temper.

"Tymon isn't a man to waste his own time," she says. "Why don't you tell us what's on your mind?"

"The politician is rude, and the fiery Italian is the diplomat," Zajac muses. "What a strange reversal. Will she wear the tux and you put on the dress later tonight?"

"This tux will be soaked in your blood after I cut your fucking tongue out of your mouth, old man," I growl.

"The young make threats. The old make promises…"

"Save the fortune cookie bullshit," Aida says, holding up her hand to stay me. "What do you want, Tymon? Callum has a lot of people to speak to tonight, and I don't think you were even invited."

"I want the Chicago Transit property," he says, cutting to the chase at last.

"Not happening," I tell him.

"Because you're already planning to sell it to Marty Rico?"

That gives me a moment's pause. That deal isn't even done yet, so I don't know how the fuck Zajac heard about it.

"I'm not planning anything yet," I lie. "But I can tell you it's not going to you. Not unless you've got some magic power washer for your reputation to make it all bright and sparkling new again."

The truth is I wouldn't sell it to the Butcher either way. I already have to make nice with the Italians. I'm not inviting the Polacks right into my backyard. If Zajac wants to play at being a legitimate businessman, he can do it somewhere else in the city. Not in the middle of my territory.

The Butcher holds the cigar in his thick fingers, rolling it over and over. "You Irish are so greedy. Nobody wanted you here when you came to America. It was the same for us. They put up signs, telling us not to apply for jobs. They tried to stop us from immigrating. Now that you think you're secure at the head of the table, you don't want to let anyone else join you. You don't want to share even the crumbs of your feast."

"I'm always willing to make deals," I tell him. "But you can't demand a plum piece of public property to be handed over to you. For what? What do you have to offer me in return?"

"Money," he hisses.

"I have money."

"Protection."

I let out a rude laugh. Zajac doesn't like that at all. His face flushes in anger, but I don't care. His offer is insulting.

"I don't need your protection. You were already outmatched when it was only my family against yours. Now that I've allied with the Italians, what do you possibly think you have to offer us? How dare you threaten us?"

"Be reasonable, Tymon," Aida says. "We've worked together in the past. We will again in the future. But milk before meat."

I'm shocked at how calm Aida can be when conversing with

someone from her own world. I've never seen this side of her. She had no patience for Christina Huntley-Hart, who brought out Aida's most outrageous and disdainful attitude. But with Tymon, who is infinitely more dangerous, Aida has managed to stay calmer than me.

I'm looking at her with actual respect. She sees it and rolls her eyes at me, annoyed rather than gratified.

"I always liked you, Aida," Zajac growls. "I hope you haven't made a mistake marrying this puffed-up Mick."

"The only mistake would be underestimating him," she replies coldly.

Now I really am shocked. Aida defending me? Wonders never cease.

The Butcher gives a stiff nod, which could mean anything, then turns and walks away. I'm relieved to see he seems to be leaving the party without making a scene.

I look back at Aida. "You handled that really well."

"Yeah, shocking." She tosses her head. "You know I grew up with these people. I sat under the table while my father negotiated deals with the Polish, the Ukrainians, the Germans, the Armenians—I'm not always running around nicking watches."

"He's got some balls marching in here," I say, scowling at the doorway where Zajac just disappeared.

"He certainly does." Aida frowns, twisting the ring on her finger while she's lost in thought.

My mother picked out that ring and mailed it to Aida. Looking at it on her hand, I realize it doesn't really suit her. Aida would have picked something more comfortable and casual. Maybe I should have let her choose her own or taken her to Tiffany. That would have been easy to do.

I was so angry with her after our first meeting that I never really considered what she might prefer. What might make her more comfortable with this arrangement or moving into my house.

I want to ask her what else she knows about Zajac. What deals he's done with Enzo. But I'm interrupted by my father, who wants to hear what Zajac said. Before I can include Aida in the conversation, she slips away.

My father is going on and on, grilling me about the Butcher, wanting a word-for-word accounting of everybody else I talked to tonight and what they said.

Usually, I'd go through it with him point by point. But I can't help sneaking glances over his shoulder, trying to see where Aida is in the room. What she's doing. Who she's talking to.

I finally catch sight of her out on the deck with Alan Mitts, the treasurer. He's a crusty old bastard. I don't think I've seen him smile once in all the times I've spoken to him. Yet, with Aida, he's lost in some anecdote, waving his hands around, and Aida is laughing and egging him on. When she laughs, she throws back her head, and her eyes close, and her shoulders shake. There's nothing polite about it. She's just happy.

I want to hear what's making her laugh so hard.

"Are you listening to me?" my father says sharply.

I whip my head back around. "What? Yes. I'm listening."

"What are you looking at?" He squints in the direction of the deck.

"Mitts. I have to talk to him next."

"Looks like he's already talking to Aida," my father says in his most inscrutable tone.

"Oh. Yeah."

"How has she been performing?"

"Good. Surprisingly well."

My father looks her over, giving a nod of approval. "She certainly looks better. Though the dress is too revealing."

I knew he would say that. There were more conservative options in the pile of dresses Marta brought for my approval. I chose this one because I knew it would hug Aida's curves like it was made for her.

My father is still blathering on.

"The mayor has kicked down thirty thousand dollars to your campaign and endorsed you, but he did the same to twenty-five other council allies, so I don't think his statement is as strong as…"

Oliver Castle has reappeared, buoyed by liquid courage. I can tell he's half-drunk by the flush in his sunburned face and the way he roughly cuts between Aida and Mitts. Aida tries to shake him off, heading to the opposite side of the deck. Castle follows her over, trying to get her to talk to him.

"So I think it will be most efficient and most effective if we—"

"Hold that thought, Dad."

I set my drink down before heading outside through the wide-open sliding doors. This part of the venue is only dimly lit by the lanterns overhead, the music quieter and the seating more private. Oliver is trying to pull Aida into the darkest and most distant corner, hidden behind a screen of potted Japanese maples.

I intend to interrupt them immediately, but as I draw closer, I hear Oliver's low, urgent voice pleading with Aida. My curiosity is piqued. I creep up at an angle, wanting to hear.

"I know you miss me, Aida. I know you think about me, just like I think about you…"

"I really don't," she says.

"We had good times together. Remember the night we all built that bonfire on the beach, and you and I walked out on the dunes, and you had that white bikini on, and I took the top off with my teeth…"

I'm standing in place, molten jealousy churning in my guts. I want to interrupt them, but I have this sick curiosity. I want to know exactly what went on between Oliver and Aida. He was obviously infatuated with her. Did she feel the same? Did she love him?

"Sure, I remember that weekend," she says lazily. "You got drunk and crashed your car on Cermak Road. And almost broke your hand getting in a fight with Joshua Dean. Good times."

"That was your fault," Oliver growls, trying to pin her against the deck railing. "You drive me out of my mind, Aida. You make me crazy. I only did all that shit after you left me at the Oriole."

"Yeah?" she says, looking down at the city streets below the patio. "Do you remember why I left you there, though?"

Oliver hesitates. I can tell he does remember but doesn't want to say it.

"We bumped into your uncle. He asked who I was. And you said, 'Just a friend.' Because you liked being a rebel, dating Enzo Gallo's daughter. But you didn't want to risk your trust fund or your spot at Daddy's company. You didn't have the balls to admit what you actually wanted."

"I made a mistake."

Oliver keeps trying to take Aida's hand. She moves it out of his reach.

"Aida, I learned my lesson, I promise you. I've missed you so much that I could have thrown myself off the roof of Keystone Capital a hundred times. I sit in that office, and I'm fucking miserable. I've got that picture of us on my desk, the one on the Ferris wheel where you're laughing and hanging on to my arm. That was the best day of my life, Aida. If you give me another chance, I'll prove what you mean to me. I'll put a ring on your finger and show you off to the world."

"I already have a ring on my finger," Aida says dully, holding up her hand. "I got married, remember?"

"That marriage was horseshit. I know you only did that to hurt me. You don't care about Callum fucking Griffin—he's everything you hate! You can't stand people who are stuck up and phony and show off their money. How long did you even date him? I can tell you're miserable."

"I'm not miserable."

She doesn't sound very convincing.

I know I should interrupt the two of them, but I'm riveted.

Furious at the balls on Oliver Castle, trying to seduce my wife at my own fucking fundraiser, but also perversely curious to hear how Aida will respond.

"Come meet me for dinner tomorrow night," Oliver begs her.

"No." Aida shakes her head.

"Come to my apartment, then. I know he doesn't touch you like I used to."

Is she going to agree? Does she want to fuck him still?

Oliver is trying to wrap his arms around her, trying to kiss her neck. Aida smacks his hands away. He's got her backed into a corner; she's hampered by the tight dress and heels.

"Knock it off, Oliver. Someone's going to see you—"

"I know you miss this—"

"I'm serious, stop it, or I'll—"

Oliver presses her against the railing, trying to shove his hand up her skirt. I know for a fact she doesn't have any panties on because I dressed her myself. The thought of Oliver touching her bare pussy lips is what finally makes me snap.

I've heard of people being blinded by rage. It's never happened to me before—even at my angriest, I've always maintained control.

Now, in an instant, I go from standing behind the Japanese maples to grabbing Oliver Castle around the throat, squeezing as hard as I can with my left hand. My right fist smashes into his face over and over. I hear an insane roaring sound, and I realize it's me, I'm the one howling with rage while I hit the man who put his hands on my wife. I pick him up like I'm going to throw him over the railing; I halfway throw him over that railing.

Aida, my father, and several other people grab my arms and pull me off Castle.

Castle's face is a mess of blood, his lip is split, and his dress shirt is splattered. So is mine, now that I look down at it.

The party has come to a screeching halt. Everybody inside and outside is staring at us.

"Call security," my father barks. "This man tried to attack Mrs. Griffin."

"The fuck I did," Oliver snarls. "He—"

My father silences him with another blow to the face. Fergus Griffin hasn't lost his touch—Castle's head snaps back, and he slumps to the patio floor. Two security guards hurry onto the deck to pick him up.

"Leave. Now," my father hisses at me under his breath.

"I'm going to take my wife home," I say, loud enough for everyone to hear. I take my jacket off, then wrap it around Aida's shoulders like she's had a shock.

Aida allows this because she *is* shocked. Shocked by how I attacked Oliver Castle like a rabid dog.

With my arm around her shoulders, we push through the crowd before taking the elevator back down to the ground floor.

I hustle her into the waiting limo.

15
AIDA

As soon as we're in the limo, Callum barks, "Drive," and raises the partition so we're alone in the back, cut off from the chauffeur.

His hands are covered in blood, the same with his white dress shirt. He's even got blood on his face. His hair is disarrayed, coming down over his forehead. His eyes look wild, the pupils very black against the pale blue. A thin black ring encircles the iris, making him look like a bird of prey when he stares at me like he's doing right now.

I can see the muscles of his jaw twitching and the tendons standing out on his neck.

"Are you insane!" I shout, as the limo pulls away from the curb. I shake off Callum's jacket, annoyed that I let him put it around my shoulders like I was some kind of victim.

"That greasy fuck put his hands on you."

There's an edge to his voice. I've heard him angry before—not on this level. His blood-spattered hands are shaking. I saw him try to pick up Oliver and hurl him over the railing. He was going to do it. He was going to kill him.

I might have underestimated Callum Griffin.

"I could have handled it myself," I snap. "He was just drunk. I could have gotten away from him without making a scene."

"He was trying to seduce you right in front of me," Callum snarls.

"You were spying on me!"

"You're damn right I was. You're my wife. You have no secrets from me."

I scoff. "That only goes one way, though, doesn't it? You're off all day long having secret meetings and appointments. Holed up in Daddy's office making plans."

"I'm working," Callum says through stiff lips.

I can tell he's still amped to the max, thousands of volts of pure vengeful energy running through his body. He was interrupted, taking out his aggression on Oliver. Now it has nowhere to go. He looks like he'll explode at the slightest touch.

I'm pretty fucking pissed myself. Where does he get off listening in on my private conversation? Acting like I'm his property, like he has any right to be jealous?

Oliver loved me at least, in his own stupid, immature way. Callum doesn't love me. Why should he care if some guy tries to put his hand up my skirt?

"Keep working," I hiss at him. "And stay the fuck out of my personal life. You want a pretty little accessory on your arm? I did it. I came to your stupid party, wore this ugly dress. Told Mitts he should support you. I'm holding up my end of the bargain. Who I dated before is none of your fucking business."

"Did you love him?" Callum demands.

"None of your business!" I shout. "I just fucking said that!"

"Tell me," Callum orders. "Did you love that arrogant piece of shit?"

He's got that crazed look of hunger again. Like it's driving him nuts and he has to know.

Well, I'm not telling him shit. I'm pissed he was eavesdropping, and I'm pissed he thinks he has a right to my thoughts and feelings when he hasn't earned the slightest shred of trust. "What do you care? What does it matter?"

"I need to know. Did you like how he touched you? How he fucked you?"

Without seeming to realize it, he's put his hand on my bare thigh. His fingers slide upward, under the stiff beaded skirt of the dress he made me wear.

I slap his hand away before shoving him in the chest for good measure.

"Maybe I did."

"Who fucks you better? Me or him?" Callum demands. His hand is on my thigh again. His other hand reaches for the back of my neck, trying to pull me closer. He's pressing me back against the seat, climbing on top of me.

This time I slap him across the face hard enough to split his lip.

The slap echoes in the back of the limo, loud in the silence.

For a second, it seems to shake him awake.

Then he blinks, and his eyes are more lustful than ever. Hungry as a wolf's.

He kisses me, mashing his lips against mine and shoving his tongue into my mouth. I can taste the blood from his split lip, salty and hot.

His weight crushes me against the deep leather seat. His body temperature seems like it's two hundred degrees.

I hate Callum the most when he's cold, stiff, robotic. When he walks past me in the hallway like I'm not even there. When he sleeps next to me in bed without holding me, without even touching me.

When I drive him into a rage like this, when he finally cracks and loses control…that's when I don't hate him. In fact, I almost like him a little. Because that's when I see a little more of myself.

When he has a temper, when he's angry, when he wants to kill somebody…that's when I understand him. That's when we finally have common ground.

I kiss him back, grabbing his face in my hands. My fingers thrust into his hair. His hair is wet with sweat, his scalp radiating heat.

I want to feel the rest of his body.

I fumble with the buttons of his dress shirt, which are the stupid covered kind, the kind you can never undo even when you can see them in full light.

I tear open the front of his shirt instead, like he's Superman and there's an asteroid headed right at us. I run my hands over his burning flesh, feeling the muscles twitching with arousal.

His tongue delves into my mouth so deep that it almost chokes me. The close-trimmed stubble on his face scratches my cheek. He's trying to get my dress off, but it's so stiff and tight that he can't even pull the skirt up around my waist.

Snarling with frustration, he grabs his jacket off the floor and pulls a knife out of the breast pocket. He presses a button and the blade flips up, swift and brutally sharp. It's a lot like the one Nero carries. And just like Nero, I can tell from the way Callum holds it that he knows how to use a knife.

"Hold still," he growls, pinning me against the seat.

I hold perfectly still. With five or six quick jerks, he's cut the dress off my body, leaving it in pieces on the limo floor.

I'm completely naked underneath.

Callum takes one second to devour my body with his eyes. Then he unbuttons his trousers, letting his cock spring free.

I'd never admit it to him, but Callum has a gorgeous cock. I've never seen anything quite like it. The deep cuts of his Adonis belt lead directly to the shaft, which is too thick for me to close my hand around. His skin is pale and creamy, and his cock is almost exactly the same color, with just a hint of pink on the head.

I quite enjoyed having it in my mouth that time in the shower. It was incredibly smooth, sliding in and out of my lips with ease.

In fact, I'd be willing to do it again right now. But Callum is too impatient.

He pulls me down on top of him so I'm straddling his lap. His cock stands between us, reaching almost all the way up to my belly button. I slide my pussy lips back and forth along the shaft, moistening it. Then I lower myself on the fat head, letting it slip inside me.

Callum leans his head back against the seat, letting out a deep, guttural moan as my pussy swallows his cock. His hands are wrapped tight around my waist, pulling me down.

Oh, my fucking god, it feels so good…

I've been wet all night long from the maddening friction of my bare pussy under that dress. I was horny and frustrated, wondering when the hell I was going to have sex again.

I have to admit, for a second, Oliver's offer didn't sound that bad. He's arrogant, and immature, and kind of an idiot, but at least he worshipped my body.

But when he was talking about the night we fucked on the sand dunes, a different image flashed into my head: Callum shoving me against the glass wall of the shower and sliding that beautiful thick cock inside me. I was thinking of my husband's hands all over me in the humid heat, not my ex-boyfriend's.

I haven't been able to stop thinking about it.

Now that I'm experiencing it again, it feels even better than the first time. Callum is even wilder and more ravenous than before. He's taking my breasts in his mouth, sucking them like he's starving and I'm the only thing keeping him alive. When he lets go of my nipple, he starts sucking my neck instead, so rough and so ravenous that I know I'm going to be covered in marks tomorrow.

I bounce up and down on his lap, riding his cock. The movement of the limo as it runs over rough parts in the road only increases the friction of the ride. Even the vibration of the engine adds to the sensation. I smell the rich leather of the seats, the alcohol in the minibar, the blood on Callum's shirt, and the sweat on his skin.

He grabs a handful of my hair, biting the side of my neck like the vampire I imagine him to be. It sends shivers down my body; it makes me cling to his neck and squeeze around his cock.

"Aida," he moans in my ear. "You're so fucking gorgeous."

I freeze for a second.

Callum has never complimented me before. I thought he liked girls like Christina Huntley-Hart—skinny, blond, fashionable, popular. Well-bred like a show poodle.

When he attacked Oliver, I thought it was out of pride. Annoyance that Oliver crashed his fundraiser and tried to put his hands on Callum's property.

I never imagined Callum might actually be jealous.

Is my tightly wound, stuck-up, perfectionist husband…actually into me?

I start to ride his cock again, rolling my hips so my pussy slides up and down the full length of his shaft.

Callum groans, his arms wrapped around me so tightly, I can hardly breathe.

I put my lips up against his ear, and I whisper, "Do you want me, Cal?"

"I don't want you," he moans, his voice husky and raw. "I *need* you."

His words release something inside me. That part of me that was trying to hold back my own desperate attraction because it was too intense, too dangerous to indulge. I couldn't let myself crave this man because it was pointless. I thought I had no power over him.

Now I realize he needs this as badly as I do.

I come so hard that my whole body shakes in the frame of his arms. It feels like a waterfall thundering through me. A fucking Niagara Falls of pleasure, pounding down and down and down. Unstoppable. Uninhibited.

Even after I finish climaxing, I still want more. The orgasm was incredible, but it didn't completely satisfy. I need more.

Callum lays me on my back and climbs on top of me before thrusting into me again. He looks directly into my eyes, his clear blue into my smoky gray.

Usually, when I look him in the eye, it's because I'm furious, trying to stare him down. We've never looked at each other quite like this before: open, curious, questioning.

Callum isn't a robot. He feels things as acutely as I do. Maybe even more because he's always trying to shove it down inside.

For the first time, he presses his lips against mine with gentleness. His tongue tasting and exploring.

I kiss him back, still rolling my hips under his. I can feel another climax building, the other half of the one that came before. Why do our bodies fit together so perfectly when everything else about us is completely opposite?

"You're mine, Aida," Callum growls in my ear. "I'll kill anyone who tries to touch you."

With that, he erupts inside me. I'm coming, too, the second orgasm even stronger than the first. The strongest I've ever felt, in fact.

I'm not sure I'll be alive when it's over.

16
CALLUM

Luckily, Aida and I are the first ones back to the house, because the scraps of her dress are scattered across the limo floor, and she doesn't have anything else to wear except my suit jacket.

She doesn't give a shit. Ever the free spirit, she just wraps my jacket around her body and runs inside barefoot, giving the chauffeur a jaunty salute on her way by.

I'd like to follow her, but I can feel my phone buzzing in my pocket—my father, calling to chastise me.

"What the fuck were you thinking?" he says the moment I pick up.

"That piece of shit tried to assault my wife."

"You got in a brawl at your own fundraiser. With Oliver Castle! Do you know how that looks?"

"He's lucky I didn't splatter his brains on the concrete."

"If you did, you'd be in jail right now." My father seethes. "That wasn't some frat boy you hit—Henry Castle is one of the richest men in Chicago. He donated fifty thousand to your campaign!"

"Well, he's not getting a refund."

"You're going to have to give him a hell of a lot more than a refund to keep him from torpedoing your run."

I grind my teeth so hard that my molars feel like they're about to crack in half. "What does he want?"

"You're going to find out tomorrow. Eight in the morning, at Keystone Capital. Don't be late."

Fucking hell. Henry Castle is worse than his son—bloated, arrogant, and hyperdemanding. He's going to want me to grovel and kiss his ring, while I want to castrate him to prevent him from siring any more shithead sons. "I'll be there."

"You lost control tonight," my father says. "What the fuck is going on with you and that girl?"

"Nothing."

"She's supposed to be an asset, not a liability."

"She didn't do anything. I told you it was Castle."

"Well, pull it together. You can't allow her to distract you from your goal."

I hang up, boiling with everything unsaid that I wanted to scream into the phone.

He's the one who forced me to marry Aida, and now he's pissed off because she's not a little chess piece he can shuffle around the board like he does to everybody else?

That's what I admire about her. She's wild and she's fierce. It takes everything I've got just to get her to wear a damn dress. She'd never grovel in front of Henry Castle. And neither will I.

I head upstairs to our bedroom, expecting her to be brushing her teeth and getting ready for bed. Instead, she pounces on me the minute I come inside. She kisses me deeply, pulling me toward the bed.

"Aren't you tired?" I ask her.

"It's not even midnight." She laughs. "But if you'd rather go to sleep, old man…"

"Let's see what it takes to tire you out, you fucking lunatic," I say, throwing her down on the mattress.

———————

Aida is still deep asleep when I get up for my meeting with Henry Castle. I pull the blankets up around her bare shoulders, though it seems a pity to cover all that smooth glowing skin.

She looks exhausted after the romp we had last night. We spent an hour doing something that was as close to wrestling as fucking. She was testing me, testing whether I'd let her take control, testing my energy and my stamina.

There was no fucking way I was tapping out first. Every time she tried to overpower me, I pinned her down again and fucked her ruthlessly, until we were both panting and dripping with sweat.

I could see how it excited her, feeling my strength against hers, knowing I wouldn't give an inch to her. She likes to push me, to see how far she can go before I snap. She does it in and out of the bedroom.

Well, I'm a fucking mountain that can't be pushed. She'll learn that soon enough.

And so will Henry Castle. I know he thinks I've come to his office to grovel, but that's not fucking happening.

In fact, when his receptionist tells me to sit and wait outside his door, I tell her, "Our meeting's at eight," and I sweep inside.

Just as I suspected, Henry is sitting behind his desk, doing bugger all at the moment.

He's a big man, completely bald, well muscled and fat. He wears loose suits with wide shoulders, enhancing the impression of his bulk. His eyebrows look black and out of place on his otherwise hairless head.

"Griffin," he says with a stern nod. He's trying to set a commanding tone.

Henry gestures for me to sit down opposite his desk. The chair is low and narrow, deliberately inferior to the one Henry himself sits in.

"No thanks," I say, remaining standing and leaning casually against the side of his desk. Now I'm the one looking down on him.

I can tell it annoys him. Almost immediately he stands himself, on the pretext of looking at some of the photographs on his bookshelf.

"You know Oliver is my only son." He picks up a framed photo of a boy on a beach. The boy is running toward the water. There's a house behind him—small, blue, almost more of a cottage. The sand comes right up to its steps.

"Mm." I nod noncommittally. "Where's that?"

"Chesterton," Henry says shortly. He wants to turn the conversation back on topic. I draw out the tangent instead, to increase his irritation.

"You go out there a lot?"

"We used to. Every summer. I just sold it, though. Would have done it sooner, but Oliver made a fuss. He's more sentimental than I am."

Henry sets the picture firmly back down on the shelf, turning to face me again. His thick black brows hang low over his eyes.

"You assaulted my son last night."

"He assaulted my wife."

"Aida Gallo?" Henry allows himself a small sneer. "No offense, but I wouldn't take her word for it."

"That's extremely offensive." I hold his stare. "Not to mention I saw it with my own eyes."

"You had him escorted out by security. I expect better treatment for one of your biggest donors."

I give a small snort. "Please. I've got plenty of money. I'm not going to prostitute my wife for fifty K. And in any case, my relationship is with you, not with Oliver. I doubt the fact he's a handsy drunk is a surprise, so let's cut to the chase of what's really bothering you."

"Fine," Henry snaps. His face reddens, making his bald head look shinier than ever. "I heard you're selling the Transit Authority property to Marty Rico. I want it."

Jesus Christ. I'm not even alderman yet, the property isn't for sale, yet half the men in Chicago are trying to close their grubby fists around it.

"I've got several interested parties." I tap my fingers lightly on his desk. "I'll be entertaining all bids."

"But you'll give it to me," Castle says threateningly.

He can threaten all he wants. I'm not giving anything away for free. "If the price is right."

"You don't want to make an enemy of me." Henry is back behind his desk now, standing because he wants to loom over me. Unfortunately for him, that doesn't work when you're not the tallest man in the room.

"I'm sure you'll come up with something good," I remark. "After all, it says 'capital' on the door."

His face turns darker and darker in color. He looks like he's about to burst a blood vessel. "I'll be contacting your father about this."

"Don't bother," I tell him. "Unlike your son, I speak for myself."

17

AIDA

CALLUM GETS UP EARLY, QUIETLY SLIPPING INTO THE BATHROOM and closing the door so he doesn't wake me with the noise of the shower.

When I finally come all the way awake, he's long gone, probably headed off to some meeting. I can still smell his shampoo and aftershave in the air. A scent that's becoming increasingly erotic to me.

I bask in the satisfaction of the night before.

I never would have believed Callum Griffin had the capacity to be so passionate or sensual. Frankly, it's the best sex I've ever had, with the person I like the least. What a conundrum. Because it almost makes me feel friendly toward him, and I wasn't planning on that at all.

My head is spinning. What the hell is going on? Is this Stockholm Syndrome because I've been enmeshed with the Griffins too long?

Luckily, I'm going home today so I can regain a little sanity.

I wish it were for a happier reason. It's the anniversary of my mother's death—a day I always spend with my father and brothers.

I'm looking forward to it. I haven't been back since I got married. I wonder if it will feel different now that I technically live somewhere else.

The Griffins' mansion sure as shit doesn't feel like home. There are a couple of things I like about it—mostly the theater room and the pool. Everything else is annoyingly tidy, like someone's coming to shoot a magazine spread any minute. Most of the couches look like you're not supposed to actually sit on them, barricaded with stiff pillows and devoid of comfortable accessories like books or blankets.

Plus, their house staff is enormous. Cleaning ladies, cooks, assistants, drivers, security guards… It's hard to feel comfortable when you know somebody could come creeping into the room at any moment, always retreating politely if they see the space is occupied but still reminding you that you're not alone and that you're in some awkward class above them.

I talk to "the help"—especially Marta, since I see her most often. She has a seven-year-old daughter, she listens to reggaeton, and she is the Michelangelo of makeup. She seems cool, like we could maybe be friends. Except that she's supposed to wait on me hand and foot like I'm a Griffin.

It's funny because the Gallos aren't exactly poor. But there are levels to richness just like everything else.

I'll be glad to get back to reality for a day.

Nessa kindly lends me her Jeep to drive home. I don't actually have my own car. At Papa's house, there were always enough random vehicles in the garage that I could take whatever I wanted, assuming Nero hadn't removed the engine for his own bizarre purposes. I guess I could get one now. I've got plenty of money in the bank. But I hate the idea of begging the Griffins for a parking spot.

I head over to Old Town, feeling like it's been months instead of only weeks since I was here last.

Driving up these familiar streets is like becoming myself again. I see the shops and bakeries I know so well, and I think about how crazy it is that Callum and I lived only a few miles apart from each other all this time, yet our worlds are so different.

All kinds of people have lived in Old Town over the years—when it was full of German farms, they called it the Cabbage Patch. Later, Puerto Ricans moved in, and an army of artists. Penty of Italians, too.

Our house is a grand old Victorian—emphasis on the *old*. It's four levels high, as dark and steeply gabled as a haunted house, shaded by overgrown oak trees, and backed by a walled garden.

My father hollowed out an underground parking garage for Nero's ongoing projects. I drive below street level to park before climbing the stairs to the kitchen, where I surprise Greta by throwing my arms around her thick waist.

"*Minchia!*" she shrieks, spinning around with a spoon in hand, spattering me with tomato sauce. "Aida! Why didn't you tell me you were coming home? I would have made dinner!"

"You are making dinner," I observe.

"I would have made better dinner."

"I love everything you make," I say, trying to snatch the spoon from her hand so I can taste the sauce.

She uses it to smack my knuckles instead. "It's not ready yet."

I seize her around the waist and hug her again, squeezing her tight and trying to lift her off the ground.

"*Smettila!* Stop that before you break your back. Or break mine!"

I content myself with kissing her on the cheek instead.

"I miss you. The Griffins' cook makes the shittiest food."

"They don't have a good cook, with all that money?" she says in amazement.

"It's all health food. I hate it."

Greta shudders like I said they were serving live rats. "There's nothing healthier than olive oil and red wine. You eat like an Italian, and you'll live forever. It's not good to be too skinny."

I stifle a laugh. I don't think Greta has ever been within fifty pounds of skinny, and I've never been close to a stick. So we're not exactly speaking from experience. But it looks miserable.

"Where's Papa?" I ask her.

"He's up in your mother's room."

She means the music room. My mother trained as a classical pianist before she met my father. Her grand piano still sits in the sunniest room of the topmost floor, along with all her composition books and sheet music.

I climb the two flights of stairs to find Papa. The staircases are narrow and creaking, the wooden risers barely wide enough for Dante to ascend without his shoulders brushing the walls on either side.

Papa is sitting on my mother's piano bench, looking down at the keys. He has the piano tuned and serviced every year, though Mama was the only one who played on the grand.

I remember her sitting in exactly that spot. It amazed me how quickly her hands could fly over the keys, considering she was petite and her hands were barely any larger than mine.

I don't have a lot of other memories of her. I'm jealous my brothers knew her for so much longer than I did. I was only six when she died.

She thought it was a flu. She holed up in her bedroom, not wanting to give it to the rest of us. By the time my father realized how ill she was, it was too late. She died of meningitis after being sick only two days.

My father felt horribly guilty. He still does.

In our world, you know you may lose a family member in a violent way. The Gallos have lost more than our share. But you don't expect a silent thief, disease striking a woman so young and otherwise healthy.

Papa was devastated. He loved my mother intensely.

He saw her perform in the Riviera Theatre. Then he sent flowers and perfume and jewelry to her for weeks before she agreed to have dinner with him. He was twelve years older than her and already infamous.

He wooed her for two more years before she agreed to marry him.

I don't know what she thought about his job or his family. I know she adored her children at least. She always talked about her three handsome boys and me, her last little surprise.

Dante has her focus, Nero her talent, Sebastian has her kindness…I don't know what I have—her eyes, I suppose.

I can play the piano a little. Not like her.

I see Papa's broad suited shoulders hunched over the keys. He touches middle C with a finger almost too thick to stay within the bounds of the key. Papa has a massive head that sits almost directly on his shoulders. His eyebrows are as thick as my thumb. They're still black, and so is his mustache. But his beard is gray, and his dark, curly hair has shocking streaks of white.

"Come play with me, Aida," he says without turning around.

It's impossible to sneak up on him. And not just in our house, where the stairs creak.

I sit next to him on the bench. He slides over to make room for me.

"Play your mother's song."

I spread my fingers over the keys. Every time, I think I'm going to forget it. I couldn't tell you how it starts or even hum it properly. But the body remembers much more than the brain.

She played this song over and over. It wasn't her most difficult, or even the most beautiful. Just the one that stuck in her head.

Gnossienne No. 1 by Erik Satie. An odd and haunting piece.

🎵 *Gnossienne No. 1–Erik Satie*

It starts out rhythmic, mysterious, like a question. Then it seems to answer angrily, dramatically. Then it repeats, though not quite the same.

There are no time signatures or bar divisions. You can play as you like. Mama sometimes played it faster or slower, harder or softer depending on her mood. After the second time through, it transitions into a sort of bridge—the most melancholic bit of all. Then back to the beginning once more.

"What does it mean?" I asked her when I was little. "What's a gnossienne?"

"Nobody knows," she said. "Satie invented it."

I play it for Papa.

He closes his eyes, and I know he's imagining her hands on the keys, moving much more sensitively than mine.

I see her slim frame rocking with the motion of the music, her gray eyes closed. I can smell the fresh lilacs she kept in a vase by the window.

When I open my own eyes, the room is darker than she kept it. The oak trees have grown thicker and taller since then, crowding the window. There's no vase anymore, no fresh flowers.

Nero stands in the doorway—tall, slim, his black hair falling over one eye, his face as beautiful and cruel as an avenging angel.

"You should play it," I say to him. "You're better than me."

He gives one quick shake of his head and heads back down the stairs. I'm surprised he came up here to begin with. He doesn't like reminiscing. Or displays of emotion. Or anniversaries.

Papa is looking at the ring on my left hand. It weighs my hand down and makes it hard to play.

"Are they good to you, Aida?" he says.

I hesitate, thinking of how Callum stole my clothes last night, how he pounced on me in the car and cut my dress off. How his mouth tasted. How my body responded to him.

"You know I can take care of myself, Papa," I say at last.

He nods. "I know."

"Tymon Zajac came to Callum's fundraiser last night."

Papa sucks in a sharp breath. If we were outside, he might have spit on the ground. "The Butcher. What did he want?"

"He said he wanted some Transit Authority property that's about to be auctioned off. But I don't think that was it, not really—I think he was testing Callum. And maybe me, too. To see how we'd react to a demand."

"What did Callum say?"

"Told him to fuck off."

"How did Zajac take it?"

"He left."

My father frowns. "Be careful, Aida. That won't go unanswered."

"I know. Don't worry, though—the Griffins have security everywhere."

He nods but doesn't look satisfied.

I hear a clattering in the downstairs kitchen. This house has no insulation—noise travels all over.

Next comes the rumbling sound of Dante's voice and a laugh that sounds like Sebastian.

"Your brothers are home," Papa says.

"Come on." I rest my hand on his shoulder as I stand from the piano bench.

"I'll be down in a minute."

I head downstairs. Sure enough, all three of my brothers are crammed in the small kitchen with Greta. Dante is trying to clean the shards of the plates Sebastian knocked to the floor with one of his crutches. Seb's knee is still encased in some high-tech brace that's supposed to be helpful but instead has turned him into even more of a walking disaster than usual.

At least he's walking. Sort of.

"Hey, clumsy," I say, giving him a hug.

"Was that you playing up there?" Sebastian says, hugging me back.

"Yeah."

"You sound just like her."

"No, I don't." I shake my head.

"You definitely don't," Nero agrees.

"Give me the broom," Greta demands of Dante. "You're just spreading the mess around."

While her back is turned, Nero steals one of her orange rolls and stuffs it in his mouth.

Sensing misbehavior, she whips around again and gives him a hard stare. Nero tries to keep his face perfectly still, despite the fact his cheeks are puffed out like a chipmunk's.

"Those are for lunch!" Greta shouts.

"Eh esh lunsh," Nero says around an entire orange roll.

"No, it isn't! And don't eat without your father."

Nero swallows hard. "He's not gonna eat. You know how he is today."

"Well, don't make it worse!" Greta cries. "And you." She points a finger at Sebastian. "Get out of here before you break something important."

"All right, all right." Sebastian slots his crutches back under his armpits and wheels around for the living room, just barely missing Greta's kettle, while knocking over the broom.

Nero catches the handle neatly in his right hand, snatching another orange roll with his left. He passes the broom to Greta, keeping the roll hidden behind his back. "Here, Greta. You know I only want to help."

"You'd help yourself to the shirt off my back, you devil."

"Depends. What size is it?"

She tries to whip him with a tea towel. He bolts out of the kitchen, pushing past Sebastian, who almost topples over.

Dante follows at a more leisurely pace. I leave last of all, eyeing the freshly glazed orange rolls but not wanting to risk Greta's wrath.

Eventually, we do lure Papa down by bringing out his old mah-jongg set and opening the bottle of wine Dante brought. We play a rotating tournament, in which Nero eventually emerges victorious, but not without accusations of cheating and demands to recount all the pieces in case some were "misplaced" in the course of the game.

When lunch is ready, we physically force Greta to sit and eat with us instead of working the whole time. Nero convinces her to drink one, then several glasses of wine, at which point she tells us stories about a famous writer she used to know, whom she might have slept with "once or twice," until he wrote a character based on her that offended her terribly.

"Was it Kurt Vonnegut?" Sebastian says.

"No." Greta shakes her head. "And I'm not telling you his name. He was married some of the time."

"Was it Steinbeck?" Nero grins wickedly.

"No! How old do you think I am?" Greta says, outraged.

"Maya Angelou," I say, with an expression of innocence.

"No! Stop guessing, you disrespectful little beasts."

"That's not disrespectful," Dante says. "Those are all excellent authors. Now, if we said Dan Brown…"

Greta, who loves *The DaVinci Code*, has had enough of us.

"That's it!" She rises threateningly from her seat. "I'm throwing your dessert in the trash."

Nero makes a frantic signal to me to go rescue the semifreddo from the freezer before Greta can wreak her revenge.

All in all, the day is as cheerful as I could hope for, given the occasion. The only person who isn't in as high of spirits as usual is Sebastian. He's doing his best to smile and participate in games and conversation with the rest of us, but I can tell that the weeks of inactivity and the loss of his favorite thing in the world is wearing on him. He looks thin and tired. His face is pale like he hasn't been sleeping much.

I know he doesn't want me to apologize again. But watching him try to navigate the narrow hallways and numerous staircases of the house on those damn crutches is killing me.

Even with that unhappy reminder, the afternoon ends too soon.

Once we've all eaten and cleared the table, Dante and Nero have to get back to the Oak Street Tower project; Sebastian has a biology class.

I could stay with Papa, but I know he's going to finish the wine while looking through old photo albums. I don't have the heart for it. All those pictures of Papa, Mama, and my brothers traveling in Sicily, Rome, Paris, Barcelona, while I'm not yet in existence, o at best, I'm a baby in a stroller. It just reminds me of what I missed.

I give my father a kiss and offer to help Greta with the dishes, knowing she won't let me. Then I descend to the garage and retrieve Nessa's Jeep.

I'm back at the Griffins' mansion by 3:00 in the afternoon.

I don't expect to find anybody home other than the staff. When Imogen isn't working on family business, she's spreading her influence over dozens of charities and boards or else strategically socializing with the wealthy and influential wives of Chicago's top citizens. Fergus, Callum, and Riona work long hours, and Nessa has classes almost every day—either at Loyola or at Lake City Ballet.

Yet, as I enter through the side door into the kitchen, I hear two male voices.

It's Callum and his bodyguard, sitting on the barstools in their shirtsleeves, jackets draped over the backs of their chairs.

I don't know what they're talking about, but I'm immediately enraged by the sight of the brutish boxer, who I now know is named Jackson Howell Du Pont. Callum met him at school in his Lakeside Academy days. Jack is one of the many descendants of the Du Pont family, whose members first made their fortune in gunpowder, then later by inventing nylon, Kevlar, and Teflon.

Unfortunately for Jackie-boy, the Du Ponts were a little too successful at spreading their name and their seed, because there are now about four thousand of them, and Jack's particular branch barely had enough scratch to pay for his fancy private school education, without the usual accompanying trust fund. So poor Jack is reduced to driving Callum around, running his errands, watching his back, and occasionally breaking kneecaps on his behalf. Like he did to my brother.

Fresh from the sight of Sebastian's dark circles and unhappy smile, I want to grab the closest piano wire and wrap it around Jack's throat. Callum has wisely kept his bodyguard on the back burner, away from casa Griffin and out of my sight. I guess he didn't expect me home so early.

"What the fuck is he doing here?" I snarl.

Callum and Jack have already stood, startled by my sudden appearance.

"Aida…" Callum holds up his hands in warning. "That's water under the bridge."

"Is it? Because Sebastian is still hobbling around. While this punch-drunk fuck boy is apparently still on your payroll."

Jack rolls his eyes, sauntering over to the fruit bowl on the counter and picking out a nice, juicy apple.

"Put your bitch on a leash," he says to Callum.

To my surprise, Callum turns on Jack, face still but eyes blazing. "What did you say?"

I see the dull gleam of metal inside Jack's suit jacket. A Ruger LC9 in the inside pocket, hanging over the back of his chair, instead of securely attached to his body. What a fucking amateur.

In two steps I've reached the jacket and pulled out the gun. I check that it's loaded, then slip off the safety and chamber a round.

Both Callum and Jack freeze at the sound of the bullet sliding into the chamber.

"Aida!" Callum says sharply. "Don't—"

I'm already pointing the gun at Jack.

"Leaving your weapon unattended." I click my tongue, shaking my head in mock disapproval. "Very sloppy, Jackie-boy. Where did you get your training, the Chicago Police Academy? Or was it clown college?"

"Get fucked, you lippy cunt," Jack snarls, his blocky face red with rage and his teeth bared. "If you weren't married to him—"

"You'd what? Get your teeth kicked in like last time?" I snort.

Jack is so mad that I know he'd already be charging at me if I didn't have the gun pointed right at his chest.

Callum is in a more ambivalent position. On the one hand, I can tell he's pissed I pulled a gun in his kitchen and pointed it at his bodyguard. On the other hand, he doesn't like the way Jack is talking to me. Not one bit.

"Put the gun down, Aida," he orders. But it's Jack he's looking at with cold fury in his eyes.

"I will," I say, lowering the gun so the barrel is pointed directly at Jack's knee. "After he pays for what he did to my brother."

I haven't actually shot anybody before. I've been to the range plenty of times with my brothers. We've put up those paper cutouts—sometimes a blank human silhouette, and sometimes a zombie or a burglar. I know how to aim for center mass, how to group my shots, how to squeeze the trigger instead of jerking it, and how to control the backfire.

It's strange aiming at an actual person. I can see the droplets of sweat along Jack's hairline, the way his right eye twitches slightly as he glares at me. I can see his chest rising and falling. He's an actual person, despite being a raging douche. Am I really going to put a bullet in him?

Jack decides the best way to get out of this is to intimidate me. Maybe he thinks it's reverse psychology. Or maybe he's just dumb.

"You're not gonna shoot me," He sneers. "You're just a spoiled little Mafia brat, a wannabe tough girl like your pussy-ass brother."

Callum, more perceptive than Jack, sees my intention before I even move. He dives for the gun, knocking my hands upward right as I pull the trigger.

The report is shockingly loud in the enclosure of the kitchen. It seems to echo around and around, deafening us.

Thanks to Callum's intervention, I miss Jack's leg. Instead, the bullet digs a groove along the outside of Callum's left arm before burying itself in the door of one of Imogen's custom cedar cabinets.

Like scarlet ink on paper, blood soaks through Callum's shirt-sleeve. He glances down, stoically surveying the damage before twisting my arm behind my back and pinning it tight.

"I said *don't*," he growls in my ear.

"She tried to shoot me!" Jack shouts in disbelief. "She pulled the trigger! You dirty little bitch! I'm gonna—"

"Shut your fucking mouth, and keep it shut," Callum barks.

Jack halts in place, frozen in the act of advancing upon me. His big square face looks confused.

"If you *ever* talk to my wife like that again, I'll empty that clip in your chest."

Jack opens his mouth like he's going to protest, only to shut it again when he sees the look on Callum's face.

I can't really see it myself, since Callum still has my arm twisted behind my back, rather painfully. But I can feel the heat radiating from his body. I can hear the deadly seriousness of his threat. He means it. Every word of it.

"You're…you're bleeding on the floor, boss," Jack says humbly.

Sure enough, a little puddle is forming on Callum's left side, seeping into the spotless grout between Imogen's tiles. Another thing that's really going to piss her off.

"Clean that up, please," Callum says in the direction of the doorway.

I realize that at least three members of the house staff are peeking in, trying to figure out what the hell is going on. One of the maids, Linda, seems particularly alarmed by the fact Callum has me in an armbar. Martino, the landscaper, peers in the window, looking queasy at all the blood on the floor.

"Go home," Callum orders Jack. "I'll call you in the morning."

Jack nods, chastened. He doesn't make eye contact with me as he hurries by.

I expect Callum to let go of me once Jack is gone. I assumed he was holding me like that to make sure I wasn't going to attack his bodyguard again.

Instead, he starts frog-marching me out of the kitchen, down the hallway.

"Where are we going?" I demand, trying to twist my wrist out of his grip.

Callum only holds me tighter. Pain shoots up my right arm into my shoulder. My hand has gone numb. His left arm wraps around my body, his hand clenching a fistful of the front of my shirt. My back presses against his chest. I can feel his heart pounding, furious as a war drum.

"You can let go, I'm not—*Ouch!*"

He's shoving me up the staircase, pushing me so hard and fast that my feet barely touch the ground. He keeps rocketing me along until we're all the way down the hallway and through the doorway to our room. Only then does he release me, slamming the door behind him.

He turns around to face me, his pupils contracted to pinpricks so his eyes look bluer and colder than ever. No longer vampirically pale, his skin flushes with color, his jaw rigid from how hard he's clenching it.

"Look," I say. "I know that got a little—"

He crosses the space between us in one stride, seizing a handful of my hair. He jerks my head back and kisses me ferociously.

It's the last thing I was expecting. All the defiance goes out of my body. I sink against him, limp with relief. I think he's forgiven me or that he at least understands why I did it.

I immediately realize I was very wrong in that assumption. As soon as our chests touch, I can feel his body is still burning and shaking, every muscle throbbing with the effort of containing the emotion inside him.

His tongue fills my mouth. His lips grind against mine so hard that I can feel my own lips starting to swell. He's crushing me against him, still determined to subdue me even though I already submitted. It's only when my knees are literally buckling beneath me that he picks me up and carries me to the bed.

He pulls my shirt over my head. Like a child, I cooperatively lift my arms. Once the shirt is above me, he pulls my wrists back down behind me, the cotton T-shirt still wrapped around one arm. Swiftly, Callum crosses my wrists, using the twisted shirt as a rope to knot them together.

Then he unbuttons my shorts. With one hard jerk, he pulls both shorts and panties down around my knees.

I feel very stupid standing there, my arms bound behind my back and my ankles effectively tied as well, unless I want to try to step out of my shorts without falling on my face.

"Callum," I say hesitantly. "Can you—"

Callum is in the process of unknotting his tie. He pulls it from around his neck and approaches me with the material held taut between his two hands like a garrote. I'm mildly concerned he's about to strangle me. Instead, he gags me with the tie, cutting me off midsentence and knotting the tie tightly behind my head.

I taste the raw silk against my tongue. Must be expensive.

I have a vague idea that Callum plans to tie me up and leave me here as punishment for shooting at his employee. I soon realize Callum has no intention of leaving. He sits on the edge of the bed and roughly pulls me onto his lap. He throws me over his thighs so my face is down by his shins, my bare ass up in the air.

In a flash, I realize what he's planning. I start to wriggle and squirm, trying to kick my feet free of my shorts, shouting through the gag, "*Don't you dare*—" though it comes out more like, *Der do dah*—

Callum lifts one large, strong hand and brings it whistling down on my bottom. There's a sharp cracking sound, almost as loud as the kitchen gunshot. An instant later, stinging-hot pain rushes in.

"*Erggg!*" I shriek through the gag.

SMACK!

I didn't even know he lifted his hand again, and already he's spanked me in the same spot, even harder this time.

SMACK!

SMACK!

SMACK!

His precision is vicious. Each hit is landing in precisely the same spot on my right buttock, making it feel like it's been dipped in gasoline and set aflame.

I'm kicking and trying to roll off his lap, shouting all kinds of curses. Callum has me pinned tight, his left hand bearing down between my shoulder blades while his right hand administers the punishment.

I give one particularly vigorous struggle. Callum barks, "Hold still, or you'll get twice as many!"

That only makes me kick harder. How fucking dare he try to spank me! How dare he threaten me! When I get free, I'm going to punch him right where I shot him, and then I'm going to kick him someplace worse.

SMACK!

Callum brings his palm smashing down on the left side. *Fuck!* Why does it hurt even more? How is he slapping me so hard? He's like a jockey whipping a horse!

SMACK!

SMACK!

SMACK!

I've never actually been spanked before. I can't believe how it's making my ass burn and throb.

Callum told me to hold still, but I can't. I can't help flinching away from the next blow, squeezing my legs together, and squirming on the hard surface of his trousered thighs.

This is having its own embarrassing effect.

I am naked after all. The squeezing and squirming of my bare flesh against the fine wool of Callum's trousers create a whole lot of friction in very inconvenient places…

My nipples are rock-hard inside my bra. I feel warmth and wetness between my thighs. I can't see it, but I suspect my cheeks are burning as red as my ass.

I stop struggling, mostly because I don't want to make myself any more inadvertently excited than I already am. I also don't want Callum to notice. It's fucking humiliating. If he realizes the effect this is having on me, I'll never be able to look him in the face again.

But he already knows. He's so goddamned perceptive. The moment I stop fighting him, the moment my breath changes and I tense, he stops the spanking. He pauses for a moment, his heavy palm resting on my throbbing buttocks.

Then he starts kneading my ass, gently.

The rubbing feels unutterably good. It's like the time I stole one of Dante's special brownies and ate the whole thing before getting a massage. Each squeeze of Callum's hand sends pulses of pleasure running down my neurons, making them glow like a string of Christmas lights.

Without meaning to, I moan and press my thighs against the outside of Callum's leg.

"You like that?" he growls, his voice lower and rougher than ever.

His fingertips dance down the crevice of my ass before slipping between my thighs to find confirmation of what he already suspects. Sure enough, his fingers slide easily across the slick surface of my cunt.

"I thought so," he breathes.

Without warning, he plunges two fingers inside me. I let out a deep, desperate groan. My pussy is so swollen and warm that those fingers are the most pleasurable things that have ever been inside me. They feel tailor-made, superpowered, as custom fit as one of Imogen's fucking cabinets.

Callum slides his fingers in and out, enjoying the anxious plead-ing sounds I'm making around the gag.

Oh my god, I want to be fucked.

I want it so bad, I feel like I could be willing to die after, if I could only get what I need for five straight minutes.

"Look what you did." Callum touches the wound on his left arm. When he brings his fingertips down in front of my face, I can see they're shining with fresh blood.

"I've had enough of you flying off the handle," Callum says. "It ends tonight. From now on, you're going to be the wife I was promised. Helpful. Useful. Obedient."

Hooking his arms under my body, Callum stands, lifting me off his knees. He throws me facedown on the bed, wrists still bound behind my back and knees bent under me so my ass points up in the air.

I hear a button popping and a zipper going down. Callum's strong, warm hands grip my hips, the right one disappearing momentarily as Callum lines his cock up with my entrance, then returning.

He rams inside me with one thrust of his hips. He goes all the way in, bottoming out with the front of his thighs flush against the back of mine. He grips my hips tight, letting his cock stay fully sheathed so deep that I feel the head throbbing against my cervix.

Only then does he pull out again, almost all the way, before thrusting all the way back in.

He does this several times, letting me appreciate the full length of his cock. Then he starts fucking me hard. Harder and faster, our bodies slamming together with a sound not as sharp as the spank-ings but more rapid and insistent.

To be desperately aroused and then aggressively serviced like this is just so...satisfying. On the level of Popsicles on a hot day, or a bratty kid falling on their face, I am at peak happiness. I don't just want this; I fucking need it.

Then Callum really starts to torture me.

He reaches around my hip and finds my clit with his fingers. He lightly teases me with his fingertips before gradually increasing the pressure.

I'm panting and moaning into the gag, trying to buck my hips to get more pressure on just the right spot.

Callum isn't giving it to me. He knows what I want, but he's denying it.

His arm is wrapped tightly around me. He's still thrusting into me, deeper and deeper. He leans over and growls in my ear, "Are you going to be a good girl, Aida? My good little wife?"

I'm whimpering, almost begging. I don't want to say it. God damn him, I don't want to say it!

"Tell me," Callum croons. "Tell me you'll be a good girl."

No way.

I'm not gonna do it.

I'm totally going to do it.

Squeezing my eyes tightly shut, I nod.

Callum presses hard against my clit. He rubs me in time with his thrusts, just in the right spot, just the right way to make me accelerate through the stratosphere.

Blast off. We've left the planet, ladies and gentlemen; it's pure flaming stars up here.

I'm floating, flying, zooming at a million miles, experiencing a kind of pleasure that I've never even imagined before. Hard, fast, endless.

I lose all sense of what Callum is doing. I'm just gone.

I don't come back to earth until Callum pulls me into his arms, wrapping them tightly around my body.

He's taken off the gag and the makeshift handcuffs. I'm lying naked on his chest, all his clothes stripped off, too. My body is rising and falling with the rhythm of his breaths. His chin nestles against my temple.

His breathing is steady and peaceful. His arms are warm and

gentle around me. I don't know if I've ever felt his body this relaxed. I've seen him stiff and controlled but never calm.

"Did you get there, too?"

He kisses the side of my head. "Of course."

"That was…" What, exactly? Insane? Shocking? Confusing? Breathtaking? Unforgettable?

"I know," Callum says.

There's a long pause. I can't help asking, "Have you ever done that before?"

Another long pause in which I think he won't answer.

Then, finally, he says, "Not like that."

Dear lord.

I'm a pretty opinionated girl. I thought I knew what I liked and what I didn't like.

But I might have just discovered a whole new category…

18
CALLUM

AIDA IS LYING IN MY ARMS. I CAN FEEL HOW FLUSHED AND WARM she still is. And I saw how hard she came. But I would be worried how she was feeling in the aftermath, if I weren't so distracted with my own absolute amazement.

I've tied women up and fucked them roughly before. Some of them asked for it, and other times I was just experimenting. Some girls are so boring to fuck that you might as well tie them up because they're just going to lie there either way.

In all those instances, I felt like I was going through the motions.

With Aida, it was totally different.

Sex with her always is.

Fucking used to be about release for me. It was a manual act that could be good, bad, or indifferent. I never imagined it could feel so good that it takes me over, body and brain. The sheer physical pleasure is insanely intense. Bizarrely stronger than what I'm used to.

And then there are the psychological factors. Aida attracts me in a way I can't understand. It's as if every one of her features was formed with some kind of secret code designed to burrow into my brain. The long almond shape of her smoky-gray eyes. The insane curves of her body. Her smooth cedar-colored skin. The way her teeth flash at me when she grins. The way she bites the edge of her bottom lip when she's aroused or trying not to laugh.

She loves passion of any kind. She loves to be angry, stubborn, joyful, or mischievous. The only thing she doesn't like is a lack of feeling.

Unfortunately, that's what I am. Cold. Restrained. Lacking in pleasure.

Until I'm around her. Then my senses crank up to a feverish degree. I smell and taste and see more acutely. It can almost be too much.

It scares me how I lose control around her. In the few weeks I've known Aida, I've lost my temper more times than in all the preceding years.

Yet I don't want it to stop. I can't imagine going back to dull indifference. Aida is the doorway into another world. I want to stay by her side forever.

Jesus, what am I saying?

I've never had these thoughts before, let alone allowed them to form into words.

How am I getting so wrapped up in this girl who's frankly out of her fucking mind? She tried to shoot Jack! In my kitchen! If she did that at a campaign event, I'd be royally fucked. And I wouldn't put it past her either.

I've got to calm down and keep my head on straight.

That resolution lasts about five seconds, until I press my nose against her hair and inhale that wild scent of hers, like sunshine and sea salt, dark coffee, pepper, and just a hint of honeyed sweetness. Then I feel that jolt again, the adrenaline shot that switches off the governors on every one of my impulses.

When Aida's phone rings, I almost jump out of my skin.

She jolts awake, having drifted off on my shoulder. "Who is it?" she mumbles.

"It's your phone."

She rolls out of the bed, amusingly clumsy. She doesn't even try for grace, tumbling off the edge of the mattress like a panda bear.

She roots around for the phone before finally locating it halfway under the bed.

"Dante?" She holds it against her ear.

She listens for a moment, eyebrows drawn together in a scowl rather like the default expression of the person to whom she's speaking.

"*Cavalo!*" she exclaims. "*Sei serio? Che palle!*"

I've never heard Aida speak more than a word or two in Italian. I wonder if that's what she speaks at home with her family. She's obviously fluent.

Aida has a lot of hidden talents.

I underestimated her when we met. I thought she was spoiled, careless, uneducated, unmotivated.

She's shown me several times now that she absorbed far more of her father's business than I gave her credit for. She's astute, observant, and persuasive when she wants to be. Clever and resourceful. She knows how to handle a gun—my throbbing bicep can attest to that. And she's brave as hell. The way she stared me down when she threw my grandfather's watch over the railing… It was a dick move but actually pretty smart.

She and Sebastian were outmatched. If she'd handed the watch over, I could conceivably have shot them both and walked away. By throwing it in the lake, she goaded me into acting impulsively. She created chaos and split her opponents.

Aida can be rash and rageful, but she doesn't panic. Even now on the phone with her brother, though something's obviously wrong, she hasn't lost her head. She's getting the information, responding quickly and concisely. "*Capisco. Si. Sarò lì presto.*"

She hangs up the call, turning to face me.

She glows like a bronzed goddess in the watery light coming through the shutters. She doesn't notice or care that she's completely naked.

"Dante says somebody torched the equipment on the Oak Street

Tower site. We've lost about two million in heavy machinery, plus whatever damage there is to the building itself."

"Let's go down there." I'm already climbing out of bed.

"You don't—I was going to go over, but you don't have to."

"Do you not want me to come?" I ask, standing in the doorway between the bedroom and the bathroom.

"No. I mean, yes, you can, but you don't…" She shifts uncomfortably from foot to foot. My little Aida, not embarrassed by nudity but blushing from a direct question on the topic of what she wants.

"I'm coming," I say firmly. "We're on the same team now, right?"

"Yes…" she says, unconvinced.

Then, seeming to commit to the idea, she follows me into the walk-in. I already put back her clothes—a job that took me all of five minutes.

I've ordered Marta to buy Aida a proper wardrobe of professional clothing. By the end of this week, Aida should have a full complement of gowns and cocktail dresses, slacks and sundresses, cardigans, blouses, skirts, sandals, heels, boots, and jackets. Whether she'll actually agree to wear any of it is a different question.

For now, she pulls on a pair of jean shorts and an old Cubbies T-shirt. She sits on the carpet to tie her sneakers.

I pull on my own clothes.

Aida raises a shocked eyebrow. "*Jeans?*" she says, hiding a grin.

"So what?"

"I've never seen you wear jeans. Of course they would be Balenciaga," she adds, rolling her eyes.

"Aida," I say calmly. "I do not pick out any of my clothes, including these jeans. I don't even know what Balan—what that brand even is."

"What?" Aida pauses with only one sneaker on her foot. "You don't buy your own clothes?"

"No."

"Who does?"

"Right now, Marta. Before that, it was a different assistant named Andrew. We agree on an aesthetic, and then—"

"So you never go to the mall?"

"No."

"Why not?"

"Aren't we supposed to be leaving?" I say.

"Right!" Aida pulls on her other sneaker and jumps up.

As we hurry down the stairs, she's still pestering me. "But what if you don't like the color, or—"

I hustle her into the car, saying, "Aida. I work literally all the time. Either on campaign projects or one of our numerous businesses. Some of which, as you very well know, are more difficult and hazardous than others. When I socialize, it's at events where I need to network. I can't remember the last time I ran an errand or did anything for entertainment."

Aida stays quiet longer than usual. Then she says, "That's sad."

I shake my head at her. "I like being busy. It's not sad; it's purposeful."

"What's the point, though? If you're not having any fun along the way."

I give her a sidelong look. "I don't consider *Lord of the Rings* marathons to be all that fun." I can't help taking a little poke at her because I know very well that Aida is often bored or understimulated. It's why she's always getting into trouble.

Sure enough, she doesn't retort with the usual flippant response. She bites the edge of her thumbnail, pensive rather than annoyed.

"I can do more than this, you know," she says.

"I actually do know that."

She glances over at me, checking to see if I'm mocking her.

I'm not.

"I see how smart you are. You had a better read on Madeline Breck than I did," I tell her.

"I have a lot of good ideas," she says. "Papa was always so afraid of me getting hurt, but I'm as smart as Dante or Nero. Or Seb. I'm smart enough not to get myself killed."

"As long as you can keep your temper," I say, half smiling.

"I don't—" Aida says hotly, breaking off when she sees I'm teasing her. Mostly. "I don't have a temper," she says with dignity. "You don't know what it's like to always be the smallest dog in the fight. I have to attack first and hardest."

I can't imagine her soft. It would ruin everything about her.

"Anyway," Aida says quickly. "I still don't know why you want to be alderman. The Griffins are richer than god. You've got friends all across the city. Your territory's secure. Why in the fuck do you want to sit in an office and deal with all that bullshit?"

"Why do you think people spend a half a million dollars campaigning for an alderman's seat when the salary is $122,304?" I ask her.

"Well, obviously you can fuck around with zoning and tax law and suit your business interests, as well as handing around favors to everybody else."

"Right," I say, encouraging her to go on guessing.

"It just doesn't seem worth the trouble. You can get all that shit with bribes and trading favors. Or good old-fashioned violence."

"But you're always at the mercy of somebody else," I tell her. "The incorruptible detective or the greedy politician who got a better offer from someone else. Real power isn't working the system. It's running the system. Building it yourself, even."

I pause, remembering a little of our overlapping family history.

"You remember when the Italians ran this city?" I say to her. "Capone had the mayor on his payroll. Imagine if Capone *had been* the mayor. Or the governor. Or the fucking president."

"I don't like how you use the past tense to refer to our glory days," Aida says lightly. "But I take your point. I guess it makes sense why your dad was keen to make an agreement between our families.

It's not about this election. It's about the one after. If you want to run the whole city, you really do need us."

"Yes," I say quietly.

We've pulled up to the tower, its skeletal, half-built frame jutting into the sky. Only the bottom few floors have been completed. The lot is a jumble of heavy machinery, stacks of building materials, makeshift offices, porta potties, and parked trucks.

The site would be dark and deserted if the whole north side weren't lit up by lights and sirens. I see a fire truck, two ambulances, and several police cars. Dante is speaking with a uniformed officer while another cop takes notes from a battered and bandaged security guard. I assume that's the guard who was on duty when someone torched the machines.

The air stinks of gasoline and charred metal. At least four pieces of heavy machinery are unsalvageable, including two excavators, a backhoe, and an entire crane. The blackened hulks are still smoking, the ground beneath muddied by the firemen's hoses.

"It was that fucking Polack, I know it," a voice says on Aida's opposite side.

Nero appears out of the darkness, quiet as a bat.

He's quick and fucking sneaky. He could probably steal the gun out of the nearest cop's belt without the guy noticing until he tries to disarm at the end of the night.

"How can you be sure?" Aida murmurs back. She's keeping her voice down because we don't want to draw attention to ourselves. Me because I don't want my name attached to this, and Nero because he has, at the bare minimum, a fuck ton of unpaid parking tickets.

"This is their calling card," Nero says. "They're like Russians but crazier. They love to make a scene, and they love symbolism. Besides"—he jerks his head toward the crane, where a blackened lump smolders against the base—"they left that."

"What is it?" Aida breathes.

Her face has gone pale. I know she's thinking the same thing as I am—the object has the raw, cracked look of charred flesh.

"It's a boar's head," Nero says. "The Butcher's calling card."

Dante joins us, his skin darker than ever from all the smoke in the air. Sweat has cut pale tracks on the sides of his bristled cheeks. His eyes look black and glittering, reflecting the flashing lights atop the police cars.

"The security guard is telling them it was a bunch of punk kids. We got the story straight before the cops rolled up. Luckily, the fire truck was faster than the cops, or we would have lost half the building, too."

"You don't want them to know it's Zajac?" I say.

"We don't want them in our business, period," Dante replies. In fact, he shoots a questioning look at Aida as to why I'm here.

"I asked to come," I tell him. "I feel responsible, since it was me who aggravated Zajac at the fundraiser."

"He already had it out for us," Nero says. "We've gotten into it with him twice already over his men encroaching on our territory. Ripping off our suppliers and robbing banks in our neighborhoods."

"He's intent on starting conflict, that's obvious," Dante says, his deep rumble like an idling engine. "We should—"

What he proposes is cut off by the rapid-fire pops of a semiautomatic, like a string of firecrackers but a hundred times louder. A black Land Rover roars by, three men hanging out of the rolled-down windows, guns protruding and muzzle flashes illuminating their masked faces.

The moment the shots start, Aida's brothers try to surround her. I've already wrapped my arms around her shoulders and pulled her down behind the wheel of the nearest truck.

The remaining police officers likewise dive for cover, using their radios to call for backup. Hunched behind their vehicles, a few even attempt to return fire. The SUV has already sprayed the lot with a hail of bullets before disappearing around the corner.

One of the officers was hit in the chest. Thanks to his vest, he's only knocked backward against the bumper of his cruiser. Another officer, less lucky, took a bullet to the thigh. His partner drags him behind a stack of pilings, shouting for an EMT.

"Are you hit?" Dante growls to the rest of us.

"No," Nero says at once.

"What about you?" I ask Aida, manually rubbing my hands down her bare arms and legs to make sure they're uninjured.

"I'm fine," she says firmly.

I try to actually pay attention to my body, above the rushing thud of blood in my ears and the frantic firing of my neurons. I don't think I was shot either.

"We're good," I tell Dante.

"Did you see any of the shooters?"

"They had their faces covered. I think I saw a gold watch on one of their wrists. Nothing useful."

Aida pipes up. "The end of the license plate was 48996."

"How did you see that?" Dante demands.

Aida shrugs. "I'm shorter."

"That crazy son of a bitch!" Nero shakes his head in amazement. "He really wants us to fucking obliterate him, doesn't he?"

"He's trying to provoke a response." Dante frowns.

"Don't get up!" I say sharply, seeing Nero about to rise. "We don't know if that was the only car. There could be another. Or other shooters." I nod upward to the countless windows in the high-rises surrounding the site.

"We can't stay here," Aida mutters. "The cops are gonna sweep the whole lot. Unless they're dumb enough to write that off as a coincidence, they're going to be taking this a hell of a lot more seriously now."

Moving slowly, we sneak off the opposite side of the site, making our way back toward Nero's truck. It's the closest vehicle and the one in the least well-lit area.

We all crowd into the cab so Nero can drive Aida and me around the corner to the spot where we left my car.

Dante says, "Zajac may be trying to lure us into an immediate retaliation. We need to hole up for the night. Figure out how we're going to respond. Aida, you should come home with us."

"She's staying with me," I say.

Dante frowns. "We don't know exactly who the Butcher is targeting. He hit our building site, but he came to your fundraiser. We don't know if that was for Aida or for you. Or for both."

"Exactly—which is why Aida should stay with me. If it turns out he's aiming his attacks at your family, she'll be safer with mine."

"What exactly did Zajac say to you two?" Dante asks.

I summarize the conversation. "I don't know if he really wants that CTA property or if he was just testing me. Actually, he mostly seemed annoyed about the wedding. I think he's trying to crack us before the alliance is solidified."

"Could be." Dante's forehead wrinkles in thought. "The Butcher is touchy. Insanely prideful, easily offended. He's probably angry we didn't offer Aida to him first."

Aida interjects. "Fucking gross. For one thing, he's old. For another, I'm not a fucking pog."

"Either way, it's too late," I growl. "You're mine. And whatever he wants as a consolation prize, he's not getting it."

"I still think she should come with us," Dante says. "We know the Butcher better than you do."

"Not happening," I say flatly. I'm not letting Aida out of my sight.

Dante scowls, not used to anybody contradicting his orders. But it's not all ego—I can see the concern on his face, his fear for Aida. It softens my tone, just a little.

"I'll protect her," I promise him.

Dante gives a curt nod. He believes me. "We'll ride out the night," he says. "In the morning, we'll find out where Zajac is hiding and plan our response."

"A coordinated response," I say.

"Yes," Dante agrees.

Aida and I get out of the truck, transferring over to my Audi. I can see Dante is still reluctant to let his sister leave with me.

It's Aida who convinces him. "I'll be safe with Callum." She gives her oldest brother a quick hug and squeezes Nero's arm. "I'll see you both soon."

As I pull the car away from the curb, I say, without looking at her, "I'm glad you stayed with me."

Aida examines my profile while I drive. "I want us to be partners," she says. "Not just...unwilling roommates."

"I want that, too."

Easier said than done. But it doesn't seem impossible anymore. I'm starting to believe Aida and I could actually work together. We could be stronger together than apart.

Aida sighs. "He certainly hit us where it hurts."

"Because the tower's such a big project?" I ask her.

"It's not the money exactly. It's the work—we have to provide a constant flow of contracts to the trades and unions to keep them loyal. The materials, the jobs—if you can't feed the machine, then it all grinds to a halt. And, of course"—she casts a sideways look at me—"there are the other layers of the machine. The shipments that carry more than lumber. The businesses that wash money for the other businesses. It's a web, all interconnected, all reliant on the smooth operation of the individual parts."

I nod. "We work the same."

Our businesses may differ, but the strategies are similar.

"The election is only a couple of days away," Aida muses. "I wonder if Zajac will try to blow that up, too."

My hands tighten around the steering wheel. "If he tries, the Butcher's going to find himself on the wrong end of the cleaver this time around."

19

AIDA

I HAVE TO LEAVE EARLY THE NEXT MORNING BECAUSE I'VE GOT A literature class I don't want to miss. I've been buckling down this semester, actually passing my classes. I think it's time to quit fucking around and finish my degree.

Callum doesn't want me going anywhere until this thing with Zajac has come to a head, but he finally relents under the condition that Nessa and I have one of his men drive us to school.

Unfortunately, the only person available is Jack.

Under orders from Callum, he opens the car door for me with forced politeness. Waves of loathing roll off us both. The tension in the car is so thick that poor Nessa is wide-eyed and confused, too uncomfortable to engage in her usual stream of cheerful conversation.

"So, uh, did you guys see there's supposed to be some kind of meteor shower tonight?" she asks us.

Jack grunts from the driver's seat.

I'm looking at the back of his head, wondering if it would be worth another fight with Callum to just pop Jack once in the ear when we pull up to campus.

"What?" I say to Nessa.

"I said—Oh, never mind."

Jack drops us off in front of the Cudahy library, his eyes fixed rigidly ahead as he waits for us to get out of the car.

"Thank you, Jack," Nessa says politely as she climbs out.

"Yeah, thanks, Jeeves," I mutter to him on my way out the door.

I see his knuckles whiten on the steering wheel and practically hear his molars grinding. I slam the door behind me just to annoy him more and head off to class, hoping Jack will be too irritated to pick me up again afterward.

I keep sneaking my phone out during class to see if my brothers have texted me or if Cal has. I know they're hunting down the Butcher.

I hope they're all together, whatever they're doing. Zajac scares me. I know where he came from. There's a difference between growing up in a criminal family and fighting your way up in the criminal world. The Butcher is playing this game to win or to die. There's no middle ground for him.

I'm glad my brothers aren't alone in this. But I'm annoyed that, yet again, I'm being left out of the action. This morning, I demanded Cal take me with him. He refused before the words were even out of my mouth.

"No, Aida. We have no idea where the Butcher is or how far he plans to take this. We could be walking into an ambush everywhere we go."

"Then why are *you* going? Send someone else. Like Jack," I said hopefully.

"This isn't an errand boy kind of job. Zajac isn't fucking around. He didn't just shoot at us last night. He hit two cops. We have no idea how far he plans to take this."

"I know people who know his people. I can help," I insisted.

Callum seized me by the arm hard enough to hurt. His blue eyes cut into me, narrow and unblinking. "You're not going anywhere near this. So help me god, I will lock you in that closet for a month before I let you wander around Little Ukraine talking to bartenders and strippers."

Whenever anybody tells me what I *can't* do, it makes me about a hundred times more determined.

Callum saw the flare of rebellion in my eyes and sighed, loosening his grip on my arm just a little. "I promise, as soon as I hear anything, I will call you."

"Or text."

Callum nodded. "I promise."

So I let him go and didn't immediately slough off my classes to head to Little Ukraine. That's not where I'd go anyway if I wanted info on the Butcher—I have a much better lead than that.

For now I'm stuck in comparative literature, completely ignoring the analysis of feminist characters in Austen's novels. Instead, I'm wondering what Nero meant when he texted me,

We found the shooter. Got a tip on the old bastard, too.

I text him back, but he doesn't send me anything else.

The class ends abruptly—or so it seems to me as I stare out the window totally distracted.

I snatch up an armful of books, not bothering to stow them in my bag, then head outside, trotting across campus in the direction of the west lot where I'm supposed to meet Nessa and our detestable chauffeur.

When I'm almost at the right spot, I hear a male voice say, "Do you need help carrying all those books, little lady?"

For a second, I think it's Callum. I don't know why—he doesn't do corny impressions, like some helpful cowboy. When I turn around, I'm met with Oliver's grinning tanned face. He's bruised where Callum tuned him up. A dark line down the center of his lip marks the place where it split.

"Oh," I say, annoyed. "It's you."

"Not exactly the enthusiastic greeting I was hoping for," Oliver says, keeping pace at my side.

"What are you doing here?" He's years out of school; there's no reason for him to be hanging around here.

"I came to talk to you."

I take a false step on a stone hidden in the grass, my ankle bending uncomfortably under me. "Ouch! Fuck!" I hiss, stumbling a little.

"Careful." Oliver catches my elbow.

"I'm fine." I try to pull my arm away. I'm limping slightly now. I don't think it's sprained; it's just that thing where it's tender and wonky and you have to baby it for a minute.

"Come over here," Oliver says. "Sit down a second."

He steers me away from the parking lot, over to an underground walkway with a stone bench, partially hidden under an overhang.

Oliver is so big and overbearing that I can't really pull away, not without hurting myself. I sink onto the bench. Oliver sits right next to me, almost forced to put his arm around me because of the tightness of the space. I can smell that cologne he always wears, pleasant but a little overpowering.

"I can't stay," I tell him. "Somebody's picking me up." I pull off my sneaker and massage my ankle, trying to work out the kink.

"They can wait a minute."

He takes my socked foot and pulls it into his lap, kneading and massaging my ankle. It feels good, but I don't want him to get the wrong idea. So, after a minute, I say, "That's good, thanks," and take my foot back.

Oliver looks down at me with his big brown eyes, his expression reproachful. "Aida, what you did cut me to the bone. Do you know how painful that was to see a picture of you on fucking Facebook wearing a goddamned wedding dress? Standing next to *him*?"

I take a deep breath, trying to be patient. "I'm sorry, Oliver. It was sudden. I was pretty fucking surprised myself." I don't know how to explain it without telling him too much. All I can say, lamely, is, "I didn't do it to hurt you."

"But you did hurt me. You're still hurting me. You're killing me every day."

I let out a breath, both guilty and annoyed. Oliver can be a bit...
dramatic.

"I didn't even know you were dating him!" he cries.

I press my knuckles into my forehead. My ankle is throbbing.
It's actually kind of cold here, out of the sunshine and close to the
chilly cement tunnel.

I feel bad about the way I dumped Oliver. I really do. It was the
weirdest thing. He never did anything wrong, exactly. He took me
on trips, bought me about a thousand gifts, told me how desperately
infatuated he was with me.

It started out as a casual fling. I didn't think some country club,
uber-capitalist trust-funder would pursue me so aggressively. I
figured Oliver just wanted to get fucked by a bad girl. Tired of the
Madisons and the Harpers of the world refusing to make eye contact
during a BJ.

We happened to be at the same party two summers ago. We
drunkenly kissed in the boathouse. Then he tried to put his hand
down my bikini bottoms, and I shoved him in the lake.

A couple of weeks later, we met again at a party in Wicker Park.
He gave me shit about the lake thing, and I told him he was lucky
we were swimming, not mountain climbing.

The next day he sent a bouquet of three hundred pink roses to
my father's house.

That's how it was from then on. He kept chasing after me with
these grand gestures, and I went along with it for a while. Dinners,
dancing, weekend trips. But I didn't take it seriously. I never thought
he'd want to bring a gangster's daughter home to meet Mr. and Mrs.
Castle. Even around his friends, I could tell he was sometimes proud
to show me off, sometimes nervous like I might pull out a switch-
blade and shank somebody.

I was tempted a time or two. I already knew some of Oliver's
friends from running in the overlapping circles of the party crowd,
the criminal crowd, and the wealthy heirs of Chicago.

They weren't all bad. But some of the would-be upper crust made me want to puncture my own eardrums just to avoid the sound of their idiocy.

Plus, it kinda freaked me out how Oliver told me he loved me after only a couple of weeks. He called me a goddess, an angel, the only real person on earth.

I'm no angel.

To me he was just another guy—sometimes fun, sometimes good in bed, but barely a boyfriend, let alone a best friend or soul mate.

I felt like Oliver didn't really know me at all. He loved some exaggerated version of me in his mind.

I tried to break up with him a few times. He'd follow me around, finding me at every party, begging me to take him back. Once he even flew all the way to Malta to surprise me on a trip.

He could be persuasive. He was handsome, considerate, a decent lover. When I was going through a dry spell, he made it so easy to fall back into his arms.

But I knew I had to break it off for good. Because if he really did love me, I couldn't drag it out—not without feeling the same way in return. So I finally dumped him, as brutally and finally as I could. Trying to make him get the message at last.

After that, I pretty much had to turn myself into a hermit for a few months. No parties or dinners or dancing or even fucking bowling because I knew Oliver would be watching, trying to find a way to "bump into me" again.

I had to block him everywhere, change my number. And finally, *finally*, after months of messages, flowers, missed calls, and even fucking letters, Oliver stopped. He stopped for almost two whole months. So it was pretty jarring seeing him again at the engagement party. And then again at the fundraiser.

This is the most uncomfortable meeting of all. Because how, exactly, did Oliver even know I was here? Does he have my class schedule?

"Oliver, cut the shit. You need to quit stalking me."

He makes that wounded face. Like he's a giant puppy and I keep kicking him.

"I'm not *stalking* you, Aida. I'm visiting Marcus's little sister. I promised to take her out for lunch on her birthday."

Hm. Possible. The attempt to make me jealous is misguided, however.

"Okay, I believe you, but you still better quit trying to make conversation everywhere I go. My husband is kinda the jealous type, if you didn't notice."

"I know exactly what Callum Griffin is like," Oliver hisses. "That stuck-up, arrogant, dirty-money piece of shit. No offense," he adds, remembering my money is just as "dirty" as Callum's. And also that I'm married to the guy.

"I can't believe he puts his cold, dead hands on you every night." Oliver's eyes are feverishly bright. "How in the fuck did this happen, Aida? How did he make you fall in love with him when I couldn't?"

That actually makes me feel bad, at least a little bit. I didn't fall in love with Callum. It's cruel to let Oliver think I did. "It wasn't... it's not..." I lick my lips. "It's not about love, exactly."

"I knew it," Oliver breathes. "I knew it as soon as I realized what his family is. They're fucking Mafia, just like yours."

I wince. I never spilled any secrets to Oliver. But it's not exactly classified information that the Gallos have been Chicago gangsters for the past six generations. "Our families have a...relationship. I think you'll agree Callum and I are a better match culturally than you and I would have been. So there's no point—"

"That's bullshit." He's trying to take my hands, and I'm pulling them away like we're playing Red Hands. "I know they forced you to do this. I know you would have come back to me, Aida—"

"No," I say sharply. "We weren't getting back together, Oliver. We're never going to. With or without Callum in the picture."

"We'll see," Oliver says.

I'm about to stand. I'm definitely late—Nessa will have been waiting at least ten minutes. Oliver grabs my wrist, pulling me back down to the bench. He holds me tight, looking into my eyes. "I know how you feel about me, Aida. Whether you can admit it or not." He looks down at my chest where my nipples are poking through my T-shirt.

"That's not—it's just fucking cold on this bench!" I shout.

Oliver silences me with his mouth, kissing me hard and wet.

I shove him off as quickly as possible, jumping up from the bench and immediately stumbling again on that stupid ankle.

"Don't!" I say, holding out my hand to stop him as he stands, too. "I have to get back. Don't follow me. Don't call me. And definitely don't fucking kiss me anymore."

Oliver doesn't reply. He just stands there, his brows furrowed, his hands stuffed in his pockets.

I hobble back in the direction of the car, stomping on my one good foot and fuming over that encounter.

I'm pissed that he kissed me! My marriage to Callum may not be exactly real, but I'm not ready to be unfaithful. Especially not with Oliver, who's really starting to creep me out.

When I get to the lot, I see Nessa standing on the sidewalk with her bag slung over her shoulder.

"Where's Jack?" I ask her.

"The car's there." Nessa points to a nearby parking stall. "But it's locked and empty."

I get out my phone, planning to text Jack's phone with something polite and simple—maybe one of those middle finger emojis.

He pops up next to me, saying, "You ready to go?"

"Yes!" Nessa says sweetly.

"We've been ready to go for twenty minutes," I lie. "Where were you?"

"Taking a leak." He holds open the back door so Ness and I can slide inside. I lean back against the leather seat, not really believing him.

I'm quiet on the drive back to the Griffins' mansion, wondering how in the fuck I'm going to avoid Oliver Castle in the future. About halfway home, I get a text from Callum saying,

Come meet me in the library when you get back.

I get out of the car as soon as it stops moving, hurrying into the pleasantly cool house and heading directly up the stairs to the library.

Callum is sitting in one of the new armchairs—cream leather this time instead of brown. I take a seat in the chair opposite.

He looks pale and composed in his dark suit. I can already tell he found something from the resolute set of his shoulders.

Before he says anything, I want to tell him about Oliver showing up on campus. The problem is that Oliver groping me the other night was the one and only time I've seen Callum lose his temper violently. It's a sore subject between us. I'm not exactly looking forward to bringing it up. Especially when we've been working so well together.

Before I can start, Callum says, "We found one of the shooters. Not the Butcher, though. Your brothers think we should smash up Zajac's casino tonight. Try to flush him out."

"Are you going with them?" I ask.

He steels himself and says, "Yes. And you could come, too. If you wanted."

I can tell it's not what *he* wants at all, but he's offering it, not even waiting for me to make the demand.

Now I definitely don't want to tell him about Oliver.

Instead, I say, "I do want to come."

Callum looks slightly pained but doesn't take his offer back.

It's funny that he invited me into the library. I haven't stepped foot in here since the first night we met.

The restored portrait of his great-great—however many

greats—grandmother is back above the mantel. Also the carriage clock and the hourglass. But no watch anymore.

Callum already knows what I'm looking at.

"The watch was mine, the clock is Riona's, and the hourglass is Nessa's," he says.

"What do they mean?" I ask him, not sure if I even want to know.

"My grandfather passed them down to us when we were born. He said, 'All we have is time.'"

"Were you close to him?"

"Yeah." Callum nods. "Closer than anyone."

Fuck, I hate feeling guilty. Why did I grab that fucking watch? If I'd never touched it... Then I wouldn't be here right now, I guess. Looking at Callum's handsome lean face.

"I'm...sorry about that," I say.

Callum shakes his head like he forgot it was even lost. "That's in the past, Aida. Let's concern ourselves with tonight."

20
CALLUM

As we start hunting down the Butcher, I have to admit, I'm pretty fucking glad I've got Aida's brothers on my side. My father might have been right that I was too arrogant, too sure of our dominance. I'm spread thin trying to secure deals, whip up votes, and put a lid on Zajac all at the same time.

Funnily enough, I'm quite enjoying having Aida on my team, too. When she's not setting our library on fire or chucking my most beloved possession over a railing, she's actually pretty fucking helpful. I use the license plate number she spotted to track down one of Zajac's men, the one who owns the Land Rover used in the drive-by. His name is Jan Kowalski, but everybody calls him Rollie.

I call Dante and Nero so we can run him down together.

We find him at a used-car dealership in East Garfield. The Butcher owns several car dealerships and repair shops. He can kill two birds with one stone, laundering money through car sales while chopping up and reselling the cars stolen by his minions.

Nero goes around back while Dante and I walk through the front door looking for Rollie. I already know what he looks like, having had minor dealings with him in the past. Thanks to his idiotically public social media, Dante and Nero have also had the pleasure of scrolling through pictures of Rollie getting smashed at the pub, Rollie showing off the new pair of Yeezys he probably stole, and Rollie receiving the world's worst tattoo of a pair of praying hands.

So we recognize him fairly easily in the service bay of the dealership. He's wearing coveralls. A filthy bandana ties back his longish sandy-colored hair. As soon as he sees Dante's bulk in the doorway, he chucks away the oil pan from the F-150 he's servicing and tries to sprint out the bay doors like a fucking jackrabbit.

Unfortunately for him, Nero is already lying in wait behind a stack of tires. If Rollie is a rabbit, Nero is a greyhound—lean, swift, and utterly ruthless. He hooks Rollie's legs with a tire iron, then pounces on his back, pinning him to the ground.

Dante knocks out the manager with a brutal right cross, and I do a quick sweep of the shop to make sure we haven't missed any other employees.

I find a mechanic crouched behind a BMW. He's older and lacks any of the usual markers of the Polish Mafia—tattoos, gold chains, and gaudy rings. I assume he just works on the cars and isn't one of the Butcher's soldiers.

I search him anyway, then lock him in the office after ripping the phone cord out of the wall.

Dante and Nero are already tuning up Rollie. It doesn't take much to get him talking. He gives us the phone the Butcher uses to contact him, as well as several locations where Zajac "might" be.

"I don't care where he *might* be," Nero hisses. "Tell us where he is right now."

"I don't know!" Rollie shouts, swiping the back of his hand across the bloody nose Nero already gave him. "I'm not, like, one of his top guys."

"He sent you to shoot up the construction site last night," I say.

Rollie darts his eyes between Nero and me, licking his lips nervously. "I didn't know who was there. I didn't know I was shooting at you guys. He told us to spray the lot, hit the cops, and make a ruckus."

"Horseshit," Dante growls, his voice rough as gravel. "You knew that work site was ours."

"You don't know what he's like!" Rollie babbles. "It's not like with other bosses where you can take a job or not. He gives an order, and you have to do it. If you fuck up, you get one warning. Fuck up again, and that's it."

"What's the warning?" Dante asks.

Rollie holds up his right hand. He's missing the pinky finger, severed cleanly at the base. The stretched pink skin shows this is a relatively recent injury.

"I don't care if he's the fucking boogeyman." Nero seizes the front of Rollie's coveralls and jerks him close. "There's only one name you should be afraid of in this city. Whatever Zajac does to you, I'll do ten times worse. If he shoots you in the face, I'll drag your screaming soul back from hell just to kill you again."

Nero's eyes look flat and dark in the shadows of the car bay. In some ways he's the "prettiest" of Aida's brothers—high cheekbones, full lips. It makes the viciousness of his expression all the more disturbing.

Nero pulls a knife from his pocket and flicks up the blade so quickly, it seems to appear out of nowhere. He presses the point against the jumping pulse in Rollie's throat. "Tell me where Zajac is, or I'll nick this artery. Then you'll have about twelve seconds to answer me before you bleed out on the floor."

He's not threatening Rollie. His expression is hopeful—hoping Rollie won't talk so Nero can let his hand do what it's obviously itching to do.

"I don't know! I swear—"

With one swift slash, Nero cuts the length of Rollie's forearm, from the rolled-up sleeve of his coverall down to his wrist. The blade is wickedly sharp. Blood runs down in a sheet, pattering on the bare cement floor.

"Agh, fuck me! Knock it off!" Rollie howls, trying to cover the wound with his grease-stained hand.

"Last warning," Nero says, readying his blade again.

"I don't know! Wait, wait!" Rollie howls as Nero's knife comes at his neck. "I do know one thing…a girl he's been seeing."

"Go on," I say.

"She works at the Pole. She's got an apartment somewhere in Lawndale that he pays for. That's all I know, I swear!"

"I believe you," Nero says.

He sends the blade slashing toward Rollie's throat anyway. He would have slit it wide open if not for Dante catching his wrist. The point of the knife trembles a millimeter from Rollie's neck.

"That's not necessary," Dante says. "He told us what he knows."

"He also tried to shoot us, in case you forgot."

"I remember," Dante says before letting go of his brother's wrist.

As soon as Dante drops his hand, Nero strikes again, slashing Rollie's cheek instead of his throat.

Rollie yelps, clapping his hand over the long cut from ear to jaw.

"That's a reminder for you," Nero says. "Next time you want to shoot at somebody, either improve your aim or stay home."

Dante scowls but lets this pass.

We're about to leave when I hear a crashing sound. Shattering glass, then a howl as somebody runs straight at me, swinging a baseball bat.

I duck, the bat whistling over my head. Instinctively, I punch the man right in the gut. When he doubles over, I wrench the bat out of his hand, then hit him again across the jaw.

It's the mechanic. He's got something wrapped around his knuckles, some sort of rag, which didn't prevent him from getting a handful of glass when he punched through the office window. His whole arm is bleeding. All the fight has gone out of him now that he doesn't have his baseball bat. I'm guessing he was only propelled by desperation to begin with, since he had no chance of besting me, Dante, and Nero in a fight.

Now he's panting and wheezing, trying to decide if he's required to put up any further resistance.

"Stay the fuck down there," Nero says, shoving him down on the ground next to Rollie. "In fact, lie down on your face and count to a hundred before you get up, or I'll put a bullet in the back of your skull."

I don't know if Nero actually has a gun on him, but the two men lie obediently facedown, and Rollie starts counting. We leave them there, jogging back toward our cars.

"Didn't know you could fight, rich boy," Nero says, looking at me in mild surprise.

"That wasn't much of a challenge." The mechanic has to be at least fifty and a good six inches shorter than me.

Shows how terrified he must be of Zajac. He preferred to face the three of us rather than explain himself to the Butcher.

"Still," Dante says, "that was pretty fast."

"Shaking hands and slapping backs is new for me." I shrug. "I still remember how to get my hands dirty."

"Fergus knows how to fight," Dante says. "They used to call him the Bone Doctor, didn't they?"

He's referring to my father's stint as a debt collector and enforcer before he took control of what remained of the Griffin family.

"That's right."

My father could put a spiral fracture down a man's arm with a twist of his wrist, if that's what was required to enforce the payment plan.

He definitely taught me a few things. The number one thing was never to fight when you can negotiate instead. Because the outcome of a fight is never certain.

The problem is I don't think Zajac wants to negotiate. Not without spilling a little blood.

Aida arrives home only a little after I do. She comes up to the library, and I fill her in on what we've been doing.

I can tell she's annoyed at being left out of the morning's activities, but I'll keep my promise and bring her along tonight, if that's what she really wants.

When she heads into our bedroom to drop off her books, Jack pokes his head into the library. "Can I talk to you for a minute, boss?"

Jack and I have been friends for a long time. Back in our college days, he got himself in trouble. He was dealing Molly at parties to pay for the trust fund lifestyle without actually having the trust fund. When the cops raided his dorm, he had to flush about twenty-eight thousand dollars of product. I paid off his supplier, then had Jack come work for me instead.

He's been a good employee and a good friend, if a little overzealous at times. Like with Aida's brother on the pier. And sometimes with Aida herself. Aida may drive me up the fucking wall, but she's still my wife. If Jack didn't learn his lesson down in the kitchen, I'll be quick to educate him again.

"I picked the girls up at school," he says.

"Good."

"Aida was talking to someone."

I give him a sharp look in case he's trying to start shit again. "She's allowed to do that."

"It was Oliver Castle."

My stomach clenches in a knot. If he had said any other name, I would have ignored it. But I can't help feeling jealous of that shit-for-brains wannabe playboy. As far as I know, he's the only actual boyfriend Aida's ever had, and for some reason, that eats me alive. The thought of them swimming on some tropical beach together, laughing and talking, Aida in a bikini with her skin more tanned than ever...

It makes me want to rip Castle's face off his skull.

Plus, I know damn well he doesn't go to Loyola. He was on campus for one reason only.

"What did he say?"

"I don't know," Jack says. "I couldn't get close enough to hear. But they were talking a while."

I can feel my eye twitch. Aida didn't mention anything about Oliver. Didn't mention seeing him. "You're sure it was Castle?"

"One hundred percent. He left right after they talked. I followed him back to his car—the gray Maserati."

That's definitely him.

"And there's something else," Jack says.

"What?"

"They kissed."

The floor seems to drop out from under me.

I completely forget about Zajac. All my anger, all my desire for violence and revenge is turned on Castle instead. If he were in the room right now, I'd shoot him in the face.

"Thank you for telling me," I say through stiff lips.

She kissed him. Then she came home to me, cheerful as ever, like nothing happened.

Maybe to her, it is nothing.

After all, we never really talked about this. We never promised to be faithful to each other. Our marriage is a business arrangement; I can't forget that. The vows we spoke mean nothing, not really. The only real promises were the ones made by my father and hers.

Still, it gnaws at me.

Is she meeting up with him secretly? Are they fucking? Does she love him still?

I'm going to ask her.

I stride down the hallway to our bedroom, determined to confront her.

When I push my way through the door, she's typing something on her phone. She closes out of it abruptly, swiping upward to change apps, then flips her phone over and lays it facedown on the bed.

"What's up?" she says.

"What were you doing?"

"What do you mean?"

"Just now. On your phone."

"Oh," she says, cheeks slightly pink. "Just adding some new songs on Spotify. Gotta make a victory playlist for after the election."

She's lying. She was typing a message, I'm sure of it.

I should grab her phone, demand to see what she was doing.

It has a password, though, and Aida is stubborn as fuck. She won't give it to me. It'll turn into a battle.

Better to wait. I'll steal her password, then go through her phone uninterrupted without tipping her off.

I force my face to be calm and inexpressive and say, "Okay. We should eat something before we head out."

"What do you want to eat?" she asks, relieved I dropped the subject.

"I don't care."

21
AIDA

CAL INTERRUPTED ME IN THE MIDDLE OF SOMETHING I'D RATHER not show him—not yet, at least. Now he's acting weird. We're downstairs, eating two of the meals the chef left in the fridge. Cal is chewing his meat like he can't even taste it, looking moodily out the kitchen window to the pool.

"What's going on?" I ask him, taking a bite of braised short rib and grilled carrot. This is about as decadent as it gets in Casa Griffin, so I'm trying to enjoy my meal. Hard to do with Callum sitting stone-faced right next to me.

"Nothing," he says shortly.

"What are you all wound up about? Poking a stick in the hornet's nest?"

I'm aware someone named the Butcher isn't the best target to antagonize. Still, I'm excited at the prospect of hunting down Zajac. I've been playing the good girl for weeks now. It's time to get in a little trouble.

"Yes," Callum says testily. "I'm concerned about teeing up against an unhinged gangster. Especially two days before the election."

"Maybe we should hold off, then," I tell him. "Wait until after to slap back at him."

"If we don't find him tonight, then that's what I'll do," Callum says. "But I'd rather deal with it sooner than later."

Callum's phone buzzes with a message. He glances at it, saying, "Your brothers are here."

A minute later they pull up in front of the house, parking and getting out of Dante's Escalade warily. They haven't been here since Nessa's party. I can tell they feel awkward coming in through the kitchen door.

"Nice house," Dante says politely, as if he hasn't seen it before.

"Yeah, very nice." Nero stuffs his hands in his pockets, looking all around the gleaming modern kitchen. His eye catches on the one thing out of place. He bends over for a closer look, saying, "Is that a—"

"*Yes,*" I tell him. "And we don't need to talk about it."

Imogen already read me the riot act about the bullet hole in her cabinet door. I think she was angrier than when I'd poisoned her son. This house is her actual favorite child. It would have gotten ugly if Callum hadn't covered for me, telling her it was an accident. She didn't look convinced.

"How am I even going to get someone to fix it?" she demanded, eyes blazing. "How am I going to explain to some carpenter that he needs to dig a bullet out before he can fill in the hole?"

"You could act totally surprised," I said helpfully.

Callum shot me a look telling me to shut up immediately. "I could get the bullet out first," he said.

"No!" Imogen snapped. "Don't touch it. You two have done enough."

It still hasn't been fixed, and it's another sore subject that I don't need Nero bringing up right before we're supposed to head out.

But then Sore Subject Number Three comes strolling into the kitchen.

"Car's out front," Jack says, holding up the keys.

"Don't tell me he's coming," I say to Callum.

"He is."

"We don't need—"

Callum interrupts me. "We're not going in shorthanded. Your brothers brought someone, too."

"Gabriel's in the car," Dante confirms.

Gabriel is our cousin and one of my brothers' enforcers. He looks like a big gruff teddy bear, but he can be a killer when he has to be.

"Fine," I say, with only a hint of annoyance. "And what's the plan?"

"Well…" Callum exchanges a look with my brothers. "There are two options. One, we try to follow this lead about the girl Zajac's been fucking."

"But we don't have her address," Nero says, obviously not a fan of this option. "And we don't know how often he sees her."

"*Or,*" Callum continues, as if he hadn't been interrupted, "we could hit one of his businesses. Smash his shit up, maybe take something, then wait for him to call us."

"We're leaning toward his casino because it's remote and cash heavy," Dante says.

"Why not both?" I say. "Are you talking about Francie Ross? She works at Pole, right?"

"Do you know her?" Callum asks quickly.

"No. But I know a girl who knows her. That's what I was trying to tell you earlier."

Callum gives me a look, half-annoyed and half-curious. "Does your friend know where Francie lives?"

"Maybe. We should ask her."

"Why bother?" Nero snaps. "Who cares about finding Zajac? We need to hit him back for what he did to our job site. We don't need to look him in the eye to kick him in the balls."

Dante looks like he could go either way. "The casino seems like more of a sure bet," he says.

"Well…" Callum glances over at me. "Let's do both. You guys can hit the casino while Aida and I talk to her friend."

"You think three people is enough?" Dante says to Nero.

"Of course."

"Take Jack, too," Callum says.

"Then it'll just be you and Aida…" Dante says.

"We don't need an army." I snort "We're just talking to a waitress."

Dante reaches inside his jacket. He passes me a Glock, loaded.

"Is that wise?" Jack says, eyeing the gun as Dante puts it in my hand.

"Don't worry," I say sweetly. "I won't leave it lying around like an *idiot.*"

Jack looks like he wants to retort but drops it since Callum is standing right there.

"Everybody else got what they need?" Dante asks.

We all nod.

"Let's head out, then."

Dante and Nero get back in the Escalade. I wave to Gabriel through the window. He grins and gives me a little salute. Jack climbs in the back seat next to him, introducing himself with a grunt and a curt nod.

I'm extremely pleased not to have to spend any more time cooped up in a car with him and even more pleased that Cal and I are running down my lead. Well, sort of his, too—but I thought of it first.

Anyway, I like when Cal drives. It lets me sneak glances at him while his attention is fixed on the road.

Every time we're alone together, the energy seems to shift. There's a thick tension in the air, and my mind inevitably wanders back to what we did the last time we were alone.

Since I'm thinking of such pleasant things, I'm startled when Callum says, "Why did you break up with Oliver Castle?"

It jolts me and makes me remember how Oliver accosted me on campus earlier. How does he keep running into me like that? At first, when he would find me at every party, I assumed my friends were texting him. But even later—

Callum interrupts. "Well?"

I sigh, annoyed to be talking about this again. And without the likelihood of kinky jealousy-fueled sex afterward.

"It just never felt right," I say. "It was like putting a shoe on the wrong foot. Right away, it was awkward, and the longer it went on, the worse it got."

"So you weren't in love with him? When we met?" Callum asks.

There's the tiniest hint of vulnerability in his question.

I've never heard Callum be vulnerable. Not even 1 percent. I desperately want to look at him, but I use all my willpower to keep my eyes pointed forward. I feel like we're actually being honest for a minute, and I don't want to ruin it.

"I never loved him," I tell Cal, my voice steady and sure.

He exhales, relief in his sigh.

I have to smile, thinking of something poetic.

"What?" Callum asks.

"Well, ironically, when I broke up with Oliver, I thought I should find someone more compatible. Someone more like me."

Cal has to laugh, too. "Instead, you got the exact opposite."

Opposites have a kind of symmetry. Fire and ice. Stern and playful. Impulsive and restrained. In a way, they belong together.

Oliver and I were more like two objects selected at random: a pen and an owl. A cookie and a shovel.

That's why there was no emotion on my side, just indifference. You need push and pull to feel love. Or hate.

We pull up in front of Pole. It's a cabaret club on the west end of the city, dark, low-ceilinged, sprawling, and seedy. But also wildly popular because it's not your run-of-the-mill strip club. The performances are kinky and fetish based. Some of the dancers are semifamous in Chicago, including Francie Ross, who's one of the headliners. It doesn't surprise me that she caught Zajac's eye.

"Have you been here before?" I ask Callum.

"No," he says carelessly. "Is it good?"

"You'll see." I grin.

The bouncers check our IDs as we head inside.

The thumping bass makes the air feel thick. I smell the sharp scent of alcohol and the earthy tones of vape pens. The light is deep red, making everything else look like shades of black and gray.

The interior feels like a gothic dollhouse. Plush booths, botanical wallpaper, ornate mirrors. The waitresses are dressed in strappy leather harnesses, some with leather animal ears and matching fur tails—bunnies, foxes, and cats, mostly.

I spy a table emptying out close to the stage, and I drag Callum over before someone else can snag it.

"Shouldn't we be looking for your friend?" he says.

"We may be in her section. If not, I'll go find her."

He looks around at the busty waitresses and the bartenders in their skintight pleather bodysuits unzipped to the navel.

"So this is what Zajac's into, huh?"

"I think everybody's into this, to one degree or another," I reply, biting the edge of my lip and grinning just a little.

"Oh yeah?" Callum's looking at me, curious and more than a little distracted. "Tell me more."

I nod to the corner of our booth, where a pair of silver handcuffs dangle from a hook. "I could see you making good use of those."

"Depends," Callum growls, his eyes dark, "on how you behave yourself tonight…"

Before I can answer, our waitress comes to take our order. It's not my friend Jada. But she says Jada is working.

"Can you send her over?" I ask.

"Sure." The girl nods.

While we wait, the lights lower even further, and the DJ drops the music.

"Ladies and gentlemen," he croons. "Please welcome to the stage the one…the only…Eduardo!"

"Oh, you're going to like this," I whisper to Callum.

"Who's Eduardo?" he mutters back.

"Shh!"

A spotlight follows a slim young man who poses for a moment in its light, then saunters down to the stage. He's wearing a fedora and zoot suit—well tailored, with exaggerated shoulders. He has a pencil mustache and a cigarette dangling from his mouth.

His presence is magnetic. Every eye in the room is fixed on him and his outrageous swagger.

Right before he ascends to the stage, he pauses next to a pretty blond in the front row. Despite her protests and obvious shyness, he grabs her hand and drags her up onstage.

He goes through a little comedy routine where he instructs the girl to hold a flower for him. The top of the flower immediately falls off, tumbling down the front of the girl's blouse. Eduardo plucks it out again before she can move, making her shriek. Then he teaches her a dance routine, a seductive tango, which he performs master-fully, whipping her around like a mannequin.

All the while he's keeping up a patter of jokes and insults, making the audience howl with laughter. He has a low, smooth voice and a slight accent.

Finally, he tells the girl that he's finished and asks for a kiss on the cheek. When she reluctantly puckers up her lips, he holds out his cheek to her, then turns his head at the last minute, kissing her square on the mouth.

The crowd eats it up, cheering and chanting, "Eduardo! Eduardo!"

"Thank you, my friends. But before I go—one last dance!" he shouts.

As the music plays, he dances across the stage, swift and sharp. He grabs his fedora and yanks it off his head, letting down a spill of white-blond hair. He tears off his mustache, then rips open the front of his suit to reveal two absolutely spectacular breasts, full and bare, except for a pair of red tassels covering the nipples. "Eduardo" hops and shimmies to make the tassels spin, then blows the crowd a kiss, bows, and leaves the stage.

Callum looks like he got slapped in the face. I'm laughing so hard that tears are running down my cheeks. I've seen Francie's show three times now, and it still blows me away. Her ability to walk and dance and speak like a man, even laugh like one, is just incredible. She never breaks character for a second, not until the very end.

"That's Francie Ross," I say to Callum, in case he still hasn't figured it out.

"That's the Butcher's girlfriend?" he says in astonishment.

"Yup. If the rumors are true."

I get my chance to ask Jada when she brings over our drinks. She passes a whiskey on the rocks to Callum, a vodka cranberry to me.

"Hey!" she says, "I haven't seen you in forever."

"I know!" I grin up at her. "It's been crazy."

"So I heard," Jada says, casting a significant glance in Callum's direction. Jada has dyed-black hair, a multitude of piercings, and plum-colored lips. Her father worked for mine until he was sent to prison for unrelated mischief. Specifically, he tried to scam the state lottery. It was going great until he accidentally won twice in a row, which kinda tipped them off.

"Did you see the show?" Jada asks me.

"Yes! Francie's the best." I lean a little closer, keeping my voice low so it's covered by the music. "Is it true she's dating that Polish gangster?"

"I don't know." Jada picks up an empty glass from the table next to ours and sets it on her tray. She's not meeting my eyes.

"Come on," I coax her. "I know you two are tight."

"She might be," she says noncommittally.

"Does he come in here to see her?"

"No," Jada says. "Not that I've seen."

She obviously doesn't like this line of questioning. But I don't want to drop it just yet.

Callum reaches under the table, smoothly pressing a folded bill into Jada's palm. "Where does she live?"

Jada hesitates. She sneaks a glance down at her palm to see the denomination. "The yellow building on Cherry Street," she says at last. "Third-floor walk-up. He goes there Tuesday nights. That's when she's off work."

"There you go," I mutter to Callum after Jada leaves. "If he doesn't make contact after we fuck up his casino, then we'll get him on Tuesday."

"Yeah," Callum agrees. "It's still early—text your brothers and see if they need us over at the casino."

I'm about to do so when Jada brings us another round of drinks.

"On me," she says, friendlier now that I've stopped grilling her. "Don't be a stranger so long next time."

She slides a fresh vodka cranberry toward me. I didn't really want a second, but if it's free...

"Thanks," I say, raising it in a cheers motion.

"Roxy Rotten's up next," Jada says. "You want to stay for that one."

As I raise the straw to my lips, I see a strange sheen on the surface on my drink. I set it down again, looking at the cocktail. Maybe it's just the red light on my red drink. But the surface looks a little oily. Like the glass wasn't washed well enough.

"What?" Callum says.

I'm not sure I should drink it.

I'm about to tell Callum to check his own drink, but he's already slugged it back in a gulp.

The lights lower again, and the DJ introduces Roxy Rotten. Roxy performs her striptease in zombie makeup under black lights, which give the illusion that she loses several limbs over the course of her routine. Finally, her head seems to fall off. The lights go up again and Roxy stands center stage, miraculously whole again, displaying her lovely green-painted figure to the crowd.

"Should we go?" I say to Callum.

"Did your brothers reply?"

I check my phone. "Not yet."

"Let's leash, then. I mean leave." He shakes his head. "Are you gonna finish that first?" he points to my second drink.

"Uh…no." I pour half the new drink into my old glass so Jada won't be offended. "Let's go."

I stand first, slinging my bag over my arm. When Callum stands, he stumbles slightly.

"Are you okay?"

"Yeah," he grunts. "Just a headache."

I can see how unsteady he is on his feet. It's not the whiskey—he only had two shots, which I know from experience will barely get him tipsy.

I see Jada standing next to the bar, arms crossed. She looks like a malevolent gargoyle with her leather fox ears, her lips painted dark purple.

"Let's get out of here," I mutter to Callum, slinging his arm over my shoulder.

I'm reminded horribly of the day we met, when I had to carry Sebastian down the pier like this. Callum is just as heavy, slumping more and more with every step. He's trying to say something, but his eyes are rolled back, his voice mushy and incoherent.

If I can get him into the car, I can drive us someplace safe and call my brothers.

Just like on the pier, the door seems a million miles away. I'm wading through sand, and I'm never going to make it.

As I reach the exit at last, the bouncers surround me.

"Is there a problem, miss?"

I'm about to tell them I need someone to help carry Callum over to the car. Then I realize they're not coming to help us. They're blocking the door.

I look around at the semicircle of burly, looming men.

No time to call my brothers.

I do the only thing I can think of.

I slump like I'm passing out, hoping it won't hurt too bad when I hit the floor.

22
CALLUM

I wake up with my hands tied over my head, suspended from a meat hook.

This is not a great position for me. I'm a big dude, and all that weight hanging from my arms for god knows how long makes them feel like they're about to be pulled out of the sockets.

Plus, my head is fucking banging.

The last thing I remember is some dude who wasn't actually a dude doing the tango across the stage.

Now I'm in a warehouse that stinks of rust and dirt. Under that, a cold, wet, rotting smell.

And it really is fucking cold. Even in my suit jacket, I'm shivering.

Maybe it's the aftereffects of the drugs. My muscles feel weak and shaky. My vision keeps switching from fuzzy to clear like a pair of binoculars going in and out of focus.

Drugs. Someone drugged my drink. When I was sitting with…
Aida!

I whip my head around, looking for her.

Thankfully, she's not hanging from a hook right next to me. I don't see her anywhere in the deserted space. All I see is a table covered with a stained white cloth. Which is not, generally, a good sign.

I want to yell for Aida. But I also don't want to draw attention to the fact she's gone. I don't know how I got here, and I don't know if she was with me or not.

My shoulders are screaming. My feet can almost, but not quite, touch the ground.

I twist my wrists, turning them against the rough rope to see if there's any chance of wriggling free. The movement makes me rotate slightly, like a bird on a spit, but doesn't seem to loosen the knot.

The only good thing is that I don't have long to wait.

The Butcher enters the warehouse, flanked by two of his soldiers. One is slim, with white-blond hair and tattoos down both arms. The other looks familiar—he might have been one of the bouncers at Pole. Oh, fuck. He probably was.

But it's the Butcher who draws my attention. He fixes me with his furious stare, one eyebrow permanently quirked a little higher than the other. His nose looks beakier than ever under the harsh light, his cheeks hollow. The pitted scars along the sides of his face look too deep to be from acne—they could be shrapnel wounds from some explosion long ago.

Zajac pauses in front of me, almost directly under the single overhead light. He lifts one finger and touches my chest. Then he pushes, making me swing helplessly back and forth from the hook.

I can't help grunting at the increased pressure on my arms. The Butcher gives a small smile. He's amused by my discomfort.

He steps back again, giving a nod to the bouncer from the club. The bouncer strips off Zajac's coat.

Zajac looks smaller without it. But as he rolls up the sleeves of his striped dress shirt, I can see his forearms are thick with the kind of muscle built doing practical things.

As he rolls up his left sleeve with deft, sure motions, he says, "People think I got my nickname because of Bogota. But it isn't true. They called me the Butcher long before that."

He rolls up the right sleeve until it matches the left precisely. Then he strides over to the covered table. He pulls back the cloth, revealing exactly what I expected to see: a set of freshly sharpened butcher's knives, their blades arranged by shape and size. Cleavers, scimitars, and chef's knives—blades for boning, filleting, carving, slicing, and chopping.

"Before we were criminals, the Zajacs had a family trade. What we learned, we passed down. I can butcher a hog in forty-two minutes." He lifts a long slender knife, touching the ball of his thumb to the blade. Without any pressure at all, the skin parts, and a bead of blood wells up against the steel. "What do you think I could do to you in an hour?" he muses, looking up and down my stretched-out frame.

"Maybe you could explain what the fuck you want, for a start," I say. "This can't be about transit property."

"No," Zajac whispers, his eyes colorless in the stark light.

"What is it, then?"

"It's about respect, of course," he replies. "I've lived in this city for twelve years now. My family has been here for three generations. But you don't know that, do you, Mr. Griffin? Because you haven't even paid me the compliment of curiosity."

He sets down the knife he's holding and selects another. Though his fingers are thick and stubby, he handles his weapon as dexterously as Nero.

"The Griffins, and the Gallos…" he says, approaching me with a blade in hand. "Both alike in your arrogance. The Gallos bury two of my men under cement and think that's the end of it. You take my donation and then refuse to even meet with me face-to-face. Then you two make a marriage agreement without even considering my sons. Or issuing an invitation."

"The wedding was on short notice," I say through clenched teeth. My shoulders are on fire. I don't like how close Zajac is getting with that knife.

"I know exactly why the wedding happened," he says. "I know everything…"

I want to demand where Aida is right now if he knows so much.

But I'm still wary of giving her away. She might have managed to escape. If so, I hope to god she's calling the cops or her brothers.

Unfortunately, I don't think anybody is going to get here in time. If they even know where to find me.

"This was a slaughterhouse," Zajac says, gesturing around the empty warehouse with the point of his knife. "They used to kill a thousand hogs a day here. The blood ran down there"—he points down the length of a metal grate that runs below my feet—"down that pipe, then straight into the river. The water was red for a mile downriver from the plants."

I can't actually see the pipe he's referencing, but I can smell the dank and dirty water.

"A little farther down, people swam in the water," he says, his eyes fixed on the blade of his knife. "It looked clean enough by then."

"Is there a point to this metaphor?" I say impatiently. My shoulders are fucking burning. If Zajac's going to kill me, I'd rather he go ahead and do it already. "Am I supposed to be the person swimming in the dirty water?"

"No!" he snaps, eyes on my face now. "That's everyone in Chicago, who wants to think their city is clean. You're the person who eats the bacon, thinking you're better than the man who butchered it."

I sigh, trying to pretend to be interested, while actually scanning the room. I'm eyeballing the two bodyguards, looking for some way out of this mess. All the while I'm chaffing my wrists inside the rope, trying to twist them free bit by bit. Or else just rubbing my skin off—it's hard to tell.

Zajac is done monologuing. He cuts off my suit jacket and shirt with a dozen quick slashes. Parts of the sleeves still hang off my arms, but my torso is bare, bleeding from five or six shallow cuts. The Butcher is skilled enough that he could have done that without touching my skin. He slashed me on purpose. Whetting his knife.

He presses the point against the lower right-hand side of my abdomen.

"Do you know what's right there?" he says.

I don't want to play this game with him. "No."

"Your appendix. A little three-and-a-half-inch tube of tissue, extending from your large intestine. Likely vestigial for the modern human, but sometimes brought to prominence when it becomes infected or inflamed. I don't see any laparoscopy scars, so I assume yours is still intact."

I stay stubbornly silent, refusing to play along.

The Butcher rests the flat of the blade on the palm of his hand. "I intended to wait until after the election for this, but you had to make a nuisance of yourselves, smashing up my casino and bothering my mistress in her place of work. So here's what we're going to do. The Gallos are going to return the money they stole from my casino."

I don't know how much they got, but I hope it was a fuck ton of cash.

"You're going to sell me the transit property at a steep discount."

Nope. Also not happening.

"And you're going to provide me with a city government position of my choice, after your election."

When pigs fucking fly.

"As a down payment on these services, I'm going to take your appendix," Zajac says. "You won't miss it. The surgery, though painful in the absence of anesthetic, won't be fatal."

He raises the point of the knife once more, positioning it directly above the apparently nonessential portion of my guts. He takes a breath, readying himself to slice into my flesh. Then he presses the knife into my belly.

He pushes it in agonizingly slowly.

I grind my teeth together as hard as I can, keeping my eyes closed, but I can't help letting out a strangled yell.

It really fucking hurts. I've heard that being stabbed is more painful than being shot. Having recently been grazed in the arm by my loving wife, I can definitely attest that having a knife slowly, torturously burrowed into your guts is about a hundred times worse. My face is sweating, my muscles shaking. The knife is only an inch or two into my flesh.

"Don't worry." The Butcher hisses, "I should be done in an hour or so…"

"Wait a second, wait a second…" I pant.

He pauses without taking the knife out of my stomach.

"Could you take a break for a second and scratch my nose? I've got an itch, and it's driving me crazy."

Zajac gives an irritated snort, tensing his arm to drive the knife deeper into my body.

At that moment, a bottle comes flying through the doorway, a smoking rag stuffed in its neck. The bottle shatters on the cement floor, and the flaming liquor spreads in a pool, shards of fiery glass spinning outward. One catches the bouncer's sleeve. He spins around, trying to slap it out.

There's another smashing sound, then an explosion, loud and close.

"Deal with that," Zajac hisses to his men.

The blond one splits off at once, skirting the wreckage of the Molotov cocktail and heading through a side door. The bouncer heads straight for the main door, only to catch a bullet in the shoulder the second he walks through.

"*Kurwa mać!*" the Butcher barks. He jumps behind me in case the shooter is about to come through the door.

We wait. No one walks through. I can see Zajac is torn—on the one hand, he doesn't want to leave me here alone. On the other, he's now unprotected. He has no idea how many people are storming the warehouse. He doesn't want to be caught in here if it's my men who come barging through the door.

As the seconds tick by, we hear the confusing sounds of shouting, running, and something else smashing. It's impossible to tell what's going on. The Molotov is still burning—in fact, the flames are spreading across the cement floor somehow. Perhaps the paint is burning. Clouds of acrid black smoke make us sweat and cough.

Zajac curses. He strides over to the table, seizing a cleaver in one hand and a machete in the other. He hurries out through the same side door through which his blond lieutenant disappeared.

The moment I'm alone, I start wrenching and working on those ropes. My left arm is almost totally numb, but I can still move the right one. I pull as hard as I can. My hands, my wrists, my arms, and my shoulders are all screaming. It feels like I'm going to dislocate my thumb. But finally, I twist the right hand free.

A figure comes sprinting barefoot through the door, jumping over the fallen body of the bouncer who was shot in the shoulder.

Aida's dark hair streams behind her as she flies across the cement. She nimbly avoids the flames and shattered glass, pausing only to grab a knife off the table. She presses it into my palm.

"Cut the rope!" she cries. "It's too high for me to reach!" She's got blood running down the right side of her face. Her left hand is wrapped in a rag.

"Are you okay?" I reach overhead to saw at the rope still holding my left hand in place. "Where are your brothers?"

"I have no idea—those goons took my phone. Took my gun, too, so Dante's gonna be pissed. I'm the only one here!"

"What? What the hell was all that noise, then?"

"A diversion!" Aida says gleefully. "Now hurry up, before—"

The rope parts, and I tumble onto the concrete. My arms feel like they're not attached to my body. My legs are throbbing, too. Not to mention the puncture on my right side.

"What did they do to you?" Aida asks, her voice shaking.

"I'm fine," I tell her. "But we'd better—"

At that moment the blond soldier returns with another of Zajac's men. They're both armed, standing in the doorway with their guns pointed right at us.

"Don't move," the blond lieutenant says.

The air is thick with smoke. I'm not sure how well he can actually see us—well enough to shoot us, I'm sure. I grab Aida's arm and start inching backward.

We're following the metal grate along the floor, back to the dumping spot where butchers used to off-load the blood and viscera into the river.

"Stop!" the lieutenant shouts, advancing on us through the smoke. He raises his AR, fitting it against his side.

I hear a dull clang as I step on a hinged grate.

Keeping my eye on Zajac's men, I press the toe of my shoe against the corner of the grate, trying to lift it without using my hands.

It's heavy, but it starts to move upward, enough that I can get my whole foot under.

"Stay there and keep your hands up," the blond soldier barks, closing in on us.

I kick the grate all the way open.

I wrap my arms around Aida, murmuring, "Take a deep breath."

Her body tenses.

I kick the grate all the way open.

Then I sweep her up and jump through the grate, down into a four-feet-wide pipe that leads to god knows where.

We plunge into the filthy icy water.

The current is swift, dragging us along.

It's dark, so dark that it makes no difference if my eyes are open or shut. Keeping an iron grip on Aida, I reach up with one hand to see if there's air above our heads. My hand swipes the pipe, no space between water and metal.

That means we need to get through as quickly as possible. The current is moving us along. I kick with my feet, propelling us faster.

We've probably been down here thirty seconds so far. I can hold my breath for two minutes. I can't expect Aida to manage more than a minute or so.

She's not struggling in my arms, not fighting me. But I can feel how rigid and terrified she is. She trusts me. God, I hope I didn't make the worst kind of mistake.

We rocket along, with me kicking all the harder. Then we shoot out an outlet pipe, falling five feet right into the Chicago River.

The current drags us to the center of the river, about twenty feet from either bank. That's not where I want to be in case any boats come along, but I'm not sure which way I should be taking us. I look around, trying to figure out exactly where we are.

Aida clings to my neck, only paddling with one hand. She isn't a very strong swimmer, and the current is powerful. She's shivering. So am I.

"How'd you know we could get out there?" she asks me, her teeth chattering.

"I didn't," I say. "How in the fuck did you come find me?"

"Oh, I was with you the whole time!" Aida says. "That backstabbing bitch Jada drugged our drinks, but I didn't actually drink mine 'cause it looked weird."

"Why didn't you tell me that?"

"I was going to! You'd already slugged it down. I don't want to make this a cultural critique, but you Irish could learn to sip a drink once in a while. Not everything is a shot."

I roll my eyes.

"Anyway," she says, "I tried to get you out to the car, but you were stumbling and slurring, and the bouncers closed me in. So, when you passed out, I pretended like I was passed out, too. I was so floppy, you would have been amazed by my acting. Even when the big one slammed my hand in the trunk, I didn't break character."

I'm staring at her in amazement. While I was knocked out, she was plotting and planning.

"They brought us to the warehouse and carried us inside. They took you away and put me in some kind of office room. The guy hadn't tied me up 'cause he thought I was still out cold. He left me alone for just a second. Locked the door, though. I didn't have a phone—he took my purse and Dante's gun. So, instead, I went up into the air vent—"

"You what?"

"Yeah." She grins. "I used my fingernail to turn the screw, got the cover off, climbed right out. Remembered to put the cover back on, too. I wish I could've stayed to see the guard's face when he came back—he probably thought I pulled some kind of Houdini move. I lost my shoes along the way; they were making too much noise in the vent. Then I dropped into a little kitchen—it had a fridge, freezer, full liquor cabinet. That's how I made the Molotovs. There was all kinds of stuff in there—Zajac must work out of this building a lot, not just when he's torturing people."

She pauses, eyebrows pinched with concern. "Did he cut you? You were bleeding…"

"I'm fine," I assure her. "He just poked me a little."

She says, "I heard the guards freaking out. They didn't want to tell him I escaped. They're all completely terrified of him. So that gave me some extra time to run around raising a ruckus. I stole a gun and shot one of them. A different one grabbed me from behind, shoved my head into the wall. I had to shoot at his foot like nine times before I hit it. Then I didn't have any more bullets. But I found you right after!"

I'm staring at her in absolute astonishment. Her eyes are bright with excitement, her face alight with the thrill of what she accomplished.

It's crazy and hectic, and we could have been killed, but I've never felt more alive. The freezing water, the night air, the stars overhead, the light reflected in Aida's gray eyes…I feel it all with painful clarity. It's absolutely fucking beautiful.

I grab Aida's face and kiss her. I kiss her so long and so hard that we sink under the water and then rise to the surface again, our mouths still locked together.

"You're incredible," I tell her. "Also completely insane. You should have just run!"

Aida fixes me with her most serious expression. "I would never abandon you."

We're spinning slightly in the current, the city lights rotating around us. We're holding each other, looking into each other's eyes, while our feet tread water.

"Neither would I," I promise her. "I'll always find you, Aida."

She kisses me again, her lips chilly and trembling but still the softest thing I've ever touched.

23
AIDA

THE ELECTION TAKES PLACE TWO DAYS LATER.

Cal is all patched up. He needed stitches for a couple of the slashes. Now you'd hardly know he'd been in a fight. I, on the other hand, have to wear a giant cast, since apparently that idiot bouncer broke two of my fingers when he slammed the trunk on my hand. Makes me extra glad I shot him.

It's making it damn hard to type anything on my phone, which is annoying because I have a very important project in the works, and I don't want it getting all fucked up because I can't check my email.

"I can help you with that," Cal says, reaching out to take my phone. "You can dictate, and I'll type."

"No!" I say, snatching it back. "I don't need help."

"What are you doing?" he asks suspiciously.

"None of your business." I tuck the phone back in my pocket.

He frowns. He's already on edge because we're supposed to be getting the election results any minute. I really shouldn't bait him.

His phone rings, and he almost jumps out of his skin. He holds it to his ear, listening.

I watch as the relief pours over him. He hangs up the call, grinning.

"Congratulations!" I shout.

He picks me up and spins me around until I lock my legs around his waist and kiss him for a very long time.

"You did it," I say.

He sets me down again, his bright blue eyes boring into mine. "We did it together, Aida. We really did. You got me the extra support I needed from the Italians. You helped me win over the right people. I want you to come work with me. Every day. Once you graduate, I mean."

My heart gives a funny little flutter.

That's crazy. A couple of weeks ago, I hardly thought Callum and I could share a room without murdering each other.

"Roommates *and* coworkers?" I say teasingly.

"Why not?" Callum frowns. "You'd get sick of me?"

"No. You're not exactly the chatty type." I laugh. "Actually, you're pretty…calming to be around."

It's true. When Cal's not driving me into a rage, he steadies me. I feel safe around him.

"What are we going to do about Zajac, though?" I ask him.

Dante and Nero made off with about five hundred thousand dollars in cash from the Butcher's casino, as well as smashed up a bunch of his machines. We haven't heard anything since. Which seems like it must be the calm before the storm.

"Well, Nero thinks we should—"

We're interrupted by Fergus and Imogen, who heard the news. They burst into Cal's office, wanting to celebrate with champagne.

I try to sidle out to leave them alone together, but Imogen puts her arm around my shoulders and pulls me back in again.

"Don't you want a drink? We're celebrating you, too, Aida. A husband's achievement belongs to the wife, and vice versa."

Imogen has apparently forgiven me for murdering her cabinet. In fact, she insists we all go to dinner to celebrate, including Nessa and Riona. I notice our reservation at Everest is already set. I have to smile at Imogen's confidence in her son.

His parents leave us. The silence between us is warm.

"I guess you want me to change, then," I say to Callum.

He looks down at my T-shirt and shorts.

"I don't know." He gives me a little half smile. "You look pretty cute as is."

I raise my eyebrows in astonishment. "Who are you, and what have you done with my husband?"

Cal shrugs. "You look beautiful in everything. I'm not going to boss you around about it."

I give him a sideways smirk and whisper up to him, "But what if I kind of like it when you boss me around?"

He grabs my arm and growls into my ear. "Then go put on that little blue sundress I bought for you, and see how I reward you."

As soon as he gets that controlling tone, the tiny hairs rise on my arms, and I get a warm, throbbing, nervous feeling.

Part of me wants to disobey him.

The other part wants to see what will happen if I play along.

So I go into the walk-in closet, find the requested dress, and put it on. Then I brush my hair, pin it back with a clip, put on some earrings shaped like little white daisies, and slip my feet into sandals.

By the time I finish, Callum's waiting downstairs for me. I descend the staircase like a prom queen, trailing my hand along the railing, trying to look graceful.

Callum grins up at me, looking extremely handsome in his pale blue dress shirt and slacks. He's shaved his face clean, making his jaw look sharper than ever. Now I can see the flawless shape of his lips, the way they smile just a little even when his eyes look stern.

"Where's everybody else?" I ask him.

"I told them to go ahead in the other car. Jack's driving us." He takes my hand, pulling me close. "Nothing under that skirt, I hope."

"Of course not," I say primly.

Jack is already waiting by the town car, holding the door. He's been marginally nicer to me since robbing the casino with my brothers and cousin. I don't know if it's because he likes my family or because he's scared of them. He hasn't made a single rude comment since, and I haven't had to shoot him at all.

Callum and I slide into the back seat. I can see Cal already put the partition up. He turns on the music, too, louder than usual.

"How far is the restaurant?"

"I think I'll have just enough time..." Not bothering with his seat belt, he gets down in front of me and puts his head under the skirt of my sundress. I gasp and turn the music up a little more. Then I lie back against the seat.

Callum licks my pussy with long, slow strokes. His mouth feels incredibly soft with the fresh shave. His lips caress my skin, his tongue sliding between my folds, warm and wet and sensual.

I love fucking him in the car. I never knew why people had chauffeurs. Now I realize it's 100 percent for this reason—so you can turn a boring commute into the best part of your day. Someday, when we all have robot cars, you'll look into the other windows, and all you'll see will be people banging.

I'm starting to get a Pavlovian response to the smell of leather conditioner—suddenly it's the most erotic scent in the world.

I love the feel of the seats against my bare skin, the way the motion of the car rocks me and presses me all the tighter against Callum's tongue. He's so fucking good at this. He looks cold and stiff, but actually his hands and mouth are warm like butter. He knows exactly how hard to lick and suck, providing maximum stimulation without ever tipping over into too much.

I'm rocking my hips, riding his face, trying hard not to make any noise. I may have given up my vendetta with Jack, but that doesn't mean I want to put on a show for him.

But it's impossible to stay quiet when Cal slips his fingers inside me. He gently twists and slides in motion with his tongue, teasing out all my most sensitive spots.

I squeeze around his fingers, my breath quickening and my skin tingling. Warmth spirals outward from my belly. My pussy is soaking wet and extra sensitive.

With his other hand, Callum reaches up and pulls down the front of my dress. Freeing one of my breasts, he caresses it with his hand, gently pinching and tugging on the nipple.

He gradually increases the pressure until he's roughly squeezing my tits, pinching and pulling at the nipples. For some reason, this feels fucking fantastic. Maybe it's because I'm already so aroused, or maybe it's just because I like when Cal is a little rough in bed. There's so much tension between us that it gives relief to the aggression. It gives us somewhere to channel it.

I've never had a relationship quite like this. There were always people I hated and people I liked, and those two categories were polar opposites. My boyfriends fell in the "sweet and fun" category, not the "drive me fucking insane" one.

Callum is becoming a little bit of both. And somehow that makes my attraction to him ten times stronger. He captures all my emotions: resentment, jealousy, rebelliousness, desire, anger, curiosity, playfulness, and even respect. He bundles it all into one package. The result is absolutely irresistible. It captivates me entirely.

Cal keeps licking my pussy, fingering me, and squeezing my tits all at the same time. Stimulating every part of me until I'm squirming and grinding against him, ready to explode.

I can feel the car turning, starting to slow.

It's now or never.

I let go, coming over and over on the flat of Cal's tongue. The rolling waves of pleasure crash over me. I have to bite my lip and squeeze my eyes tightly shut to keep from screaming.

The car stops. Cal sits up, wiping his mouth on the back of his hand. "Just in time."

I'm panting like I ran a mile. "Your hair is crazy," I tell him.

He smooths it with the palm of his hand, smirking at me.

"Yes, yes, you did a great job," I say, laughing.

"I know," he says. He takes my hand to help me out of the car.

We take the elevator up to the fortieth floor of the Stock Exchange building. I haven't actually been up here before, though I know the restaurant is supposed to be nice.

The view is stunning. Imogen has, naturally, snagged the best table in the place. Below is a sprawling panorama of city lights and the inky void of the lake.

The others are already seated. Nessa's wearing a flowered romper, her light-brown hair pulled up in a high ponytail. She's got more freckles now that it's getting hotter. Riona has her hair down—unusual for her. She really does have the most stunning hair I've ever seen, thick, wavy, deeply hued. I think she dislikes how vivid it looks. How much attention it steals.

Tonight, however, she's almost in as good a mood as everybody else. We're all talking and laughing, ordering decadent things off the menu. I look around at Cal's family, and for the first time, I don't feel like a stranger. I feel comfortable at the table. Happy to be there, even.

We're talking about the longest book we've ever read.

"I read *War and Peace!*" I tell them. "I'm the only person who ever did, I think. I was stuck at this cabin, and it was the only book on the shelf."

"I think *The Stand* may be my longest," Riona muses. "Unabridged version, obviously."

"You read Stephen King?" I ask her in astonishment.

"I've read every one," Riona says. "Until his most recent because I haven't had time—"

"She was so scared of *It*," Callum says. "She's still terrified of clowns."

"I'm not *scared* of them," Riona says loftily. "I just don't like them. There's a difference…"

"Do you want more wine?" Cal asks me, holding up the bottle.

I nod, and he refills my glass.

When he sets the bottle down, he drops his hand to my lap. He finds my hand—the one not in a cast—and intertwines his fingers with mine.

His hand is warm and strong, squeezing just the right amount. His thumb gently strokes mine, then goes still again.

Cal and I have fucked plenty of times. We've kissed, too. But this is the first time we've ever held hands. He's not doing it for show because we're at an event. And he's not grabbing me to pull me close. He's holding my hand because he wants to.

Our relationship has proceeded in such a funny, backward way. Marriage first. Then sex. Then getting to know each other. And finally…whatever this is. A feeling of warmth and desire and affection and connection spreads through my chest, a feeling that grows stronger by the moment, especially when I glance over at the man sitting next to me.

I can't believe it.

I think I'm falling in love.

24

CALLUM

I'M SITTING AT THE TABLE SURROUNDED BY MY FAMILY, BASKING IN the glow of victory. My parents look happier and prouder than I've ever seen them. My sisters are in good spirits, laughing and joking about some guy who's been chasing after Nessa.

It's a scene I've been working toward for months.

And yet I find myself tuning out of the conversation because I want to look at Aida instead.

I can't believe she stayed at Zajac's warehouse for me.

She could have been killed or, at the very least, recaptured and held hostage until her brothers returned the money they stole.

She could have just run the moment she escaped the office. But she didn't. Because she knew I was somewhere in the building, probably being tortured, possibly being killed.

That would have been an easy way for her to get out of our marriage contract.

I'm not sure she wants to get out of it anymore. Or at least not as much as before.

I know I don't want to lose her.

I've come to respect Aida and like her, too. I like the effect she has on me. She makes me more reckless but also more focused. Before I met her, I was going through the motions. Doing what I was supposed to without really caring.

Now I want to achieve all the same things, but I want them so much more. I want to do it all with Aida by my side, bringing life to the whole enterprise.

I take her hand and hold it, gently running my thumb over hers. She looks up, surprised but not annoyed. She smiles at me, squeezing my hand in return.

Her phone buzzes. She sneaks it out of her bag to read the message. She's looking at it under the table so I can't see the screen. But I notice the immediate change in her expression—how she sucks in a little breath of excitement, her cheeks flushing with color.

"What is it?"

"Oh, nothing," she says. "Just a text from my brother."

She quickly stows the phone away. I can tell she's lit up with excitement, barely able to sit still.

I take my hand back and drink my wine, trying not to let my irritation show.

What would it take to make Aida be completely honest with me? When will she open up to me and stop treating me like an annoying overseer?

She's too happy to notice the change in my mood. "We should order dessert! What's your favorite?"

"I don't eat sweets," I say sulkily.

"They have a grapefruit gelato," she teases. "That's pretty much health food."

"Maybe I'll have a bit of yours," I say, relenting.

"I'm not eating that." Aida laughs. "I'm getting chocolate soufflé."

The next afternoon, I'm supposed to go see my new office at city hall. I swing by the house to see if Aida wants to come along with me. To my surprise, she's already dressed, holding the keys to Nessa's Jeep.

"Where are you going?"

"I've got some errands to run," she says vaguely.

"What kind of errands?"

"All kinds," she says, climbing into the car and closing the door.

She's wearing a little crop top and cutoff shorts, her hair pulled up in a ponytail and heart-shaped sunglasses perched on her head. By Aida's standards, this is fairly dressed up. My curiosity is inflamed.

I lean against the windowsill, annoyed she's not coming with me. I wanted to show her all of city hall and maybe go for a late lunch together.

"Can't it wait?" I ask her.

"No," she says regretfully. "Actually, I've got to get going…"

I step back, letting her start the engine. "What's the hurry?"

"No hurry. See you tonight!" she calls, putting the car in reverse.

Aida is fucking maddening when she won't answer my questions.

I can't help thinking she looks way too cute just to be running to the post office. And what kind of errands could she possibly have that are time sensitive?

And who messaged her last night? Could it be Oliver Castle? Could she be going to meet with him right now?

I'm burning with jealousy.

I know I should just talk to her when she comes home tonight, but I don't want to wait until then.

I wish I'd remembered to steal her phone. I figured out her pass code by watching over her shoulder while she entered it—it's 1799, not hard to remember. But in the craziness of our encounter with Zajac and the election right after, I forgot to look through her messages.

I should have done it last night while she was sleeping.

Now it's fucking eating me alive.

I grab my own phone out of my pocket and call Jack. He picks up immediately.

"What's up, boss?"

"Where are you right now?"

"Ravenswood."

"Is there a GPS tracker on Nessa's Jeep?"

"Yeah. Your dad's got them on all the vehicles."

I let out a sigh of relief. "Good. I want you to follow it. Aida's running errands—I want you to see what she's doing, where she goes."

"You got it," Jack says. He doesn't ask why, but I'm sure he can guess.

"Keep me posted. Tell me everything she does. And don't lose track of her."

"Understood."

I hang up the phone.

I don't feel great about siccing Jack on Aida—especially knowing how she feels about him. But I have to know what she's doing. I have to know, once and for all, if Aida's heart belongs to someone else or if it might be available. Maybe even for me.

I still have to go to city hall, so I take my father instead. He's already talking about how we'll parlay this into a mayoral campaign in a couple of years. Not to mention all the ways we can use the aldermanship to enrich ourselves in the meantime.

I can barely pay attention. My hand keeps sneaking back into my pocket, clenching my phone so I can pick it up the moment Jack calls.

After about forty minutes, he texts me to say:

She's somewhere around Jackson Park. I see the car, but I haven't found her yet. Looking in the shops and cafes.

I'm strung tighter than a wire.

What's in Jackson Park? Who's she meeting? I know she's meeting someone; I can feel it.

My father puts his hand on my shoulder, startling me. "You don't look pleased. What's wrong? You don't like the office?"

"No." I shake my head. "It's great."

"What is it, then?"

I hesitate. My relationship with my father is based off work. All our conversations center the family business: problems we need to fix, deals we need to make, ways we can expand. We don't talk about personal things. Emotions. Feelings.

Still, I need advice.

"I think I might have made a mistake with Aida."

He peers at me through his glasses, thrown off-balance. That's not what he expected me to say. "What do you mean?"

"I was cold and demanding. Cruel, even. Now it may be too late to start over..."

My father crosses his arms, leaning against the desk. He probably doesn't want to talk about this. I don't want to talk about it either. But it's eating me alive.

He says, "She didn't seem to be holding a grudge last night."

I sigh, looking out the window at the high-rises opposite.

Aida always rolls with the punches. That doesn't mean she wasn't hurt. And that doesn't mean it will be easy to win her over. She's a tough nut. What will it take to truly crack her open, to find that vulnerable core inside?

"When did you fall in love with Mom?" I ask, remembering my parents' marriage wasn't exactly traditional either.

"I'm not a sentimental person," my father says. "I think we're alike in that way, you and I. I don't think much about love or what it means. But I can tell you that I came to trust your mother. She showed me I could rely on her, no matter what. That's what bonded us. That's when I knew I wasn't alone anymore. Because I could count on one person, at least."

Trust as the essence of love.

It doesn't sound romantic, not on the surface.

But it makes sense, especially in our world. Any gangster knows your friends can put a bullet in your back just as easily as your enemies—even more easily, in fact.

Trust is rarer than love.

It's putting your fate, your happiness, your life in someone's hands. Hoping they keep it safe.

My phone vibrates again.

"Give me a minute," I say to my father, stepping out into the hall to take the call.

"I saw her for a second," Jack says. "She was at a restaurant with some guy. He gave her something, a little box. She put it in her bag."

"Who was the guy?" I ask, my mouth dry and my hand clenched tight around the phone.

"I don't know," Jack says apologetically. "I only saw the back of his head. He had dark hair."

"Was it Castle?"

"I don't know. They were sitting on the patio. I went into the restaurant—I was going to try to get a table so I could get closer and listen in. But while I was inside, they left. I haven't been able to find her again."

"Where's her car?" I demand.

"Well, that's the weird thing." I can hear Jack breathing heavily like he's walking and talking at the same time. "The Jeep is still in the same parking lot. But Aida's gone."

She must have left with the guy.

Fuck!

My heart is racing. I feel sick.

Is she with him right now? Where are they going?

"Keep looking for her," I bark into the phone.

"I will," Jack says. "There's just one other thing…"

"What?"

"I found a shoe."

I'm about to explode. Jack isn't making any sense. "What the fuck are you talking about?"

"There was a sneaker in the parking lot, over by the Jeep. It's a woman's shoe, Converse slip-on, size eight, cream colored. The left foot."

I rack my brain, trying to remember what Aida was wearing when she stepped into the Jeep. A lavender-colored crop top. Jean shorts. Bare legs. And then, down on her feet…sneakers, as usual. The kind you can slip on without tying the laces. White or cream, I'm almost certain.

"Stay there," I say into the phone. "Stay by the Jeep. Keep the shoe."

I hang up the phone, hurrying back into the office. "I've got to go," I say to my father. "Do you mind if I take the car?"

"Go ahead. I'll take a cab back to the house."

I hurry down to the main level again, mind racing.

What the fuck is going on? Who was Aida meeting? And how did she lose a shoe?

As I drive to meet Jack, I try calling Aida again and again. Her phone rings, but she doesn't pick up.

The fourth time I call, it goes straight to voicemail without even ringing. Which means her phone is switched off.

I'm starting to get worried.

Maybe I'm a fool and Aida is shacked up in some hotel room right now, ripping the clothes off some other man.

But I don't think so.

I know what the evidence looks like; I just don't believe it. I don't think she's cheating on me.

I think she's in trouble.

25
AIDA

I'm sitting across the table from my new best friend, Jeremy Parker. He passes me the little box I've been waiting and hoping for all week long, and I open the lid to peek inside.

"Oh my god, I can't believe it…"

"I know." He laughs. "This was the hardest one I've ever done. Took me three whole days."

"You're a miracle worker. Honestly."

He grins, almost as gleeful as I am. "You mind if I put the whole thing up on my YouTube channel? I was wearing my GoPro, got some great footage."

"Of course!" I say.

I close the box, still hardly believing what I'm holding in my hand, and stow it back in my purse. I give Jeremy a slim envelope of cash in return—the amount we agreed upon, plus a bonus for saving my ass.

"Well, call me if you ever need me again," he says, giving me a little salute.

"I hope I won't need you." I laugh. "No offense."

"None taken." He chuckles, raising his hand to signal for the waitress.

"I already paid for the meals," I tell him.

"Oh, thanks! You didn't have to."

"It was the least I could do."

"All right, I'm off then."

He gives me a wave and leaves through the restaurant. I cut straight through the patio, then cross the street because that's the quickest route to the lot where I left the Jeep.

It feels like my feet are barely touching the sidewalk.

This is so fucking fantastic, it's got to be some kind of sign. A bona fide miracle.

It's a gorgeous day, too. Sun beaming down, the tiniest breeze blowing in off the lake, the clouds so puffy and uniform that they look like a child's painting.

I'm dying to see Cal. I felt bad about not going to see his new office, but this couldn't wait—I couldn't chance something else going wrong. He won't be mad about it when he sees what I've got.

Nessa's Jeep looks brilliantly white in the sunshine. I washed it and filled it with gas on the way over as a thank-you to Nessa for letting me borrow it so many times. I even vacuumed the seats and threw away all her empty water bottles.

Still, the Jeep is outshone by the car parked next to it. A very familiar car.

I stop midstride, frowning.

I don't see anyone around. Probably the best thing to do is to get in the Jeep and drive away as quickly as possible.

As soon as my fingers touch the door handle, something hard and sharp pokes between my ribs.

"Hey, baby girl," a deep voice whispers in my ear.

I stand perfectly still, running through my options in my mind: Fight. Run. Scream. Dial my phone.

"Whatever you're thinking about, just don't," he growls. "I don't want to have to hurt you."

"Okay," I say, trying to keep my voice as casual as possible.

"You'll be getting in my car."

"All right."

"In the trunk."

Fuck.

I'm cooperating because it seems like the best option right now—the one most likely to keep him calm.

He presses the button on his key fob, popping open the trunk.

I try to glance around without him noticing. The lot is jumbled and half-empty. There's nobody in the immediate vicinity to see me being stuffed into the back of the car.

So I do the only thing I can think of. I slip off one of my sneakers, the left one. As I sit in the open trunk, I flip my foot to kick the shoe off under the Jeep. Then I bring my knees up and hide my bare foot beneath me so he won't notice.

"Lie down," he says. "I don't want to hit your head."

I do as he says. He slams the trunk shut, closing me in the darkness.

26
CALLUM

I'm standing in front of Nessa's Jeep, turning the sneaker over and over in my hand.

It's Aida's, I'm sure of it.

How did she lose her shoe?

It's been over an hour since Jack lost sight of her, but she hasn't come back to the Jeep. I've called her phone twenty times. It keeps going straight to voicemail.

Dante and Nero pull up in a vintage Mustang. They jump out of the car, not bothering to close their doors after them.

"Where was she?" Dante says at once.

"At that restaurant over there." I point to the patio on the far side of the street. "She was meeting a friend. After they ate, she disappeared."

"What friend?" Dante asks.

"I don't know."

He gives me a strange look.

"Maybe she left with the mystery friend," Nero says.

"Maybe," I agree. "But she lost a shoe."

I hold it up so they can look at it. They obviously recognize it because Nero frowns and Dante starts looking around like Aida might have dropped something else.

"That's weird," Nero says.

"Yeah, it is. That's why I called you."

"You think the Butcher took her?" Dante says, his voice low and rumbling.

"Then why the fuck are we standing here?" Nero looks like a current just ran through his body. He's agitated, spoiling for action.

"I don't know if it was Zajac," I say.

"Who else could it be?"

"Well…" It sounds insane, but I've got to say it. "It could be Oliver Castle."

"*Ollie?*" Nero scoffs, eyebrows so high that they're lost under his hair. "Not fucking likely."

"Why not?"

"For one, he's a little bitch. For two, Aida's done with him."

Even under the circumstances, his words give me a glow of happiness. If Aida still had feelings for her ex, her brothers would know.

"I didn't say she went with him. I said he could have taken her."

"What makes you think that?" Dante scowls.

"The shoe." I hold it up. "I think she left it as a sign. Based off something she said to me once."

Oliver and I didn't fit together. Like a shoe on the wrong foot.

It sounds crazy. I don't have to look at her brothers' faces to know they're not convinced.

"Anything's possible," Dante says. "But we need to focus on the biggest danger first, which is Zajac."

"It's Tuesday," Nero says.

"So?"

"So that means the Butcher is visiting his girlfriend."

"Assuming he stuck to his normal schedule and isn't taking a night off to murder our sister," Dante says grimly.

"Aida's friend gave us the address," I remind them. "Assuming she was telling the truth. She did drug us right after…"

"I'll go to the apartment," Dante says. "Nero, you can check Zajac's pawn stores and chop shops. Cal—"

"I'm going to look for Castle."

I can tell Dante thinks that's a waste of time. He glances over at Jack, his expression wary. He suspects I sent Jack to follow Aida. He thinks I'm jealous and irrational.

He may be right.

But I can't shake the feeling Aida was trying to tell me something with this shoe.

"I'm going to Castle's apartment," I say firmly.

But then I pause, really trying to think this through. Oliver lives in a high-rise in the middle of the city. Would he kidnap Aida and take her there? One scream, and his neighbors would call the cops.

"Jack, you go to his apartment," I say, changing my mind. "I'm going to check a different place."

"Everybody, stay in contact," Dante says. "Keep trying to call Aida, too. As soon as someone finds her, let the others know, and we'll all go in together."

We all nod in agreement.

I already know if I find Aida, I'm not waiting a moment for anybody else. I'm going in to get my wife back.

"Here, take my car," I say to Dante, throwing him the keys. "I'll take the Jeep."

Dante and Nero split off, and Jack heads back to his truck. I climb into the Jeep, smelling the familiar feminine scent of my little sister—vanilla, lilac, lemon. And then, fainter but perfectly clear, the cinnamon spice scent of Aida herself.

I leave the city, heading south on I-90. I hope I'm not making a horrible mistake. The place I'm going is over an hour away. If I'm wrong, I'll be too far away from wherever Aida actually is to help her. But I feel propelled in this direction, pulled by an invisible magnet.

Aida is calling to me.

She left me a sign.

Oliver Castle took her, I know it.

And I think I know exactly where he's headed—the little beach house Henry Castle just sold. The one Oliver loved. The one that's completely empty right now, without anyone around.

27

AIDA

I WOULDN'T HAVE GOTTEN IN THE FUCKING TRUNK IF I'D KNOWN how far Oliver was going to drive. I feel like I've been in here forever. Also, I drank a lot of water with lunch, and I really have to pee. Also, I'm worried about what Oliver might have done with my purse. He wasn't stupid enough to put it in here with me, unfortunately. I'm anxious that he just chucked it out the window or something, which means my precious little package is already missing again.

For a long time, I can feel we're on the freeway—smooth, steady progress in the same direction. Eventually, we turn off and drive slowly and erratically down roads that are obviously narrower and less well maintained. A couple of times, the car jolts hard enough that I hit my head on the top of the trunk.

I've been hunting around in the dark, looking for anything useful. If there was a tire iron back here, I'd use it to brain Oliver the second he opened the trunk.

At last, the car slows. I think we've arrived wherever the hell we were going. I haven't found any weapons, but that's not going to hold me back. I wait, crouched and ready, for Oliver to pop the trunk.

The tires crunch over gravel and roll to a stop. I hear the car door opening and feel the suspension lift as Oliver removes his considerable bulk from the front seat. Then I hear him walking around to the back of the car.

The trunk pops open.

Even though the sun is going down, the light is still brilliant compared to the darkness of the trunk. My eyes are dazzled. Still, I kick out with both feet, as hard as I can, right toward Oliver's crotch.

He jumps backward, my feet barely making contact with his thigh. Those goddamned athlete reflexes.

"So predictable, Aida." He sighs. "Always fighting."

He grabs my foot and yanks me halfway out of the trunk. He pauses when he notices the lack of a sneaker on one foot. "What happened to your shoe?"

"How should I know? I was busy being kidnapped and stuffed in a trunk. You better not have lost my purse, too."

"I didn't," Oliver says.

He lets go of my foot. I stand, looking around.

We're parked in front of a little blue beach house. The water is only a hundred yards away across smooth cream-colored sand. The house is bracketed by thick stands of trees, the view down to the water clear from the back.

I've never been here before. Still, I know exactly where we are. Oliver talked about it all the time—it's his family's cabin.

He wanted to bring me here. We'd been to another cabin, right on the edge of Indiana Dunes State Park. That was the night Oliver talked about at the fundraiser—when I wore the white bikini and we had sex out on the sand.

Apparently, he thinks that was some magical night. To me, it was cold and uncomfortable, and I got a shit ton of mosquito bites.

Now we're back here, this time at the Castle residence. Oliver came here as a child. He said it was the only time he got to see his parents for more than ten minutes in a row. Which is sad but not sad enough to make me forget the kidnapping part.

"What do you think?" Oliver says, his expression hopeful.

"It's, uh…exactly how you described."

"I know!" Oliver says happily, ignoring my lack of enthusiasm.

"Don't forget my purse," I remind him.

He opens the driver's side door again so he can retrieve my purse from the front seat.

The moment he leans over, I sprint away from him, running down toward the water.

It would have been easier to run to the road, but then he'd find me in two seconds. I'm hoping I'll be able to hide somewhere in the trees or the dunes.

As soon as my feet hit the sand, I realize what a stupid plan this was. I don't run at all, let alone through soft, mushy sand. It's like a nightmare where you sprint as hard as you can and barely move.

Meanwhile Oliver used to run the forty in 4.55 seconds. He may have put on a few pounds since his glory days, but when he puts his head down and pumps his arms, he still charges through the sand like a linebacker.

He tackles me so hard that it knocks every last molecule of oxygen out of my lungs. They're so deflated that I make a horrible gagging sound before I can finally drag in a sweet breath of air.

My head is pounding. I'm covered in sand; it's in my hair and in my mouth. And worst of all, in my cast, which is gonna drive me fucking bonkers.

Oliver is already on his feet again, watching me with pitiless eyes.

"I don't know why you do this to yourself, Aida. You're so self-destructive."

I want to tell him I didn't fucking tackle myself, but I'm barely breathing, let alone able to speak.

While I'm gasping and gagging, Oliver rummages through my purse. He finds my phone. Kneeling in the sand, he picks up a rock the size of his fist and smashes the screen. His face is red with effort, the muscles on his arms and shoulders straining. My phone practically explodes under the rock while Oliver keeps hitting it again and again.

He picks up the broken metal and glass, then flings it into the water.

"Was that really necessary?" I ask him once I've recovered my breath.

"I don't want anyone tracking you."

"Nobody—" I break off, my mouth hanging open.

I was about to say, *Nobody has a tracker on my phone*, but I realized that isn't true.

Oliver put a tracker on my phone. He must have done it when we were dating. That's how he always knew where to find me. At restaurants, at parties—and later, at Callum's fundraiser.

That's probably how he found me today. He's been watching where I go. Most of the time, it's completely boring places like school. It still gives me a sick feeling knowing I was a little dot on a screen, always under his eye.

Oliver leaves my purse lying in the sand.

"Come on," he says. "Back to the house."

I don't want to get up, but I don't really want him to carry me either. So I drag myself up and shuffle after him, with only one shoe and an itchy sand-filled cast that's already driving me crazy.

I try to shake it out.

Oliver says, "What happened to you?"

"Got my hand slammed in a trunk." A perverse giggle bursts out of me as I realize I've been shoved in a trunk twice this week. A new record over the zero times it happened before this.

Oliver watches me, unsmiling. "I knew this would happen," he says. "I knew he wouldn't be able to take care of you."

I scowl, stomping through the sand. I never wanted anybody to "take care" of me. Oliver was always trying to do it, and that's one of the things that annoyed me about him. Once, we played pickleball with another couple, and Oliver almost got in a fistfight because the guy slammed the ball right at me. Oliver wanted a chivalrous game. I wanted a challenge.

He was always calling me *princess* and *angel.* And I always thought, *Who in the fuck are you talking about? Because that sure ain't me.*

I guess I misread Oliver, too. Because I never thought he'd do something as crazy as this.

I follow him up to the back of the beach house. We climb the weatherworn steps. Oliver holds the door for me.

I'm surprised to find the house almost entirely empty. We're in the living/dining/kitchen area, but there's no table nor chairs nor couches. Just a bare mattress on the floor with a blanket on top.

I can't say I like the look of that any better.

"Why's it so empty in here?"

Oliver looks around resentfully, as if counting all the missing things.

"My father sold the house. I asked him not to, but he said the value is as high as it's going to get, and now's the time to sell, before they build more properties in Chesterton. As if he needs the money!"

He gives a harsh, barking laugh. "This place didn't mean anything to him," he says darkly. "I was the only one who cared about coming here."

I'm very familiar with Oliver's spoiled-yet-neglected only-child upbringing. He had no siblings and no real friends either—just the schoolmates he was "supposed" to associate with. He told me how jealous he was that I had brothers. He never met my brothers, though—I couldn't see them getting along.

"Well," I say, trying to mollify him, "I'm glad I got to see it, finally."

He turns to look at me, his pupils huge in the dim light. His face looks masklike. He's gained probably thirty pounds since we dated, which has made his face wider and older looking, more like his father's. He's still big and muscular—in fact, the extra weight makes it all the easier for him to overpower me, as evidenced by our short-lived struggle on the beach. I'm not sure how the fuck I'm going to get away from him when he's stronger and faster than me.

"I wish you could have seen it how it used to be," Oliver says. "With all the pictures and books. And couches. It's all right, though. I brought this here so we'd have somewhere to sit, at least."

He sinks onto the mattress. It creaks beneath his weight.

"Come on, sit," he says, patting the space beside him.

"Uh, actually, I've got to pee really bad," I say.

It's true. My bladder feels like it's about to burst, especially after Oliver body-slammed me on the beach.

He stares at me suspiciously like he doesn't believe me. I shift my weight from my bare foot to the one with the shoe, not exaggerating my discomfort.

"The bathroom's over here," Oliver says at last, standing again.

He leads me down the hall to a pretty little bathroom with wainscoting all over the walls and a shell-shaped sink. I'm sure there were nautical-themed towels and soap in here when the house was furnished.

When I try to close the door, Oliver stops it with one meaty hand. "I don't think so."

"I need to pee," I tell him again, like he forgot.

"You can do it with the door open."

I glare at him, in a standoff between his stubbornness and my throbbing bladder.

I can only last a few seconds. I drop my shorts and sit on the toilet, letting go. The pee comes thundering out with more pain than relief.

Oliver stands in the doorway watching me. There's a tiny smile at the corners of his mouth. His eyes look hooded and pleased.

I wish he would turn the fuck around and give me some privacy. Or at the very least, I wish I weren't peeing so long. It seems to go on forever, and it's fucking humiliating.

He's right, though—if he'd left me alone in the bathroom, I would have climbed out the window in five seconds.

When I'm finished, I pull up my shorts and wash my hands, wiping them dry on my clothes since there aren't any towels.

Oliver watches this with a scowling expression. I think he's looking at the cast again. Then I realize he's actually looking at my left hand, at my engagement ring.

I've started wearing it more often, not just when I'm going to an event with Cal.

I can tell Oliver hates the sight of it. In fact, as soon as we're back in the living room, he barks, "Take that off."

"This?" I say, holding up my left hand.

"Yes," he hisses.

Reluctantly, I slip it off my finger.

I hated that ring when I first got it, but I don't mind it so much anymore. It's kind of pretty, how it sparkles in the sunshine. And it doesn't look as strange and false to me as it did at first.

I'm about to slip it in my pocket for safekeeping when Oliver says, "No. Give it to me."

I don't want to hand it over to him. It feels like a betrayal. But if I refuse, it's not like I can stop him from wrenching it out of my hand. So I pass it to him silently.

There's a tool bag sitting on the kitchen floor next to a slightly paler patch of wall that probably had water damage until someone fixed it.

Oliver opens the bag, then takes out a hammer. He sets my ring on the kitchen countertop. Like he did to my phone, he smashes it over and over.

The metal bends, the claws coming loose around the diamonds and the stones scattering. Still, he keeps hitting it until the band is twisted and ruined and the main stone has rolled away.

It hurts more than I expected seeing that ring destroyed.

But what really disturbs me is how the hammer is taking huge chunks out of the butcher-block countertop. Oliver doesn't give a damn how much damage he's doing. Knowing how he feels about this house, that can't be a good thing.

He swings the hammer, his fury terrifying. His eyes are glittering,

his face flushed. He's sweating, dark patches showing through on the chest, back, and underarms of his T-shirt. He hits the ring about a hundred times.

Finally, he stops. He's standing there panting, looking at me. Still holding the hammer.

He takes a step toward me. I take a step back, heart racing.

I really think he's losing it.

When I knew Oliver before, he seemed like a nice enough guy. Sometimes a little shallow. Sometimes a little clingy. But mostly normal, with only small swings into oddness.

Now it's the opposite—he seems to be dangling on the precipice of madness, only hanging on by a thread. I'm not sure what that thread is—is it this house? Is it his affection for me? Or is it just the appearance of calm—fragile and easily shattered?

He takes one more step, then seems to remember he's holding the hammer. He sets it on the counter before pulling his phone out of his pocket instead. "Let's have a little music."

He scrolls through his playlist, selecting a song and setting the phone down on the counter to play.

The tinny sound of "Make You Feel My Love" fills the little room.

Oliver advances on me. There's not really any way to refuse. He takes my cast in his left hand, putting his other hand around my waist. He sways us back and forth, a little off the beat.

I can feel the heat radiating off his body. His hand is sweaty wrapped around mine. There's a slightly metallic tang to his sweat. I don't know if it was always like that or if this is new.

In sharp contrast to our apparently romantic position, every muscle of my body is tense, every nerve screaming that I'm in danger, that I need to get away from this man.

There's nothing romantic about this at all. I'm struggling to understand how I ever dated Oliver. I guess I never paid that much attention to him. I was looking for fun; he was along for the ride.

Now that I'm really looking into his eyes, I don't like what I see: need, resentment, and a spark of insanity.

"We never went dancing together," Oliver says sulkily. "You always wanted to go with your friends."

"Oliver, I'm sorry that—"

"You used to call me 'Ollie.' I like that much better than 'Oliver.'"

I swallow uncomfortably. "Everybody called you that."

"But it sounded so beautiful when you said it…"

He's pulling me closer against his body. I try to keep the space between us, but it's like swimming against the tide. He's so much stronger than me.

He pulls me right up against his chest so I have to crane my neck to look up at him.

"Say it," he orders. "Call me 'Ollie.'"

"Okay…Ollie…" I say.

"Perfect," he sighs.

He bends his head down to kiss me. His lips feel thick and rubbery against mine. They're too wet. That metallic note is in his saliva as well.

I can't do it. I can't kiss him.

I shove him away from me, wiping my mouth on the back of my arm.

Oliver folds his arms over his broad chest, frowning. "Why do you always have to be so difficult? I know you're miserable with the Griffins. I took you away from that. I brought you here instead, to the most beautiful place in the state. Look at that view!"

He gestures out the window to the pale moonlit sand and the dark water beyond.

"You won't kiss me, but you kiss him, don't you? You've probably fucked him, too. Haven't you? HAVEN'T YOU?"

I know it's only going to make him angrier, but there's no point lying about it. "We're married," I remind him.

"But you don't love him," Oliver says, eyes gleaming. "Say you don't love him."

I should just go along with it. The hammer is still lying on the counter, only a couple of feet away. Oliver could snatch it up again. He could bring it down on my skull with the same fury he applied to the ring.

I should say whatever he wants. Do whatever he wants. I never told Callum I loved him—it shouldn't be hard to say I don't.

I open my mouth. Nothing comes out.

"No," Oliver says, shaking his head slowly. "No, that's not true. You don't love him. You only married him because you had to. You don't care about him, not really."

I press my lips together hard.

I'm thinking about Callum pushing me back against the leather seats and putting his face between my thighs in the back of the town car. I'm thinking about how he wrapped his arms around me and jumped into that pipe when the Butcher's men had their guns pointed at us. I'm thinking about how he said we should work together every day. And how he took my hand at dinner last night.

"Actually…" I say slowly. "I do love him."

"NO, YOU DON'T!" Oliver roars.

He backhands me across the face. It's like being swiped by a bear paw. There's so much force behind it that my whole body goes limp, and I barely catch myself before I hit the floor.

I taste iron in my mouth. My ears are ringing. I spit out a little blood.

"Just take me home," I mutter. "You're not going to get what you want."

"You're not going home," Oliver says flatly. "You're all the same. You, my father, fucking Callum Griffin…you think you can just give somebody something and let them have it and use it and believe it's theirs forever. Then you rip it out of their hands again, just because you feel like it. Well, that's not happening. Not again."

Oliver goes back to his tool bag and pulls out a coiled rope.

I don't think that's a tool bag, not really. Because why the fuck does it have rope in it?

I think Oliver's been planning much more than a home repair for quite a while now.

I try to run, but I can barely stand. It's easy for Oliver to truss me up like a chicken and stuff a rag in my mouth.

He crouches in front of me, his face inches from mine.

"Here's what you have to understand, Aida," he says, his voice low and crooning. "I can't make you be mine. But I can stop you from belonging to anyone else."

I mutter something around the gag.

"What?" Oliver says.

I say it again, no louder than before. Oliver leans in even closer.

I rear my head back and smash my forehead into his nose as hard as I can.

"Owww, fuck!" Oliver howls, cupping his hand over his nose as blood pours through his fingers. "Fuck, Aida, you bitch!"

Oliver hits me again. This time when I topple over, I sink right through the floor into thick, quiet darkness.

28
CALLUM

I don't have the exact address for the Castles' cabin, but I know it's outside of Chesterton, and I know its rough position to the lake. I'm hoping I'll be able to spot it from the color and general location.

Unfortunately, there are a fuck ton of little blue beach houses along this stretch of the lake. Plus, it's getting dark, and there aren't that many streetlights along this route. I can barely tell which houses are blue and which are gray or green.

Now I'm searching for Oliver's Maserati, hoping he wasn't driving something else.

I can at least bypass the places lit up with noise and laughter—wherever Aida is, the house will quiet and relatively secluded, I'm sure of it.

I roll down the window to get a better look at some of the cabins that are set back from the road, half-hidden in trees.

Some of the driveways are so faint, I can barely see them. In fact, I almost pass one by, failing to see the faint tracks through the grass. Until I smell a hint of smoke.

It's so mild that I hardly know what scent I caught. Then I feel the automatic reaction—the hair on the back of my neck standing and my heart starting to race. It's a primal, terrifying smell. A warning of danger.

I slam on the brakes, whipping the wheel to the left. Then I follow the winding path toward a double stand of trees. Between those trees sits the small blue beach house I've seen once before in a battered photograph.

Oliver's silver Maserati is parked alongside the house. The trunk stands open.

I fucking knew it.

I stop my car, hoping Oliver hasn't already heard the engine or seen me driving up the road. I slip out of the driver's side, then crouch behind the car, trying to peer around at the house.

I send a quick text to Aida's brothers. I'm an hour outside Chicago. They won't be getting here anytime soon.

I smell smoke for certain now. In fact, over the sound of the wind in the trees, I think I hear the crackling of wood burning. All the lights are off, an alarming orange glow emanating from the back of the house.

Fuck it, I can't wait. If Aida's in there, I have to get her out now.

I run toward the cottage, trying to stay low. I've got my Beretta with me, and I draw it. I'm leery of actually using it in the dark without knowing where Aida is. A stray bullet through a wall could accidentally hit her.

I go around the back of the house, peering in the windows. I can't see shit. So I try the back door, finding it unlocked. The moment I open it, a cloud of thick black smoke comes rolling out. I drop lower, stifling my cough in the crook of my arm.

The infusion of fresh air invigorates the fire. I hear it sucking up the oxygen, expanding in heat and size. The kitchen is ablaze, the cabinets, countertops, floor, and ceiling all burning.

Skirting the flames, I trip over something on the floor. It's relatively soft. For a second, I hope it's Aida, but then I realize it's just an old mattress.

I want to call out for her but can't risk alerting Oliver, wherever he might be. I search the main level the best I can in the billowing smoke, unable to get near the kitchen or the hallway beyond.

She's got to be upstairs. She's got to be because otherwise this whole place is going to burn down before I find her, and I can't think about that.

I pull my shirt partly over my face and run up the stairs, thinking only of Aida.

I let my guard down. I'm not holding my gun up.

Oliver charges me from the side with all the speed and technique of the athlete he once was. He barrels into me so hard that we slam into the opposite wall, smashing into the drywall. My gun goes spinning off down the hallway, hitting the doorjamb and disappearing into one of the rooms.

Oliver pummels me with both fists, throwing wild haymakers and body shots. By bad luck, one of his blows lands directly on my amateur appendectomy, ripping open the stitches and making me roar with pain.

He's an inch shorter than me but probably thirty pounds heavier. Plus, he's been in plenty of frat-boy brawls.

He's not a trained fighter, though. After the initial shock and the wild onslaught, I get my hands up and block several of his punches before hitting him in the stomach and jaw.

The blows barely seem to faze him. His face is almost unrecognizable, his hair a tangled mess, a manic gleam in his eyes, and dried blood crusted on him like a macabre goatee.

"Where is she, you fucking psychopath?" I shout, fists up.

Oliver swipes the back of his hand across his face as fresh blood seeps from his nose. "She belonged to me first, and she'll belong to me last."

"She was never yours!"

Oliver dives at me again, grabbing for my knees. He's so reckless and inflamed that he knocks me backward down the stairs. We go tumbling end over end, the side of my head slamming against one of the bare wood steps.

Oliver gets the worst of it. He's on the bottom when we crash on the landing. It knocks him out cold. Or so it appears.

The smoke in the air is thicker than ever, and I'm breathing hard from the fight. I double over with a fit of coughing, hacking so hard that I feel a sharp pain in my ribs like I just popped one out of place. Or Oliver broke it when he threw his giant body at me.

I drag myself back up the steps, shouting, "*Aida!* Aida, where are you?"

The shouting scratches my smoke-filled throat. I cough harder than ever, tears streaming out of my eyes.

Oliver seizes my ankle and yanks, pulling my feet out from under me. I fall straight down on the top stair, slamming my jaw against the wooden edge. I kick out hard with my foot, wrenching it out of Castle's grasp and ramming the heel of my dress shoe directly into his eye. Oliver goes tumbling backward, back down to the landing.

I'm scrambling up the steps again. The upper part of the house is filling with smoke. I can feel the heat rising from the kitchen. The fire must be all across the first floor now. I don't know if we'll be able to get back down the stairs—assuming Aida is even up here.

She's got to be up here. Because if she's anywhere else in the house, she's already dead.

I run down the hallway, opening every door and looking in every room I pass. Bathroom. Linen closet. Empty bedroom. Then, at last, at the end of the hall, I find the master suite. It's devoid of furniture like all the rooms, the house cleared out for sale. But there's a figure lying in the middle of the floor, her hands tied in front of her, her feet bound with rope, her head propped up on a pillow. I'm glad he made sure she was comfy before he tried to burn her alive.

I run over to Aida before lifting her head and turning her face so I can make sure she's all right.

I press my fingers against the side of her throat; I can feel her pulse at least. As I tilt up her face, her lashes flutter against her cheek.

"Aida!" I cry, stroking her cheek with my thumb. "I'm here!"

Her eyes open, clouded and dazed but definitely alive. "Cal?" she croaks.

There's no time to untie her. I pick her up and throw her over my shoulder. As I turn toward the doorway, a hulking shape blocks our way.

Gently, I set Aida back on the bare floorboards. I feel the heat radiating upward, and the fire is getting louder and louder. We must be right over the kitchen. The wallpaper is starting to blacken and curl. The fire's in the walls, too.

"It's enough, Oliver," I tell him, holding up my hands. "We have to get out of here before the whole house collapses."

Oliver gives his head a weird twitching shake like there's a fly buzzing around his ear. He's hunched over, limping a little on one leg. Still, his eyes are fixed on me, his fists balled at his sides.

"None of us are leaving," he says.

He charges at me one more time. His shoulder hits my chest like an anvil. We're grappling and clawing at each other. I'm swinging punches at his face, his ear, his kidneys—any part of him I can reach.

Out of the corner of my eye, I see Aida slamming her hands against the windowsill. No, not her hands—her cast. She's trying to break the cast off her right hand. Grunting with pain, she bashes the cast down one more time, breaking the plaster. Now she can pull her hand loose from the rope. She fumbles with the ties around her ankles, her broken fingers clumsy and the knots too tight.

I lose sight of her as Oliver and I roll again, each of us grappling with all our might. We're both big men—I feel the floor groaning dangerously beneath us. It's getting hotter by the minute, the air so black and dense that I can barely see Aida at all.

She jumps to her feet. I shout, "Get the gun, Aida! It's in one of the rooms…"

She won't be able to find it, though. I couldn't see it before, and it's ten times smokier now.

Really, I just want her out of here. The fire rages beneath us. I have a feeling I'm about to plunge down to hell.

I get my hands around Castle's throat, and I pin him down, squeezing as hard as I can. His eyes are popping. He claws at my arms, raining blows on my face and body, weaker and weaker each time. I tighten my grip even as I feel the floor starting to shift and groan beneath us.

The whole corner of the room gives way. The floor becomes a tilted platform, a slide leading from the door into the fiery pit that's opened beneath us. We're sliding down, Oliver Castle and me on top of him, sliding and falling into the bonfire that once was a kitchen.

I let go of Castle and try to scramble backward, too late. I'm sliding faster than I can climb; there's no way to save myself. Until something seizes my sleeve.

Aida clings to the doorframe with one hand and my wrist with the other. Her teeth are bared with effort, her face a rictus of pain as she tries to hang on to the frame with her broken hand.

I don't grab her arm because I can see how weak her grip is. I'm not dragging her down with me.

"I love you, Aida," I say.

"Don't you fucking dare!" she yells back at me. "You grab my arm, or I'll jump in after you!"

With anyone else, it would be an idle threat. Aida is the only person I know who's stubborn enough to actually do it.

I grab her arm and haul myself upward, right as the joists give way and the whole room collapses. Oliver howls as he tumbles into the flames. Aida and I fling ourselves through the doorway, scrambling down the hallway hand in hand. There's no going down the stairs again, that much is obvious. We run to the opposite end of the house instead, finding a child's room with sailboat decals still stuck to the walls. Oliver's old room.

I wrench up the windowsill and climb out, releasing a fresh pillar of smoke. I hang from the window frame and drop, then put up my hands to catch Aida.

She jumps into my arms, still only wearing one shoe.

As we sprint away from the house, I hear the distant wail of sirens.

I'm pulling Aida down the drive to the Jeep. She yanks her hand out of my grip, yelling, "Wait!"

She runs in the opposite direction, past the inferno of the house, out on the sand toward the water.

She pauses, stooping to pick something up—her purse.

Then she runs back to me, her white teeth brilliant against her filthy face as she grins. "Got it!" she says triumphantly.

"I can buy you a new purse," I tell her.

"I know."

I'm about to start the engine, but there's something I can't wait another second to do either.

I grab Aida and I kiss her, tasting blood and smoke on her lips.

I kiss her like I'll never let her go.

Because I won't. Not ever.

29
AIDA

CALLUM AND I TURN ONTO THE MAIN ROAD RIGHT AS THE FIRE truck comes roaring up the lane, headed for the Castles' beach house—or what's left of it.

I can see the firemen's faces as our car passes their truck—they're looking down at us, eyebrows raised, unable to stop us from fleeing the scene.

"What a fucking trip!" I shout, my heart still galloping like a racehorse. "Did you know Oliver was that crazy? I thought he was just normal crazy, like 'I don't want my food to touch' or 'talking to yourself in the shower' crazy, not like full-on *Shining*."

Callum is driving way too fast, his hands locked on the steering wheel. Improbably, he's grinning almost as much as I am. Could my uptight husband actually be starting to enjoy our adventures?

"I can't believe I found you," he says.

"Yeah, holy shit! Did you find my shoe?"

"Yes, I found it! And I remembered."

He looks over at me, his blue eyes brilliant against his smoky skin. I don't know how I ever thought his eyes were cold. They're fucking beautiful. The most stunning eyes I've ever seen.

Even more striking is the fact he understood me, that he remembered our conversation. It almost means more to me than the fact he came to rescue me.

"Actually, I've got the other one in here somewhere," Cal says, twisting around to search the back seat.

"Eyes on the road!" I tell him. I find the sneaker a minute later, then slip it back on my foot. It's comically cleaner than the other now, so they no longer look like a matching set.

"There," I say. "Fully dressed again."

Cal's eyes alight on my bare left hand. "Not entirely," he says.

"Oh, fuck," I groan. "I forgot about that."

"Is it back at the house?" Cal asks.

"Yes. But Oliver smashed it."

"I don't think it would have survived either way," Cal says. He squeezes my thigh. "Don't worry about it. I wanted to get you another anyway. You know I didn't pick that one out."

"I know." I grin. "I'm getting to know Imogen's taste pretty well."

Cal turns onto the highway, heading north toward the city again. "You better call your brothers," he says. "They thought Zajac stole you."

"I might have been better off if he had." I wrinkle my nose. "Honestly, I think his villain speeches were better. He's a proper badass, you know? Whereas Oliver was so whiny, putting on the guilt trips…like, Jesus, dude, hop on Tinder, and get over it."

Callum stares at me for a second, and then he starts laughing so hard that his shoulders shake. "Aida, you're out of your fucking mind."

I shrug. "Just a helpful critique."

I borrow Callum's phone to dial Dante. It's Nero who picks up.

"Aida?" he says.

"Yeah, it's me."

"Thank fucking hell. I thought I was gonna have to drive over there in a second."

"Why, where are you?"

"At the hospital. Dante's been shot. He's all right, though! Zajac got him in the side—didn't hit anything crucial."

"That filthy shit!" I seethe. "He'll pay for that."

"He already did," Nero says blandly. "Dante's got better aim than the Butcher."

"He's dead? Are you sure?"

Cal looks over at me, following my side of the conversation but equally disbelieving.

"Totally sure," Nero says firmly. "Unless he's got a spare head lying around somewhere, he's done for."

"Well, shit," I say, leaning back against my seat. This really was an eventful night.

I look over at Callum, his face pale beneath the soot. He's got a nasty cut over his right eyebrow, and he winces a little every time he takes a deep breath.

Come to think of it, I'm not exactly in tip-top shape myself. My hand is throbbing in time with my heartbeat, and my ring and pinky fingers have swollen again. I'm probably going to need another cast.

"What hospital are you at?" I ask Nero. "We may need to join you."

———————

It takes a couple of hours for Callum and me to get cleaned up and patched up at Saint Joseph's. Dante will be there for a few days at least—they had to put three pints of blood back into him. Jack and Nero are keeping him company. I'm shocked to see their bruised and battered faces.

"What the hell happened to you?"

"While Dante was having a shoot-out at the mistress's apartment, Jack and I were *not* finding the Butcher and getting our asses kicked by his lieutenant instead."

"Not *just* the lieutenant," Jack says. He's got a black eye so bad, he can't even see on the left side. "There were at least four of them."

"Jack here is a serious brawler," Nero says in an impressed tone. "He gave 'em the old ground and pound, didn't ya, Jackie-boy?"

"I guess he's not so bad when he's on our side," I say.

Jack gives me a half grin—only half because the other side of his face is too swollen to move. "Was that a compliment?"

"Don't let it go to your head."

"You two aren't looking so hot either," Nero informs me.

"Well, that's where you're wrong." I snicker. "If we were any hotter, we'd have been charcoal briquettes."

Fergus Griffin comes to pick us up even though we have the Jeep parked outside.

"Two hospital visits in one week," he says, giving Cal and me a stern look through his horn-rimmed glasses. "I hope this isn't becoming a hobby for you two."

"No," Cal says, wrapping his arm around my shoulders in the back seat of the Beamer. "I don't think we're going to do anything too crazy next week. Except maybe look for an apartment."

"Oh?" Fergus pauses before putting the car in reverse. He glances back at us in the rearview mirror. "You want to get your own place together?"

Callum looks down at me. "Yeah," he says. "I think it's time."

My heart feels heavy and warm in my chest. I love the idea of finding a place with Cal—not my house or his but one we chose together.

"That's good," Fergus says, nodding. "I'm glad to hear it, Son."

Funnily enough, when we pull up in front of the Griffin mansion, for the first time, it actually feels like home. I get that wash of comfort. I know it's a safe place to lay my head. And damn, am I exhausted all of a sudden.

I stumble a little getting out of the car. I've gotten stiff and sore all over from sitting. Even though I know he's just as exhausted and probably more injured than I am, Cal scoops me up in his arms and carries me into the house like a groom carrying his bride over the threshold.

"Shouldn't you save that for our new apartment?" I tease.

"I'm going to carry you everywhere like this," Cal says. "For one, I like it. And for another, it will keep anybody else from snatching you."

"You got snatched, too, one of those times," I remind him.

He carries me all the way up the stairs.

"You're going to break your ribs again!"

"Oh, they're still broken right now," he assures me. "They didn't do much about it at the hospital. Didn't even tape me up. Just gave me a couple Tylenols."

"Did that help?"

"Not a fucking bit," he says, puffing and groaning as we finally reach the top of the stairs.

When he sets me down, I stretch up on tiptoe to kiss him softly on the lips. "Thank you," I say.

"I'm not done taking care of you yet. You still need to get cleaned up."

"Oh nooooo," I moan, remembering I'm utterly filthy. "Just let me go to bed. I'll sleep on the floor."

"At least brush your teeth," he says. "Or you'll hate yourself in the morning."

Grumbling, I head into the bathroom to brush and floss. By the time I finish, Cal has the shower running and fresh fluffy towels waiting for us.

He soaps my whole body, lathering me up until the suds running down the drain switch from black to gray to white. His fingers knead into my stiff neck and shoulders. Together with the hot water, he works out all the tense and knotted bits until I feel like a wet spaghetti noodle instead of a pretzel.

By the time we're both completely clean, I'm not tired anymore. Actually, parts of me are very much awake.

"My turn," I say, rubbing Cal with his towel. I run it down the curve of his broad back, then over his perfect ass, the bulges of his hamstrings, and his calves.

He's covered in bruises, scratches, welts, as well as the deeper cuts from the Butcher. Yet I've never seen a more flawless body. This man is perfect—perfect for me. I love the shape of him, his smell, the way his arms feel wrapped around me.

I turn him around and start drying the front side of him, starting at his feet and working my way upward. As I pass his thighs, I come to that thick, swollen cock, warm and clean from the shower. I take it in my hand, feeling it expand inside my grip. The skin is phenomenally soft. I stroke my fingertips down its length. His cock strains toward my hand, almost as if it has a mind of its own. I squeeze the shaft right below the head, making Cal moan.

He pulls me close. "I'm supposed to be taking care of you," he growls.

"You can. In a minute."

I take his cock in my mouth, gently sucking on the head. It fills to its fullest extent, so hard that the skin stretches tight. I run my tongue up and down its length in long smooth strokes and then in light teasing flicks. I take as much as I can in my mouth again and try to force the head backward, down into my throat.

It's damn hard dealing with a cock this size. I'm developing a new respect for porn stars. How on earth do they get the whole thing in there, all the way down to the base? I'd have to be a bloody sword-swallower.

I get about halfway down the shaft before I gag and have to come back up.

Callum doesn't seem to mind. I think he'd let me practice on him all night long. I've already learned a few things—I know he loves when I gently tug on and stroke his balls while I'm sliding my lips up and down his shaft. It makes him groan so deep that it's almost a rumble in his chest.

I really could do this all night. There's nothing more intimate and trusting than having the most vulnerable part of yourself in the other person's mouth. I've never wanted to make someone feel good more than I do right now, in this moment. Callum saved my life tonight. I would have burned to death, maybe without even waking up. The least I can do is give him the best release he's ever known.

Cal found me just like he'd promised. It wasn't my father or my brothers. It was my husband. This man I didn't even want. Now I can't imagine being without him.

I should worship his body all night long. Kiss every scrape and bruise.

But as usual, Cal has plans of his own. He pulls me down on the bed so we're lying side by side, his head to my toes. He puts his head between my thighs and starts eating my pussy like he's starving.

I go back to work on his cock at the same time. If anything, it's even harder to service him from this upside-down angle, but it doesn't matter. I'm pleasuring him and he's pleasuring me, I'm running my tongue over his smooth, soft skin, feeling the same warmth and wetness on myself. It's intimate and connected. And most of all, it feels like we're equals. That we're both learning to give, both learning to receive.

I didn't think Cal would find me. I didn't think anyone would.

But in the future, if I ever get myself in trouble again, I'll know my husband will come for me.

God, he's so good at this. I can already feel the pulses of pleasure zipping through me, growing stronger by the minute.

I don't want to come like this, though. I want to feel him inside me.

So I flip around and climb on him, straddling his hips, before lowering myself on his cock. It slides inside me easily, moistened from my own saliva as I am by his.

I look down into his stern, handsome face. The intensity of those blue eyes used to frighten me. Now I crave the feeling of them fixed on my face. It lights up my neurons, making me feel anxious and wild and daring. I feel like I'd do anything to keep his attention, to spark that look of hunger in his eyes.

He puts his hands on my hips, gripping me with those long, strong fingers. I'm getting flushed, and I want to ride him harder and faster. He forces me to slow down, to keep the same steady pace.

My climax is building again, my pussy clenching around his cock. My body demands to increase the pressure, to push me over the edge. Callum is thrusting his hips upward, fucking me deep. I've got my palms flat on his chest, my arms rigid from the effort of riding him.

Cal switches his hands from my hips to my breasts. He kneads them in his hands. Now I can speed up just a little, rolling my hips to slide my pussy up and down on his cock.

His hands keep pace with my motions. He's squeezing my breasts, sliding his fingers all the way down to my nipples with each squeeze. I start to come, throwing my head back and grinding my clit hard against his body.

Callum pinches my nipples, one long, drawn-out squeeze that sends a jolt of pleasure ricocheting back and forth from breast to groin. It intensifies the orgasm as it rebounds it over and over.

It's so strong that I can't even stay on top of him anymore. My pussy is throbbing, pulsing with the aftermath of that climax.

But I'm not done yet. I want to finish what I started before.

I climb off Callum and kneel between his legs. I put his cock back in my mouth, tasting myself on his skin. It's a warm, musky, mildly sweet taste that blends well with the scent of his skin and the slight saltiness of the clear fluid leaking from the head of his cock.

I want more.

I suck him off even more enthusiastically than before. My lips are swollen and sensitive from my climax. I feel every little ridge and vein of his cock against my tongue. I can feel his pulse and how his cock tenses and throbs as he gets closer and closer to the edge.

Gripping the base of his cock, I suck hard on the head, tipping him over.

"Oh, Jesus, Aida!" he cries out as he explodes into my mouth.

His come is thick and slippery and warm. I love how it tastes mixed with my own wetness. We're meant to be together, he and I. Salty and sweet.

When I've drained every last drop out of him, he wraps me in his arms again, our legs entwined beneath the sheets. I think I can even feel our hearts beating in tandem.

30

CALLUM

THE VERY NEXT DAY, I TAKE AIDA HOUSE HUNTING ALL AROUND the Gold Coast, and Old Town as well, in case she prefers to be in her old neighborhood. We look at town houses, penthouses, walk-ups, fancy apartments in posh buildings, and trendy converted lofts. Anything and everything I think she might like.

In the end we pick something in the middle: an old church that's been converted into flats. Our apartment is on the top floor, so it includes an entire rose window inside a pointed arch, making up almost the entirety of the living room wall.

Aida loves it so much that we put down a deposit on the spot.

After that, we fix the other thing missing in our marriage—I take Aida to pick out a proper ring. One she chooses herself to fit her own tastes and preferences. I'm expecting her to go with a simple band. She surprises me by choosing a small emerald-cut center stone with filigreed baguettes. It has clean lines and a hint of the old world about it. It suits her perfectly.

When I slip it on her finger, I repeat the vows I spoke so carelessly the first time around.

Now I savor every word, speaking from the heart.

"I, Callum Griffin, take you, Aida Gallo, to be my wife. I promise to be true to you in good times and in bad. In sickness and in health. I will love you and honor you all the days of my life. I promise you that, Aida. I will always be there for you. I'll never let you down."

"I know that," she says, looking up at me. "I know exactly what you'd do for me."

To celebrate the beginning of our new life together, I take her for lunch at Blackbird.

When we sit down, Aida sets her purse on the table between us, smiling gleefully. "I actually have something for you, too," she says.

"What is it?" I ask her, without the tiniest guess in my mind. I don't know if I've ever gotten a gift I was actually excited about. I'm used to putting on a fake smile for presents of cuff links or cologne.

"I almost feel stupid giving it to you," Aida says, passing me a small flat box. "Since it's already yours."

I lift the box, which is surprisingly heavy. When I open the lid, I see a gold pocket watch. It looks exactly like my grandfather's watch, but I know it can't be. She must have had a replica made somehow.

"How did you do it?" I ask her in amazement. "It looks exactly like it. Even a bit worn…"

"More worn than it was, probably," Aida says guilty. "It's been at the bottom of the lake for weeks."

"What?" I say in disbelief. "This isn't the same watch."

"It absolutely is," Aida says triumphantly.

"How?"

"Have you ever seen Jeremy Parker?"

"No. Who's that?"

"He makes these YouTube videos about finding sunken treasure. He's a scuba diver. Anyway, I saw this video where he found a lady's earring that she'd dropped in a river. And I thought, if he can do that…"

"So you called him?"

"That's right," Aida says triumphantly. "I mean, I paid him, obviously. And he gets to use it for his channel. Took him three whole days and two different metal detectors, but he found it!"

I turn the watch over in my hands, unable to believe it even while I'm holding it.

I look up at Aida's hopeful, guilty face.

Only Aida would believe she could get the watch back. I never even considered if it might be possible. You might as well drain the whole damn lake before you could get her to give up.

I love this woman. The day she set my house on fire was the luckiest day of my life. It truly is the luck of the Irish: Perverse. Inexplicable. And utterly fantastic.

"Do you forgive me for losing it in the first place?" she asks me, slipping her slim little hand into mine.

"I shouldn't tell you how much you could get away with, Aida," I say, shaking my head. "But you already know I'd forgive anything you do."

"Anything?" she says, grinning mischievously.

"Yes," I say. "But please don't test that theory."

Aida leans across the table to kiss me. She pulls back just a little so her nose is touching mine.

"I love you," she says. "Did I tell you that yet?"

"No." I grin. "Tell me again."

BONUS EPILOGUE
CALLUM

ONE YEAR LATER

F̲RIDAY IS A̲IDA'S BIRTHDAY.

I want to do something special for her. Really special.

Last month was shit. I was working too much, she was sick. I don't think we went out together one single night doing something we actually enjoy.

On Wednesday, I take Enzo down to the park to grill him over one of the stone chessboards. He wants to play even in the most godawful weather. I hold a big golfing umbrella over both of us.

I ask him for ideas, if Aida's mentioned anything she wants. He tells me I should take her mother's piano down out of the attic music room and bring it to our new place.

I act like I could never, though of course I instantly want it. Aida loves that thing like it's got her mother's soul locked inside it.

I don't want to give Enzo a heart attack, though. Definitely not *before* Aida's birthday.

"Are you sure? Don't you like to go up there and, uh, see it sometimes?"

Enzo doesn't actually play the piano, he just sits on the bench and touches the keys.

"Too often," Enzo says, staring at nothing.

Fuck.

Enzo is the living personification of my worst nightmare. Thinking about Aida dying and me living alone in our house the rest of my life gives me a panic attack. Every single time.

"You're sweating," Enzo says. "Worried you're going to lose again?"

"I won last time."

"And lost the three before."

"Am I getting better or are you getting senile?"

Enzo snorts. "Today may tell."

He touches his bishop, then moves his queen. He does that to fuck with me. I still double-check all his bishop's potential moves.

"Dante will help you move it," Enzo says, returning to the piano.

"I can't take it."

"It's already decided." Enzo advances his knight.

"Spoken like a godfather," I say to wind him up.

"Your father used to make that joke," Enzo retorts, because he knows exactly how much that will piss me off. He always has to have the last word.

And then he made a daughter who has to have it twice, and I fucking married her. So…I win?

I think of Aida's naughty grin peeking up at me this morning before she dove under the blankets and swallowed me whole.

Yes, I definitely win.

"What are you smirking about?" Enzo says.

"This." I slide my rook into place. "Check."

"Take the piano," Enzo says, moving his bishop to block. "I'll come to your place to hear Aida play it."

I thank him and let him take my king, high on how happy Aida's going to be.

As I drop him off at his doorstep, Enzo croaks, "I was going to win anyway."

_____

Friday morning I wake Aida up with my head between her thighs. She's sleepy and warm, groaning with pleasure before she's fully awake.

I lift my head to say, "You taste like you're dreaming something dirty..."

"I am," Aida laughs, arching her back and letting her knees fall apart. She thrusts her hands in my hair, pulling my mouth against her. "Keep going."

"Is it *my* birthday?"

I dive in deep.

Aida smells like cinnamon and oranges, probably because she was eating cinnamon toast and mandarins in bed last night.

The fuzz on her pussy is soft like the outside of a kiwifruit. I nuzzle my face against it, making her giggle and shriek.

I pin her legs down, licking her pussy in long strokes. I cover her in pillows and blankets, only exposing little bits of her at once. I pull her shirt up, baring her breasts, licking and sucking her nipples while the rest of her smothers in goose down. That drives her crazy, squirming and yelping, wrestling me until we're both panting.

She pounces on me, catching my cock in her mouth. I'm already hard. The first time I ever held Aida in my arms was when I tried to drown her in my parents' pool. Fucked as it may be, it still turns me on to feel how strong she fights.

We roll onto our sides, my face buried in her pussy, her mouth locked around my cock. Her thighs sandwich my ears, soft and pillowy. I scoop my arms around her legs, grabbing her ass in both hands, pulling her cheeks apart so I can delve my tongue deeper.

She moans around my cock, making eager sounds. She bobs her head up and down and I mimic her pace and pressure. She goes faster, harder, I match her lick for lick, stroke for stroke. Her pussy tastes warm and musky and delicious. I'm addicted to eating her for breakfast.

I suck gently on her clit, nibbling it lightly with my lips, softly sucking while my tongue strokes underneath. My cock slides deep in her throat.

We come together, slow and warm and wet, me pumping into her mouth and her riding my tongue.

All night long my balls have been boiling, my cock getting soft and then hard again every time Aida's bare thigh slides against mine, or I catch the scent of her hair right at the scalp.

She swallows the morning load I've been building all night long. I dive my tongue deep in her softness, making her come with her mouth around my cock, each twitch of her hips matched by the clenching of her throat.

We roll onto our backs, panting, our naked skin tinted with a kaleidoscope of colors from the stained-glass window on the wall.

"Happy birthday, baby," I say, kissing her.

The kiss starts sweet but turns filthy when I taste myself in her mouth.

Half an hour later, we've finished round two and we're in desperate need of a shower.

Aida soaps my back where I can't reach, and I wash her hair because she loves the feeling.

She grins up at me. "So what are we doing for Absolute Aida Day?"

"I thought we agreed on Awesome Aida Day."

"What about Angelic Aida Day?" She frames her face with her hands and tries to look innocent.

"I'd love to see that."

"No you wouldn't."

"Definitely not." I pull her close and kiss her again, my hand sliding down to grope her soapy breast.

"Round three?" Aida teases, her eyes alight. "It really *is* my birthday."

"I don't want to make you late."

"For what, for what?" She's giddy with anticipation.

"I booked you a spa day."

Her smile disappears. "*Hell* no. I'm not falling for that again."

"I thought you might say that…so I booked all the same treatments for Nessa."

"Pervert."

I smack her ass, making her yelp. "It means you're perfectly safe."

My real intent is to keep Aida occupied so I can get that damn piano moved to our place.

That's how I find myself on the top floor of the Gallo's decrepit mansion, trying to hoist a two thousand-pound instrument through a window.

Dante is sweating like a bull, Seb and Nero taking the opposite end. I'm working the pulley rig.

The ancient piano groans, wood creaking, strings straining. We've got rope wrapped all around it, trying to hold it together, but the soundboard is bowing.

"You can't lift it that way!" Nero bellows. "You'll crack it in half!"

"*You're* not lifting at all!" Dante shouts back. "I've got the whole damn thing on my shoulders!"

"I don't think it's gonna fit through that window," Seb remarks.

"It'll fit," I say, doggedly.

It does not fit. Not even after we remove the entire window and frame. And it's definitely not going through the door.

"How the fuck did you get that thing in up here in the first place?" I demand.

"It's been here since the house was built," Seb says. "They probably assembled it up here."

That makes sense. The grand looks older than all of us put together, covered in carvings and scrolls, birds, flowers, and vines. The woodwork used to be painted, but only flecks of faded turquoise remain.

We set the piano down again. Three of the strings snap.

"*Fuuuck.*" I cover my face with my hands, deeply disappointed.

"I don't think we can get it out without destroying it," Seb says, regretfully. He adores Aida and jumped at the chance to deliver the piano, despite his bum knee.

Even Nero looks gloomy, examining the dusty hulk of the immovable piano.

"What now?" Dante swipes a beefy arm across his dripping forehead.

"Get her a different piano," Nero says.

I shake my head. "I don't want to give her any old piano."

"You know..." Seb muses. "They have one kinda like this on campus..."

Sebastian still attends Chicago State, though I fucked up his basketball scholarship. He told me it's all water under the bridge, but I still feel like shit every time I see his limp.

"Where is it?"

"In the art museum."

"The museum!" Nero scoffs. "It's probably an antique. They're not gonna just give it to us."

Seb grins. "Who said anything about giving?"

An hour later, Nero distracts the museum docent while I disable the cameras on the back side of the building and bribe the security guard to take an extra-long lunch.

Dante pulls up at the loading dock with a moving truck held together by wire and rust.

"Where'd you get that janky-looking thing?" Seb says.

"Beggars can't be choosers," Dante grunts.

"But they *can* be thieves," I say, wheeling the dolly containing a two-hundred-year-old piano pilfered from the Early Musicians exhibit. It's not nearly as large as Aida's mother's grand, but Seb was right, it really does have the same turquoise-painted woodwork, and the same beautifully scrolled stand where the sheet music sits.

"How come this one looks better than ours?" Nero says, smoothing his hair back with both hands.

"Probably because it hasn't had three generations of kids climbing all over it," Seb says. "Did you just fuck that docent?"

"You said distract her."

"With *conversation*."

"Then I'd have to talk to her."

Seb shakes his head at Nero. "Maybe you should try it sometime."

"When I need dating advice from my little brother, I'll wake up and return to the reality where I don't need dating advice from my little brother."

"Seb's right," Dante growls

"Oh, shut the fuck up," Nero snaps. "At least I actually *want* to be single. I don't want to hear shit from you two sad sacks."

I stay out of it, because even though I'm the only one of us in a relationship, I agree with Nero that it's best for womankind if he stays single.

We load the piano into the moving van.

Right as we're about to close the back doors, the docent comes running out of the Renaissance exhibit, her hair a mess and her shirt buttoned up wrong. She spots Nero and the piano and starts shrieking as she sprints toward us.

"Go, go!" Nero bellows to Dante, slamming the van doors.

As we pull away, I hear the wavering cry, "*I'll get you for this, Greg!*"

I look at Nero, hunkered down by the stolen piano.

"Did you tell her your name was Greg?"

Nero shrugs. "So?"

Seb snorts through his fingers. "Why Greg?"

"I dunno." I swear Nero's blushing slightly. "It was the first name that popped in my head."

The idea of Nero as "Greg" has us all in stitches, even Dante.

"How's that any weirder a name than my actual name?" Nero demands, fully pissed.

"It just is," Dante chortles.

I'm crouched in the back with Nero and Seb, holding the piano steady while Dante takes wide turns in the rickety van.

"Let's get this back to the apartment," I say. "Before something else goes wrong."

I know better than to say shit like that out loud.

Before I've even finished my sentence, something hits us from the side and the whole world explodes.

AIDA

My spa day with Nessa is just as delightful as Cal promised. We spend all morning having our feet massaged and our nails painted, soaking in mud baths and eating bowls of frozen grapes.

I tell Nessa the story of my very first spa appointment. She laughs until tears run down her face.

"I can't believe you two didn't kill each other."

I grin. "Not for lack of trying."

Nessa presents me with a giant box wrapped in red ribbon.

"Happy birthday!"

I say, "Don't you want to give that to me later?"

Cal's family and mine are coming over for a party at the house— just cake and champagne, and a playlist of music that Imogen will absolutely *not* be allowed to fuck with. I'm not listening to Brahms on my birthday.

"Actually, it's for the party," Nessa smiles.

"Well, in that case…"

I gleefully rip apart the paper and ribbon, tearing into the box like a rabid raccoon.

Inside I find a mass of puffy crimson tulle, spangled with glittering red strawberries.

"It's a dress," Nessa says, helpfully.

I lift it out of the box, already giggling with delight. "Cal's gonna lose his mind."

"Don't tell him it's from me," Nessa snickers.

She helps me with my makeup. I've gotten way better at dolling up with all the practice I've had attending Cal's events, but I don't know if I'll ever have the steady hand eyeliner requires.

Nessa takes a step back and whistles with appreciation. "Red's your color. Does it fit okay?"

"It's a bit tight," I admit.

"I can exchange it—"

"No, you got the right size. I should probably stop eating pumpkin pie for breakfast."

Nessa laughs. "Where do you even get pumpkin pie this time of year?"

"Made it myself. I was in the mood and I couldn't wait for November. I've got a bit left, you should come try it. I put orange juice in the filling, it'll change your life—"

I break off 'cause Nessa's looking at me funny.

"What?" I say.

She tilts her head, frowning slightly. "You look…"

"Edible? Unhinged?"

She laughs. "I was going to say…radiant."

"Now I know you're lying."

Our aesthetician returns with a chilled bucket of Moët and two glasses.

"Courtesy of your husband." She smiles at me, popping the cork and pouring the drinks, handing us each a bubbling flute.

"What should we toast to?" I ask Nessa, holding my glass aloft.

She sets hers down untouched.

"I want to ask you something first…"

———————

Nessa drops me off at my apartment an hour later, my heart racing and my head buzzing. I'm so anxious to see Cal that I forget I'm still wearing the strawberry dress.

He pulls our door open as soon as he hears my key in the lock.

"Aida!" He sweeps me into his arms. "Oh my god, that dress… you look one hundred percent worth a trip to the ER."

I'm staring at him in shock because it looks like my husband just *came* from the ER.

"*Cal, what happened?*"

He looks down at himself, at his torn shirt, the gash on his arm, the cuts all over his hands. "It's…a long story."

He takes my hand, leading me into the living room.

There I find a pile of kindling that might once have been a piano. Two of the legs are broken off, the keyboard's cracked in half, and strings poke up in all directions.

I can't help laughing. "What's this?"

"Your birthday present," Cal says miserably.

I pull him down on the couch, kissing his poor bruised forehead, his bloodied lips and filthy cheeks.

"What happened, my love?"

He tells me the whole story, starting with the crane he rented to try to get my mother's piano out through the window, and finishing with the bakery truck that ran a red light and smashed up the second piano, along with my beloved husband and all three of my brothers.

"Is everyone okay?"

"Yeah, they're fine. I mean, they look pretty much like this," Cal gestures to himself, "but nothing's broken."

"Besides the piano," I snort.

"Yes, besides the piano," Cal says, without smiling at all. "I wanted to make today special for you. But everything went wrong."

His shoulders slump and his head hangs down.

My poor perfectionist husband. The trouble he went to trying to make me happy fills me with a joy that's almost painful. My chest is tight and my eyes burn.

I put my arm around his shoulders, kissing the side of his head. "I love my new piano. We'll tell everyone it's modern art."

Cal mumbles, "I wanted it to be the most perfect birthday…"

I take his face in my hands and make him look at me. "My love…it *is* the most perfect birthday."

"You're just trying to make me feel better."

"No, I'm not."

I can't hold back my glee. Cal searches my face, his mood already lightening though I haven't told him yet.

"What's going on…"

"I've got a present for you."

"It's supposed to be *your* birthday."

"This is for both of us."

He looks in my eyes. I see understanding dawn, bright as the sun in the morning.

"You don't mean—"

I grip his hands tight. "We're having a baby."

Cal makes a sound like a laugh and a sob. "Aida!"

He leaps up from the couch, grabbing me, swinging me around. Then he remembers and sets me down with extreme gentleness, like I'm priceless.

"When did you find out?"

"About an hour ago." I laugh. "Actually, it was your sister who told me—guess Nessa paid better attention in sex ed."

"This is…" Cal's voice cracks. "The best news I've ever gotten. I can't believe it Aida, god I'm so happy—"

He hugs me again, the kind of hug that feels like all our feelings flow into each other until we're full to the brim.

When we pull apart, he holds me by the shoulders, looking me up and down.

"I should have known—you're glowing."

Cal looks like he went through a hurricane, but he's glowing too, eyes wet and glittering, grin shining bright.

He says, "Do you think it's a boy or a girl?"

"Whichever it is, you better hope they take after their father."

Cal links his fingers through mine.

"I hope they're like both of us—we're better together."

BRUTAL PRINCE BONUS

Can't get enough of Callum and Aida?
Download one more steamy bonus chapter:

PATREON

Want to see uncensored NSFW art and stories too hot for the printed page? Check out my Patreon:

Read on for an excerpt of

STOLEN HEIR,

featuring Miko and Nessa

SOPHIE LARK

I ORDER KLARA TO GET NESSA DRESSED FOR DINNER. I INTEND to tempt her with food, and if that fails, to forcibly stuff it down her throat.

I wanted to see her in person again anyway. As a figure on my phone screen, she amuses me, but that can't compare to the exquisite bouquet of fear and fury that she can provide in the flesh.

When Jonas drags her into the formal dining room, I see that Klara has done her job a little too well. I've only seen Nessa in dance attire or school clothes, hair pulled back and face freshly scrubbed. When dressed to impress, Nessa Griffin is fucking stunning.

A few days without food have made her willowier than ever. The green silk dress clings to her frame, showing her every breath, down to the sudden intake of air when she spots me waiting for her. Her light-brown hair floats down around her shoulders in waves, longer and thicker than I expected it to be. It reflects the light just like the silk dress, just like her glowing skin and her big green eyes. Every bit of her is luminescent.

But incredibly fragile. The thinness of her neck, her arms and fingers, is frightening. I could snap those bird-like bones without even trying. I can see her collarbones, and her shoulder blades when she turns. The only part of her with curves is those big, soft, trembling lips.

I'm glad to see that while Klara has painted Nessa's face, she's left those lips bare. Pale pink like a ballet slipper. A raw and innocent color. I wonder if her nipples are the same shade, underneath that dress. I can still see the pale brown freckles scattered across her cheeks and the bridge of her nose. They're sweet and childish, in contrast to the surprisingly dark eyebrows that animate her face like punctuation marks. Her eyebrows swoop up like bird's wings when she's surprised, and contract plaintively when she's distressed.

Even dressed like this, at her most mature and glamorous, Nessa looks incredibly young. She's fresh and youthful, in contrast to this house where everything is old and dusty.

I don't find her innocence attractive. In fact, I find it infuriating.

How dare she walk through life like a glass sculpture, begging to be smashed? She's a burden on everyone around her—impossible to protect, impossible to keep intact.

The sooner I start the process of dismantling her, the better off everyone will be.

So I make her sit down. I make her eat.

She tries to strike her ridiculous bargain with me, and I allow it. I don't care if she wanders around the house. She really can't escape, not with the monitor around her ankle. It tracks her at all times, everywhere she goes. If she tries to break it, if it stops reading her pulse through her skin for even an instant, I'll be alerted.

I'm curious to see where she'll go, what she'll do. I've grown bored of watching her inside her room.

Buoying her up with this tiny victory will only give her further to fall. And if she actually starts to trust me a little, if she thinks I can be reasoned with . . . all the better.

Constant cruelty isn't how you worm your way inside someone's head. It's the mix of good and bad, give and take, that fucks with them. Unpredictability makes them desperate to please.

So after we've eaten, I take Nessa into the ballroom. I've watched her dance several times now—at Jungle, at Lake City Ballet, and trapped in her room, in the space next to the four-poster bed.

Dancing transforms her. The girl who blushes and can't meet my eye is not the same one who lets go of herself under the influence of music.

It's like watching a possession. As soon as I take her in my arms, her stiff and fragile body becomes as loose and liquid as the material of her dress. The music surges through her, until she's thrumming with too much energy for one tiny frame. She's vibrating under my hands. Her eyes glaze over and she doesn't seem to notice me at all anymore, other than as an apparatus to move her across the room.

It makes me almost jealous. She's disappeared somewhere that I can't reach her. She's feeling something that I can't feel.

I whirl her around faster and faster. I'm good at dancing in the way that I'm good at everything—quick and coordinated. It's how I work and how I fight. How I fuck, even.

But I don't get pleasure out of it like Nessa does. Her eyes close and her lips part. Her face bears an expression usually reserved for sexual climax. Her body presses against mine, hot and damp with sweat. I can feel her heartbeat through the thin silk; I feel her nipples stiffen against my chest.

I dip her backward, exposing the delicate column of her throat. I don't know if I want to kiss her or bite her—or wrap my hands around her neck and squeeze. I want to do something to yank her back from wherever she's gone. I want to force her attention back to me.

It's odd. I usually feel irritated by women's attention. I hate their neediness, their clinging hands. I use them for release, but I make it very clear there will be no conversation, no affection, and definitely no love.

I haven't kissed a woman in years.

Yet here I am, looking down at Nessa's closed eyes and her parted lips, thinking how easily I could crush that delicate mouth under mine and force my tongue between those lips, tasting her sweetness like the nectar of a flower.

Instead, I touch the ivory column of her throat. I run my

fingertips down her breastbone, feeling skin so soft it might have been born yesterday.

Her eyes snap open and she tears herself away from me, an expression of horror on her face.

Now she's looking at me. Now she's seeing me—with complete revulsion.

"Don't touch me!" she cries.

I feel a bitter stab of satisfaction, seeing her wrenched back down so abruptly. She thinks she can float up to heaven whenever she likes? Well, I'll drag her all the way down to hell with me.

"Go back to your room," I tell her, taking pleasure in dismissing her at my will. She's my prisoner, and she better not forget it. I might give her the run of the house, but that doesn't change our dynamic. She eats when I say. She wears what I say. She comes when I say. And she goes when I say.

She's only too happy to leave. She runs away, the hem of the green silk dress flowing behind her like a cape.

Once she's gone, I expect to return to my usual state of apathy. Nessa is just a blip on my radar a momentary jolt that disappears again just as quickly.

But not tonight. Her scent lingers in my nostrils—sweet almond and red wine. My fingertips can still feel the softness of her skin.

BRUTAL BIRTHRIGHT

Callum & Aida

Miko & Nessa

Nero & Camille

Dante & Simone

Raylan & Riona

Sebastian & Yelena

ABOUT THE AUTHOR

Sophie Lark writes intelligent and powerful characters who are allowed to be flawed. She lives in the mountain west with her husband and three children.

The Love Lark Letter: geni.us/lark-letter
The Love Lark Reader Group: geni.us/love-larks
Website: sophielark.com
Instagram: @Sophie_Lark_Author
TikTok: @sophielarkauthor
Exclusive Content: patreon.com/sophielark
Complete Works: geni.us/lark-amazon
Book Playlists: geni.us/lark-spotify